Francis Marion Crawford

Mr. Isaacs

A Tale of Modern India

Francis Marion Crawford

Mr. Isaacs
A Tale of Modern India

ISBN/EAN: 9783337023218

Printed in Europe, USA, Canada, Australia, Japan

Cover: Foto ©Andreas Hilbeck / pixelio.de

More available books at **www.hansebooks.com**

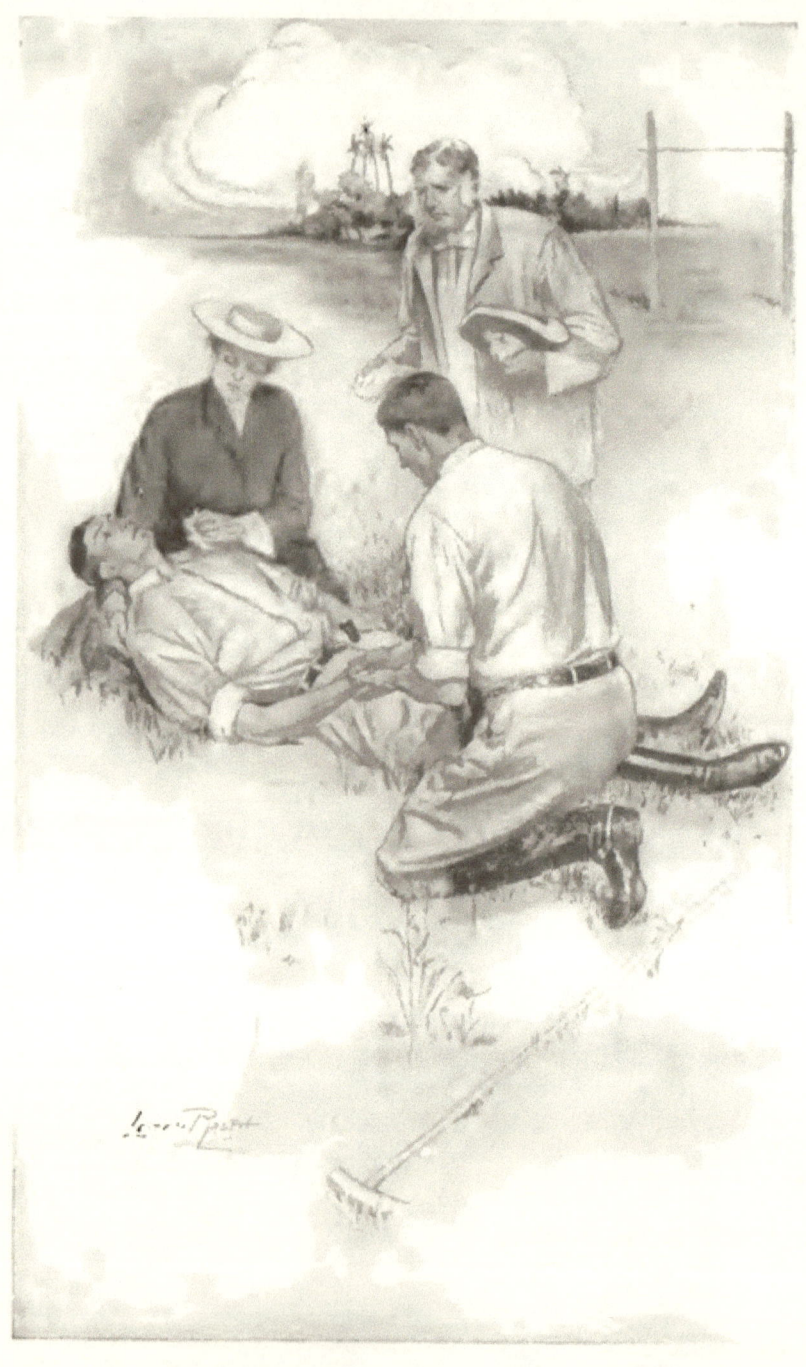

HER FACE WAS WHITER THAN HIS, THOUGH NOT A QUIVER OF
MOUTH OR EYELASH BETRAYED HER EMOTION.

—*Mr. Isaacs*

THE NOVELS OF
F. MARION CRAWFORD

MR. ISAACS
A Tale of
Modern India

BY

F. MARION CRAWFORD

WITH FRONTISPIECE

P. F. COLLIER & SON
NEW YORK

MR. ISAACS.

CHAPTER I.

IN spite of Jean-Jacques and his school, men are not everywhere born free, any more than they are everywhere in chains, unless these be of their own individual making. Especially in countries where excessive liberty or excessive tyranny favours the growth of that class most usually designated as adventurers, it is true that man, by his own dominant will, or by a still more potent servility, may rise to any grade of elevation; as by the absence of these qualities he may fall to any depth in the social scale.

Wherever freedom degenerates into license, the ruthless predatory instinct of certain bold and unscrupulous persons may, and almost certainly will, place at their disposal the goods, the honours, and the preferment justly the due of others; and in those more numerous and certainly more unhappy countries, where the rule of the tyrant is substituted for the law of God, the unwearying flatterer, patient under blows and abstemious under high-feeding, will assuredly make his way to power.

Without doubt the Eastern portion of the world, where an hereditary, or at least traditional, despotism has never ceased since the earliest social records, and where a mode of thought infinitely more degrading than any feudalism has become ingrained in the blood and soul of the chief races, presents far more favourable conditions to the growth and development of the true adventurer than are offered in any free country. For in a free country the majority can rise and overthrow the favourite of fortune, whereas in a despotic country they cannot. Of Eastern countries in this condition, Russia is the nearest to us; though perhaps we understand the Chinese character better than the Russian. The Ottoman empire and Persia are, and always have been, swayed by a clever band of flatterers acting through their nominal master; while India, under the kindly British rule, is a perfect instance of a ruthless military despotism, where neither blood nor stratagem have been spared in exacting the uttermost farthing from the miserable serfs — they are nothing else — and in robbing and defrauding the rich of their just and lawful possessions. All these countries teem with stories of adventurers risen from the ranks to the command of armies, of itinerant merchants wedded to princesses, of hardy sailors promoted to admiralties, of half-educated younger sons of English peers dying in the undisputed possession of ill-gotten millions. With the strong personal despotism of the First Napoleon began a new era of adventurers in France; not of elegant and accomplished adventurers like M. de St. Germain, Cagliostro, or the Comtesse de la Motte, but regular rag-tag-and-bobtail cut-throat moss-troopers, who carved and slashed themselves into notice by sheer animal strength and brutality.

There is infinitely more grace and romance about the Eastern adventurer. There is very little slashing and hewing to be done there, and what there is, is managed as quietly as possible. When a Sultan must be rid of the last superfluous wife, she is quietly done up in a parcel with a few shot, and dropped into the Bosphorus without more ado. The good old-fashioned Rajah of Mudpoor did his killing without scandal, and when the kindly British wish to keep a secret, the man is hanged in a quiet place where there are no reporters. As in the Greek tragedies, the butchery is done behind the scenes, and there is no glory connected with the business, only gain. The ghosts of the slain sometimes appear in the columns of the recalcitrant Indian newspapers and gibber a feeble little "Otototoi!" after the manner of the shade of Dareios, but there is very little heed paid to such visitations by the kindly British. But though the "raw head and bloody bones" type of adventurer is little in demand in the East, there is plenty of scope for the intelligent and wary flatterer, and some room for the honest man of superior gifts, who is sufficiently free from Oriental prejudice to do energetically the thing which comes in his way, distancing all competitors for the favours of fortune by sheer industry and unerring foresight.

I once knew a man in the East who was neither a flatterer nor freebooter, but who by his own masterly perseverance worked his way to immense wealth, and to such power as wealth commands, though his high view of the social aims of mankind deterred him from mixing in political questions. *Bon chien chasse de race* is a proverb which applies to horses, cattle, and men, as well as to dogs; and in this man, who was a noble type of the Aryan race, the qualities which have made that race dominant were developed in the highest degree. The sequel, indeed, might lead the ethnographer into a labyrinth of conjecture, but the story is too tempting a one for me to forego telling it, although the said ethnographer should lose his wits in striving to solve the puzzle.

In September, 1879, I was at Simla in the lower Himalayas, — at the time of the murder of Sir Louis Cavagnari at Kabul, — being called there in the interests of an Anglo-Indian newspaper, of which I was then editor. In other countries, notably in Europe and in America, there are hundreds of spots by the sea-shore, or on the mountain-side, where specific ills may be cured by their corresponding antidotes of air or water, or both. Following the aristocratic and holy example of the Bishops of Salzburg for the last eight centuries, the sovereigns of the Continent are told

that the air and waters of Hofgastein are the only
nenuphar for the over-taxed brain in labour beneath
a crown.   The self-indulgent sybarite is recom-
mended to Ems, or Wiesbaden, or Aix-la-Chapelle,
and the quasi-incurable sensualist to Aix in Savoy,
or to Karlsbad in Bohemia.   In our own magnificent
land Bethesdas abound, in every state, from the
attractive waters of lotus-eating Saratoga to the magnetic springs of Lansing, Michigan; from Virginia,
the carcanet of sources, the heaving, the warm, the
hot sulphur springs, the white sulphur, the alum, to
the hot springs of Arkansas, the Ultima Thule of our
migratory and despairing humanity.   But in India,
whatever the ailing, low fever, high fever, "brandy
pawnee" fever, malaria caught in the chase of tigers
in the Terai, or dysentery imbibed on the banks of
the Ganges, there is only one cure, the "hills;" and
chief of "hill-stations" is Simla.

On the hip rather than on the shoulder of the aspiring Himalayas, Simla — or Shumla, as the natives
call it — presents during the wet monsoon period a
concourse of pilgrims more varied even than the
Bagnères de Bigorre in the south of France, where
the gay Frenchman asks permission of the lady with
whom he is conversing to leave her abruptly, in
order to part with his remaining lung, the loss of the
first having brought him there.   "Pardon, madame,"
said he, "je m'en vais cracher mon autre poumon."

To Simla the whole surpeme Government migrates
for the summer — Viceroy, council, clerks, printers,

and hangers-on. Thither the high official from the
plains takes his wife, his daughters, and his liver.
There the journalists congregate to pick up the news
that oozes through the pent-house of Government
secrecy, and failing such scant drops of information,
to manufacture as much as is necessary to fill the
columns of their dailies. On the slopes of "Jako"
— the wooded eminence that rises above the town —
the enterprising German establishes his concert-hall
and his beer-garden; among the rhododendron trees
Madame Blavatzky, Colonel Olcott and Mr. Sinnett
move mysteriously in the performance of their wonders; and the wealthy tourist from America, the
botanist from Berlin, and the casual peer from Great
Britain, are not wanting to complete the motley
crowd. There are no roads in Simla proper where
it is possible to drive, excepting one narrow way,
reserved when I was there, and probably still set
apart, for the exclusive delectation of the Viceroy.
Every one rides — man, woman, and child; and
every variety of horseflesh may be seen in abun-
dance, from Lord Steepleton Kildare's throughbreds
to the broad-sterned equestrian vessel of Mr. Currie
Ghyrkins, the Revenue Commissioner of Mudnugger
in Bengal. But I need not now dwell long on the
description of this highly-favoured spot, where Baron
de Zach might have added force to his demonstration
of the attraction of mountains for the pendulum.
Having achieved my orientation and established my
servants and luggage in one of the reputed hotels, I

began to look about me, and, like an intelligent
American observer, as I pride myself that I am, I
found considerable pleasure in studying out the character of such of the changing crowd on the verandah
and on the mall as caught my attention.

At last the dinner-hour came. With the rest I
filed into the large dining-room and took my seat.
The place allotted to me was the last at one side of
the long table, and the chair opposite was vacant,
though two remarkably well-dressed servants, in turbans of white and gold, stood with folded arms
behind it, apparently awaiting their master. Nor was
he long in coming. I never remember to have been
so much struck by the personal appearance of any
man in my life. He sat down opposite me, and
immediately one of his two servants, or *khitmatgars*,
as they are called, retired, and came back bearing a
priceless goblet and flask of the purest old Venetian
mould. Filling the former, he ceremoniously presented his master with a brimming beaker of cold
water. A water-drinker in India is always a phenomenon, but a water-drinker who did the thing so
artistically was such a manifestation as I had never
seen. I was interested beyond the possibility of holding my peace, and as I watched the man's abstemious
meal, — for he ate little, — I contrasted him with
our neighbours at the board, who seemed to be vying,
like the captives of Circe, to ascertain by trial who
could swallow the most beef and mountain mutton,
and who could absorb the most "pegs" — those vile

concoctions of spirits, ice, and soda-water, which have destroyed so many splendid constitutions under the tropical sun. As I watched him an impression came over me that he must be an Italian. I scanned his appearance narrowly, and watched for a word that should betray his accent. He spoke to his servant in Hindustani, and I noticed at once the peculiar sound of the dental consonants, never to be acquired by a northern-born person.

Before I go farther, let me try and describe Mr. Isaacs; I certainly could not have done so satisfactorily after my first meeting, but subsequent acquaintance, and the events I am about to chronicle, threw me so often in his society, and gave me such ample opportunities of observation, that the minutest details of his form and feature, as well as the smallest peculiarities of his character and manner, are indelibly graven in my memory.

Isaacs was a man of more than medium stature, though he would never be spoken of as tall. An easy grace marked his movements at all times, whether deliberate or vehement, — and he often went to each extreme, — a grace which no one acquainted with the science of the human frame would be at a loss to explain for a moment. The perfect harmony of all the parts, the even symmetry of every muscle, the equal distribution of a strength, not colossal and overwhelming, but ever ready for action, the natural courtesy of gesture — all told of a body in which true proportion of every limb and sinew were at once the main feature and the pervading characteristic. This infinitely supple and swiftly-moving figure was but the pedestal, as it were, for the noble face and nobler brain to which it owed its life and majestic bearing. A long oval face of a wondrous transparent olive tint, and of a decidedly Oriental type. A prominent brow and arched but delicate eyebrows fitly surmouned a nose smoothly aquiline, but with the broad well-set nostrils that bespeak active courage. His mouth, often smiling, never laughed, and the lips, though closely meeting, were not thin and writhing and cunning, as one so often sees in eastern faces, but rather inclined to a generous Greek fulness, the curling lines ever ready to express a sympathy or a scorn which the commanding features above seemed to control and curb, as the stern, square-elbowed Arab checks his rebellious horse, or gives him the rein, at will.

But though Mr. Isaacs was endowed with exceptional gifts of beauty by a bountiful nature, those I have enumerated were by no means what first attracted the attention of the observer. I have spoken of his graceful figure and perfect Iranian features, but I hardly noticed either at our first meeting. I was enthralled and fascinated by his eyes. I once saw in France a jewel composed of six precious stones, each a gem of great value, so set that they appeared to form but one solid mass, yielding a strange radiance that changed its hue at every movement, and multiplied the sunlight a thousand-fold. Were I to seek a comparison for my friend's eyes, I might find an imperfect one in this masterpiece of the jeweller's art. They were dark and of remarkable size; when half closed they were long and almond-shaped; when suddenly opened in anger or surprise they had the roundness and bold keenness of the eagle's sight. There was a depth of life and vital light in them that told of the pent-up force of a hundred generations of Persian magii. They blazed with the splendour of a god-like nature, needing neither meat nor strong drink to feed its power.

My mind was made up. Between his eyes, his temperance, and his dental consonants, he certainly might be an Italian. Being myself a native of Italy, though an American by parentage, I addressed him in the language, feeling comparatively sure of his answer. To my surprise, and somewhat to my confusion, he answered in two words of modern Greek — "δεν ἐνόησα"—"I do not understand." He evidently supposed I was speaking a Greek dialect, and answered in the one phrase of that tongue which he knew, and not a good phrase at that.

"Pardon me," said I in English, "I believed you a countryman, and ventured to address you in my native tongue. May I inquire whether you speak English?"

I was not a little astonished when he answered me in pure English, and with an evident command of the language. We fell into conversation, and I found him pungent, ready, impressive, and most entertaining, thoroughly acquainted with Anglo-Indian and English topics, and apparently well read. An Indian dinner is a long affair, so that we had ample time to break the ice, an easy matter always for people who are not English, and when, after the fruit, he invited me to come down and smoke with him in his rooms, I gladly availed myself of the opportunity. We separated for a few moments, and I despatched my servant to the manager of the hotel to ascertain the name of the strange gentleman who looked like an Italian and spoke like a fellow of Balliol. Having discovered that he was a "Mr. Isaacs," I wended my way through verandahs and corridors, preceded by a *chuprassie* and followed by my pipe-bearer, till I came to his rooms.

The fashion of the hookah or narghyle in India has long disappeared from the English portion of society. Its place has been assumed and usurped by the cheroot from Burmah or Trichinopoli, by the cigarette from Egypt, or the more expensive Manilla and Havana cigars. I, however, in an early burst of Oriental enthusiasm, had ventured upon the obsolete fashion, and so charmed was I by the indolent aromatic enjoyment I got from the rather cumbrous machine, that I never gave it up while in the East. So when Mr. Isaacs invited me to come and smoke in his rooms, or rather before his rooms, for the September air was still warm in the hills, I ordered my "bearer" to bring down the apparatus and to prepare it for use. I myself passed through the glass

door in accordance with my new acquaintance's
invitation, curious to see the kind of abode in which
a man who struck me as being so unlike his fellows
spent his summer months. For some minutes after
I entered I did not speak, and indeed I hardly
breathed. It seemed to me that I was suddenly
transported into the subterranean chambers whither
the wicked magician sent Aladdin in quest of the
lamp. A soft but strong light filled the room,
though I did not immediately comprehend whence it
came, nor did I think to look, so amazed was I by
the extraordinary splendour of the objects that met
my eyes. In the first glance it appeared as if the
walls and the ceiling were lined with gold and precious stones; and in reality it was almost literally
the truth. The apartment, I soon saw, was small,
— for India at least, — and every available space,
nook and cranny, were filled with gold and jewelled
ornaments, shining weapons, or uncouth but resplen-
dent idols. There were sabres in scabbards set from
end to end with diamonds and sapphires, with cross
hilts of rubies in massive gold mounting, the spoil of
some worsted rajah or Nawab of the mutiny. There
were narghyles four feet high, crusted with gems
and curiously wrought work from Baghdad or Herat;
water flasks of gold and drinking cups of jade;
yataghans from Roum and idols from the far East.
Gorgeous lamps of the octagonal Oriental shape hung
from the ceiling, and, fed by aromatic oils, shed their
soothing light on all around. The floor was cov-

ered with a rich soft pile, and low divans were heaped with cushions of deep-tinted silk and gold. On the floor, in a corner which seemed the favourite resting-place of my host, lay open two or three superbly illuminated Arabic manuscripts, and from a chafing dish of silver near by a thin thread of snow-white smoke sent up its faint perfume through the still air. To find myself transported from the conventionalities of a stiff and starched Anglo-Indian hotel to such a scene was something novel and delicious in the extreme. No wonder I stood speechless and amazed. Mr. Isaacs remained near the door while I breathed in the strange sights to which he had introduced me. At last I turned, and from contemplating the magnificence of inanimate wealth I was riveted by the majestic face and expression of the beautiful living creature who, by a turn of his wand, or, to speak prosaically, by an invitation to smoke, had lifted me out of humdrum into a land peopled with all the effulgent phantasies and the priceless realities of the magic East. As I gazed, it seemed as if the illumination from the lamps above were caught up and flung back with the vitality of living fire by his dark eyes, in which more than ever I saw and realised the inexplicable blending of the precious stones with the burning spark of a divine soul breathing within. For some moments we stood thus; he evidently amused at my astonishment, and I fascinated and excited by the problem presented me for solution in his person and possessions.

"Yes," said Isaacs, "you are naturally surprised at my little Eldorado, so snugly hidden away in the lower story of a commonplace hotel. Perhaps you are surprised at finding me here, too. But come out into the air, your hookah is blazing, and so are the stars."

I followed him into the verandah, where the long cane chairs of the country were placed, and taking the tube of the pipe from the solemn Mussulman whose duty it was to prepare it, I stretched myself out in that indolent lazy peace which is only to be enjoyed in tropical countries. Silent and for the nonce perfectly happy, I slowly inhaled the fragrant vapour of tobacco and aromatic herbs and honey with which the hookah is filled. No sound save the monotonous bubbling and chuckling of the smoke through the water, or the gentle rustle of the leaves on the huge rhododendron-tree which reared its dusky branches to the night in the middle of the lawn. There was no moon, though the stars were bright and clear, the foaming path of the milky way stretching overhead like the wake of some great heavenly ship; a soft mellow lustre from the lamps in Isaacs' room threw a golden stain half across the verandah, and the chafing dish within, as the light breeze fanned the coals, sent out a little cloud of perfume which mingled pleasantly with the odour of the *chillum* in the pipe. The turbaned servant squatted on the edge of the steps at a little distance, peering into the dusk, as Indians will do for hours together. Isaacs lay quite still in his chair, his hands above his head, the light through the open door just falling on the jewelled mouthpiece of his narghyle. He sighed — a sigh only half regretful, half contented, and seemed about to speak, but the spirit did not move him, and the profound silence continued. For my part, I was so much absorbed in my reflections on the things I had seen that I had nothing to say, and the strange personality of the man made me wish to let him begin upon his own subject, if perchance I might gain some insight into his mind and mode of thought. There are times when silence seems to be sacred, even unaccountably so. A feeling is in us that to speak would be almost a sacrilege, though we are unable to account in any way for the pause. At such moments every one seems instinctively to feel the same influence, and the first person who breaks the spell either experiences a sensation of awkwardness, and says something very foolish, or, conscious of the odds against him, delivers himself of a sentiment of ponderous severity and sententiousness. As I smoked, watching the great flaming bowl of the water pipe, a little coal, forced up by the expansion of the heat, toppled over the edge and fell tinkling on the metal foot below. The quick ear of the servant on the steps caught the sound, and he rose and came forward to trim the fire. Though he did not speak, his act was a diversion. The spell was broken.

"The Germans," said Isaacs, "say that an angel is passing over the house. I do not believe it."

I was surprised at the remark. It did not seem quite natural for Mr. Isaacs to begin talking about the Germans, and from the tone of his voice I could almost have fancied he thought the proverb was held as an article of faith by the Teutonic races in general.

"I do not believe it," he repeated reflectively. "There is no such thing as an angel ' passing '; it is a misuse of terms. If there are such things as angels, their changes of place cannot be described as motion, seeing that from the very nature of things such changes must be instantaneous, not involving time as a necessary element. Have you ever thought much about angels? By-the-bye, pardon my abruptness, but as there is no one to introduce us, what is your name?"

"My name is Griggs — Paul Griggs. I am an American, but was born in Italy. I know your name is Isaacs; but, frankly, I do not comprehend how you came by the appellation, for I do not believe you are either English, American, or Jewish of origin."

"Quite right," he replied, "I am neither Yankee, Jew, nor beef-eater; in fact, I am not a European at all. And since you probably would not guess my nationality, I will tell you that I am a Persian, a pure Iranian, a degenerate descendant of Zoroaster, as you call him, though by religion I follow the prophet, whose name be blessed," he added, with an expression of face I did not then understand. "I call myself Isaacs for convenience in business. There is no concealment about it, as many know my story; but it has an attractive Semitic twang that suits my occupation, and is simpler and shorter for Englishmen to write than Abdul Hafizben-Isâk, which is my lawful name."

"Since you lay sufficient store by your business to have been willing to change your name, may I inquire what your business is? It seems to be a lucrative one, to judge by the accumulations of wealth you have allowed me a glimpse of."

"Yes. Wealth is my occupation. I am a dealer in precious stones and similar objects of value. Some day I will show you my diamonds; they are worth seeing."

It is no uncommon thing to meet in India men of all Asiatic nationalities buying and selling stones of worth, and enriching themselves in the business. I supposed he had come with a caravan by way of Baghdad, and had settled. But again, his perfect command of English, as pure as though he had been educated at Eton and Oxford, his extremely careful, though quiet, English dress, and especially his polished manners, argued a longer residence in the European civilisation of his adopted home than agreed with his young looks, supposing him to have come to India at sixteen or seventeen. A pardonable curiosity led me to remark this.

"You must have come here very young," I said. "A thoroughbred Persian does not learn to speak English like a university man, and to quote German

c

proverbs, in a residence of a few years; unless, indeed, he possess the secret by which the initiated absorb knowledge without effort, and assimilate it without the laborious process of intellectual digestion."

"I am older than I look — considerably. I have been in India twelve years, and with a natural talent for languages, stimulated by constant intercourse with Englishmen who know their own speech well, I have succeeded, as you say, in acquiring a certain fluency and mastery of accent. I have had an adventurous life enough. I see no reason why I should not tell you something of it, especially as you are not English, and can therefore hear me with an unprejudiced ear. But, really, do you care for a yarn?"

I begged him to proceed, and I beckoned the servant to arrange our pipes, that we might not be disturbed. When this was done, Isaacs began.

"I am going to try and make a long story short. We Persians like to listen to long stories, as we like to sit and look on at a wedding nautch. But we are radically averse to dancing or telling long tales ourselves, so I shall condense as much as possible. I was born in Persia, of Persian parents, as I told you, but I will not burden your memory with names you are not familiar with. My father was a merchant in prosperous circumstances, and a man of no mean learning in Arabic and Persian literature. I soon showed a strong taste for books, and every opportunity was given me for pursuing my inclinations in this respect. At the early age of twelve I was kidnapped by a party of slave-dealers, and carried off into Roum — Turkey you call it. I will not dwell upon my tears and indignation. We travelled rapidly, and my captors treated me well, as they invariably do their prizes, well knowing how much of the value of a slave depends on his plump and sleek condition when brought to market. In Istamboul I was soon disposed of, my fair skin and accomplishments as a writer and a singer of Persian songs fetching a high price.

"It is no uncommon thing for boys to be stolen and sold in this way. A rich pacha will pay almost anything. The fate of such slaves is not generally a happy one." Isaacs paused a moment, and drew in two or three long breaths of smoke. "Do you see that bright star in the south?" he said, pointing with his long jewel-set mouthpiece.

"Yes. It must be Sirius."

"That is my star. Do you believe in the agency of the stars in human affairs? Of course you do not; you are a European: how should you? But to proceed. The stars, or the fates or Kāli, or whatever you like to term your kismet, your portion of good and evil, allotted me a somewhat happier existence than generally falls to the share of young slaves in Roum. I was bought by an old man of great wealth and of still greater learning, who was so taken with my proficiency in Arabic and in writing that he resolved to make of me a pupil instead of a servant to carry his coffee and pipe, or a slave to bear the heavier burden of his vices. Nothing better could have happened to me. I was installed in his house and treated with exemplary kindness, though he kept me rigorously at work with my books. I need not tell you that with such a master I made fair progress, and that at the age of twenty-one I was, for a Turk, a young man of remarkably good education. Then my master died suddenly, and I was thrown into great distress. I was of course nothing but a slave, and liable to be sold at any time. I escaped. Active and enduring, though never possessing any vast muscular strength, I bore with ease the hardships of a long journey on foot with little food and scant lodging. Falling in with a band of pilgrims, I recognised the wisdom of joining them on their march to Mecca. I was, of course, a sound Mohammedan, as I am to this day, and my knowledge of the Koran soon gained me some reputation in the caravan. I was considered a creditable addition, and altogether an eligible pilgrim. My exceptional physique protected me from the disease and exhaustion of which not a few of our number died by the wayside, and the other pilgrims, in consideration of my youth and piety, gave me willingly the few handfuls of rice and dates that I needed to support life and strength.

"You have read about Mecca; and your *hadji* barber, who of course has been there, has doubtless

related his experiences to you scores of times in the
plains, as he does everywhere. As you may
imagine, I had no intention of returning towards
Roum with my companions. When I had fulfilled
all the observances required, I made my way to Yed-
dah and shipped on board an Arabian craft, touching
at Mocha, and bearing coffee to Bombay. I had to
work my passage, and as I had no experience of the
sea, save in the caïques of the Golden Horn, you
will readily conceive that the captain of the vessel
had plenty of fault to find. But my agility and
quick comprehension stood me in good stead, and in
a few days I had learned enough to haul on a rope or
to reef the great latteen sails as well as any of them.
The knowledge that I was just returning from a
pilgrimage to Mecca obtained for me also a certain
respect among the crew. It makes very little difference what the trade, business, or branch of learning; in mechanical labour, or intellectual effort, the
educated man is always superior to the common
labourer. One who is in the habit of applying his
powers in the right way will carry his system into
any occupation, and it will help him as much to
handle a rope as to write a poem.

"At last we landed in Bombay. I was in a
wretched condition. What little clothes I had had
were in tatters; hard work and little food had made
me even thinner than my youthful age and slight
frame tolerated. I had in all about three pence
money in small copper coins, carefully hoarded

against a rainy day. I could not speak a word of
the Indian dialects, still less of English, and I knew
no one save the crew of the vessel I had come in, as
poor as I, but saved from starvation by the slender
pittance allowed them on land. I wandered about
all day through the bazaars, occasionally speaking to
some solemn looking old shopkeeper or long-bearded
Mussulman, who, I hoped, might understand a little
Arabic. But not one did I find. At evening I
bathed in the tank of a temple full from the recent
rains, and I lay down supperless to sleep on the steps
of the great mosque. As I lay on the hard stones I
looked up to my star, and took comfort, and slept.
That night a dream came to me. I thought I was
still awake and lying on the steps, watching the
wondrous ruler of my fate. And as I looked he
glided down from his starry throne with an easy
swinging motion, like a soap-bubble settling to the
earth. And the star came and poised among the
branches of the palm-tree over the tank, opalescent,
unearthly, heart shaking. His face was as the face
of the prophet, whose name be blessed, and his limbs
were as the limbs of the Hameshaspenthas of old.
Garments he had none, being of heavenly birth, but
he was clothed with light as with a garment, and the
crest of his silver hair was to him a crown of glory.
And he spoke with the tongues of a thousand lutes,
sweet strong tones, that rose and fell on the night
air as the song of a lover beneath the lattice of his
mistress, the song of the mighty star wooing the

beautiful sleeping earth. And then he looked on me and said: 'Abdul Hafiz, be of good cheer. I am with thee and will not forsake thee, even to the day when thou shalt pass over the burning bridge of death. Thou shalt touch the diamond of the rivers and the pearl of the sea, and they shall abide with thee, and great shall be thy wealth. And the sunlight which is in the diamond shall warm thee and comfort thy heart; and the moonlight which is in the pearl shall give thee peace in the night-time, and thy children shall be to thee a garland of roses in the land of the unbeliever.' And the star floated down from the palm-branches and touched me with his hand, and breathed upon my lips the cool breath of the outer firmament, and departed. Then I awoke and saw him again in his place far down the horizon, and he was alone, for the dawn was in the sky and the lesser lights were extinguished. And I rose from the stony stairway that seemed like a bed of flowers for the hopeful dream, and I turned westward, and praised Allah, and went my way.

"The sun being up, all was life, and the life in me spoke of a most capacious appetite. So I cast about for a shop where I might buy a little food with my few coppers, and seeing a confectioner spreading out his wares, I went near and took stock of the queer balls of flour and sugar, and strange oily-looking sweetmeats. Having selected what I thought would be within my modest means, I addressed the shopkeeper to call his attention, though I knew he would not understand me, and I touched with my hand the article I wanted, showing with the other some of the small coins I had. As soon as I touched the sweetmeats the man became very angry, and bounding from his seat called his neighbours together, and they all shouted and screamed at me, and called a man I thought to be a soldier, though he looked more like an ape in his long loose trousers of dirty black, and his untidy red turban, under which cumbrous garments his thin and stunted frame seemed even blacker and more contemptible than nature had made them. I afterwards discovered him to be one of the Bombay police. He seized me by the arm, and I, knowing I had done no wrong, and curious to discover, if possible, what the trouble was, accompanied him whither he led me. After waiting many hours in a kind of little shed where there were more policemen, I was brought before an Englishman. Of course all attempts at explanation were useless. I could speak not a word of anything but Arabic and Persian, and no one present understood either. At last, when I was in despair, trying to muster a few words of Greek I had learned in Istamboul, and failing signally therein, an old man with a long beard looked curiously in at the door of the crowded court. Some instinct told me to appeal to him, and I addressed him in Arabic. To my infinite relief he replied in that tongue, and volunteered to be interpreter. In a few moments I learned that my crime was that I had *touched* the sweetmeats on the counter.

"In India, as you who have lived here doubtless know, it is a criminal offence, punishable by fine or imprisonment, for a non-Hindu person to defile the food of even the lowest caste man. To touch one sweetmeat in a trayful defiles the whole baking, rendering it all unfit for the use of any Hindu, no matter how mean. Knowing nothing of caste and its prejudices, it was with the greatest difficulty that the *moolah*, who was trying to help me out of my trouble, could make me comprehend wherein my wrong-doing lay, and that the English courts, being obliged in their own interest to uphold and protect the caste practices of the Hindus, at the risk of another mutiny, could not make any exception in favour of a stranger unacquainted with Indian customs. So the Englishman who presided said he would have to inflict a fine, but being a very young man, not yet hardened to the despotic ways of Eastern life, he generously paid the fine himself, and gave me a rupee as a present into the bargain. It was only two shillings, but as I had not had so much money for months I was as grateful as though it had been a hundred. If I ever meet him I will requite him, for I owe him all I now possess.

"My case being dismissed, I left the court with the old *moolah*, who took me to his house and inquired of my story, having first given me a good meal of rice and sweetmeats, and that greatest of luxuries, a little pot of fragrant Mocha coffee; he sat in silence while I ate, ministering to my wants, and evidently pleased with the good he was doing. Then he brought out a package of *birris*, those little cigarettes rolled in leaves that they smoke in Bombay, and I told him what had happened to me. I implored him to put me in the way of obtaining some work by which I could at least support life, and he promised to do so, begging me to stay with him until I should be independent. The day following I was engaged to pull a punkah in the house of an English lawyer connected with an immense lawsuit involving one of the Mohammedan principalities. For this irksome work I was to receive six rupees — twelve shillings — monthly, but before the month was up I was transferred, by the kindness of the English lawyer and the good offices of my co-religionist the *moolah*, to the retinue of the Nizam of Haiderabad, then in Bombay. Since that time I have never known want.

"I soon mastered enough of the dialects to suit my needs, and applied myself to the study of English, for which opportunities were not lacking. At the end of two years I could speak the language enough to be understood, and my accent from the first was a matter of surprise to all; I had also saved out of my gratuities about one hundred rupees. Having been conversant with the qualities of many kinds of precious stones from my youth up, I determined to invest my economies in a diamond or a pearl. Before long I struck a bargain with an old *marwarri* over a small stone, of which I thought he misjudged the value, owing to the rough cutting. The fellow was cun ning and hard in his dealings, but my superior knowledge of diamonds gave me the advantage. I paid him ninety-three rupees for the little gem, and sold it again in a month for two hundred to a young English 'collector and magistrate,' who wanted to make his wife a present. I bought a larger stone, and again made nearly a hundred per cent on the money. Then I bought two, and so on, until having accumulated sufficient capital, I bade farewell to the Court of the Nizam, where my salary never exceeded sixteen rupees a month as scribe and Arabic interpreter, and I went my way with about two thousand rupees in cash and precious stones. I came northwards, and finally settled in Delhi, where I set up as a dealer in gems and objects of intrinsic value. It is now twelve years since I landed in Bombay. I have never soiled my hands with usury, though I have twice advanced large sums at legal interest for purposes I am not at liberty to disclose; I have never cheated a customer or underrated a gem I bought of a poor man, and my wealth, as you may judge from what you have seen, is considerable. Moreover, though in constant intercourse with Hindus and English, I have not forfeited my title to be called a true believer and a follower of the prophet, whose name be blessed."

Isaacs ceased speaking, and presently the waning moon rose pathetically over the crest of the mountains with that curiously doleful look she wears after the full is past, as if weeping over the loss of her better half.   The wind rose and soughed drearily through the rhododendrons and the pines; and Kiramat Ali, the pipe-bearer, shivered audibly as he drew his long cloth uniform around him.   We rose and entered my friend's rooms, where the warmth of the lights, the soft rugs and downy cushions, invited us temptingly to sit down and continue our conversation.   But it was late, for Isaacs, like a true Oriental, had not hurried himself over his narrative, and it had been nine o'clock when we sat down to smoke.   So I bade him good-night, and, musing on all I had heard and seen, retired to my own apartments, glancing at Sirius and at the unhappy-looking moon before I turned in from the verandah.

CHAPTER II.

In India — in the plains — people rise before dawn, and it is not till after some weeks' residence in the cooler atmosphere of the mountains that they return to the pernicious habit of allowing the sun to be before them. The hours of early morning, when one either mopes about in loose flannel clothes, or goes for a gallop on the green *maidán,* are without exception the most delicious of the day. I shall have occasion hereafter to describe the morning's proceedings in the plains. On the day after the events recorded in the last chapter I awoke as usual at five o'clock, and meandered out on to the verandah to have a look at the hills, so novel and delicious a sight after the endless flats of the northwest provinces. It was still nearly dark, but there was a faint light in the east, which rapidly grew as I watched it, till, turning the angle of the house, I distinguished a snow-peak over the tops of the dark rhododendrons, and, while I gazed, the first tinge of distant dawning caught the summit, and the beautiful hill blushed, as a fair woman, at the kiss of the awakening sun. The old story, the heaven wooing the earth with a wondrous shower of gold.

"Prati 'shya sunarī janī"—the exquisite lines of
the old Vedic hymn to the dawn maiden, rose to my
lips. I had never appreciated or felt their truth
down in the dusty plains, but here, on the free hills,
the glad welcoming of the morning light seemed to
run through every fibre, as thousands of years ago
the same joyful thrill of returning life inspired the
pilgrim fathers of the Aryan race. Almost unconsciously, I softly intoned the hymn, as I had heard
my old Brahmin teacher in Allahabad when he came
and sat under the porch at daybreak, until I was
ready for him —

> The lissome heavenly maiden here,
> Forth flashing from her sister's arms,
> High heaven's daughter, now is come.
>
> In rosy garments, shining like
> A swift bay mare ; the twin knights' friend,
> Mother of all our herds of kine.
>
> Yea, thou art she, the horseman's friend ;
> Of grazing cattle mother thou,
> All wealth is thine, thou blushing dawn.
>
> Thou who hast driven the foeman back,
> With praise we call on thee to wake
> In tender reverence, beauteous one.
>
> The spreading beams of morning light
> Are countless as our hosts of kine,
> They fill the atmosphere of space.
>
> Filling the sky, thou openedst wide
> The gates of night, thou glorious dawn—
> Rejoicing run thy daily race !

The heaven above thy rays have filled,
The broad belovèd room of air,
O splendid, brightest maid of morn!

I went indoors again to attend to my correspondence, and presently a gorgeously liveried white-
bearded *chuprassie* appeared at the door, and bending
low as he touched his hand to his forehead, intimated
that "if the great lord of the earth, the protector of
the poor, would turn his ear to the humblest of his
servants, he would hear of something to his advantage."

So saying, he presented a letter from the official
with whom I had to do, an answer to my note of
the previous afternoon, requesting an interview. In
due course, therefore, the day wore on, and I trans-
acted my business, returned to "tiffin," and then
went up to my rooms for a little quiet. I might
have been there an hour, smoking and dreaming over
a book, when the servant announced a sahib who
wanted to see me, and Isaacs walked in, redolent of
the sunshine without, his luminous eyes shining
brightly in the darkened room. I was delighted, for
I felt my wits stagnating in the unwonted idleness
of the autumn afternoon, and the book I had taken
up was not conducive to wakefulness or brilliancy.
It was a pleasant surprise too. It is not often that
an hotel acquaintance pushes an intimacy much, and
besides I had feared my silence during the previous
evening might have produced the impression of indifference, on which reflection I had resolved to make
myself agreeable at our next meeting.

Truly, had I asked myself the cause of a certain attraction I felt for Mr. Isaacs, it would have been hard to find an answer. I am generally extremely shy of persons who begin an acquaintance by making confidences, and, in spite of Isaacs' charm of manner, I had certainly speculated on his reasons for suddenly telling an entire stranger his whole story. My southern birth had not modified the northern character born in me, though it gave me the more urbane veneer of the Italian; and the early study of Larochefoucauld and his school had not predisposed me to an unlimited belief in the disinterestedness of mankind. Still there was something about the man which seemed to sweep away unbelief and cynicism and petty distrust, as the bright mountain freshet sweeps away the wretched little mud puddles and the dust and impurities from the bed of a half dry stream. It was a new sensation and a novel era in my experience of humanity, and the desire to get behind that noble forehead, and see its inmost workings, was strong beyond the strength of puny doubts and preconceived prejudice. Therefore, when Isaacs appeared, looking like the sun-god for all his quiet dress of gray and his unobtrusive manner, I felt the "little thrill of pleasure" so aptly compared by Swinburne to the soft touch of a hand stroking the outer hair.

"What a glorious day after all that detestable rain!" were his first words. "Three mortal months of water, mud, and Mackintoshes, not to mention the agreeable sensation of being glued to a wet saddle with your feet in water-buckets, and mountain torrents running up and down the inside of your sleeves, in defiance of the laws of gravitation; such is life in the monsoon. Pah!" And he threw himself down on a cane chair and stretched out his dainty feet, so that the sunlight through the crack of the half-closed door might fall comfortingly on his toes, and remind him that it was fine outside.

"What have you been doing all day?" I asked, for lack of a better question, not having yet recovered from the mental stagnation induced by the last number of the serial story I had been reading.

"Oh — I don't know. Are you married?" he asked irrelevantly.

"God forbid!" I answered reverently, and with some show of feeling.

"Amen," was the answer. "As for me — I am, and my wives have been quarrelling."

"Your wives! Did I understand you to use the plural number?"

"Why, yes. I have three; that is the worst of it. If there were only two, they might get on better. You know 'two are company and three are none,' as your proverb has it." He said this reflectively, as if meditating a reduction in the number.

The application of the proverb to such a case was quite new in my recollection. As for the plurality of my friend's conjugal relations, I remembered he was a Mohammedan, and my surprise vanished.

D

Isaacs was lost in meditation. Suddenly he rose to his feet, and took a cigarette from the table.

"I wonder" — the match would not light, and he struggled a moment with another. Then he blew a great cloud of smoke, and sat down in a different chair — "I wonder whether a fourth would act as a fly-wheel," and he looked straight at me, as if asking my opinion.

I had never been in direct relations with a Mussulman of education and position. To be asked point-blank whether I thought four wives better than three on general principles, and quite independently of the contemplated spouse, was a little embarrassing. He seemed perfectly capable of marrying another before dinner for the sake of peace, and I do not believe he would have considered it by any means a bad move.

"Diamond cut diamond," I said. "You too have proverbs, and one of them is that a man is better sitting than standing; better lying than sitting; better dead than lying down. Now I should apply that same proverb to marriage. A man is, by a similar successive reasoning, better with no wife at all than with three."

His subtle mind caught the flaw instantly. "To be without a wife at all would be about as conducive to happiness as to be dead. Negative happiness, very negative."

"Negative happiness is better than positive discomfort."

"Come, come," he answered, "we are bandying terms and words, as if empty breath amounted to anything but inanity. Do you really doubt the value of the institution of marriage?"

"No. Marriage is a very good thing when two people are so poor that they depend on each other, mutually, for daily bread, or if they are rich enough to live apart. For a man in my own position marriage would be the height of folly; an act of rashness only second to deliberate suicide. Now, you are rich, and if you had but one wife, she living in Delhi and you in Simla, you would doubtless be very happy."

"There is something in that," said Isaacs. "She might mope and beat the servants, but she could not quarrel if she were alone. Besides, it is so much easier to look after one camel than three. I think I must try it."

There was a pause, during which he seemed settling the destiny of the two who were to be shelved in favour of a monogamic experiment. Presently he asked if I had brought any horses, and hearing I had not, offered me a mount, and proposed we should ride round Jako, and perhaps, if there were time, take a look at Annandale in the valley, where there was polo, and a racing-ground. I gladly accepted, and Isaacs despatched one of my servants, the faithful Kiramat Ali, to order the horses. Meantime the conversation turned on the expedition to Kabul to avenge the death of Cavagnari. I found Isaacs held

the same view that I did in regard to the whole business.   He thought the sending of four Englishmen,
with a handful of native soldiers of the guide regiment to protect them, a piece of unparalleled folly,
on a par with the whole English policy in regard to
Afghanistan.

"You English — pardon me, I forgot you did not
belong to them — the English, then, have performed
most of their great acts of valour as a direct consequence of having wantonly exposed themselves in
situations where no sane man would have placed
himself.   Look at Balaclava; think of the things
they did in the mutiny, and in the first Afghan war;
look at the mutiny itself, the result of a hair-brained
idea that a country like India could be held for ever
with no better defences than the trustworthiness of
native officers, and the gratitude of the people for
the 'kindly British rule.'   Poor Cavagnari! when he
was here last summer, before leaving on his mission,
he said several times he should never come back.
And yet no better man could have been chosen,
whether for politics or fighting; if only they had
had the sense to protect him."

Having delivered himself of this eulogy, my friend
dropped his exhausted cigarette, lit another, and
appeared again absorbed in the triangulation of his
matrimonial problem.   I imagined him weighing the
question whether he should part with Zobeida and
Zuleika and keep Amina, or send Zuleika and Amina
about their business, and keep Zobeida to be a light

in his household. At last Kiramat Ali, on the watch in the verandah, announced the saices with the horses, and we descended.

I had expected that a man of Isaacs' tastes and habits would not be stingy about his horseflesh, and so was prepared for the character of the animals that awaited us. They were two superb Arab stallions, one of them being a rare specimen of the weight-carrying kind, occasionally seen in the far East. Small head, small feet, and feather-tailed, but broad in the quarters and deep in the chest, able to carry a twelve-stone man for hours at the stretching, even gallop, that never trembles and never tires; sure-footed as a mule, and tender-tempered as a baby.

So we mounted the gentle creatures and rode away. The mountain on which Simla is situated has a double summit, like a Swiss peak, the one higher than the other. On the lower height and the neck between the two is built the town, and the bungalows used as offices and residences for the Government officials cover a very considerable area. "Jako," the higher eminence, is thickly covered with a forest of primeval rhododendrons and pines, and though there are outlying bungalows and villas scattered about among the trees near the town, they are so far back from the main road, reserved as I have said for the use of the Viceroy, as far as driving is concerned, that they are not seen in riding along the shady way; and on the opposite side, where the trees are thin, the magnificent view looks far out over the spurs of the mountains, the only human habitation visible being a Catholic convent, which rears its little Italian *campanile* against the blue sky, and rather adds to the beauty of the scene than otherwise. As we rode along we continued our talk about the new Afghan war, though neither of us was very much in the humour for animated conversation. The sweet scent of the pines, the matchless motion of the Arab, and the joyous feeling that the worst part of the tropical year was passed, were enough for me, and I drank in the high, rarefied air, with the intense delight of a man who has been smothered with dust and heat, and then steamed to a jelly by a spring and summer in the plains of Hindustan.

The road abounds in sharp turns, and I, as the heavier mount, rode on the inside as we went round the mountain. On reaching the open part on the farther side, we drew rein for a moment to look down at the deep valleys, now dark with the early shade, at the higher peaks red with the westering sun, and at the black masses of foliage, through which some giant trunk here and there caught a lingering ray of the departing light. Then, as we felt the cool of the evening coming on, we wheeled and scampered along the level stretch, stirrup to stirrup and knee to knee. The sharp corner at the end pulled us up, but before we had quite reined in our horses, as delighted as we to have a couple of minutes' straight run, we swung past the angle and cannoned into a man ambling peaceably along with his reins on one finger and his

large gray felt hat flapping at the back of his neck.
There was a moment's confusion, profuse apologies
on our part, and some ill-concealed annoyance on the
part of the victim, who was, however, only a little
jostled and taken by surprise.

"Really, sir," he began. "Oh! Mr. Isaacs. No
harm done, I assure you, that is, not much. Bad
thing riding fast round corners. No harm, no harm,
not much. How are you?" all in a breath.

"How d'ye do! Mr. Ghyrkins; my friend Mr.
Griggs."

"The real offender," I added in a conciliatory tone,
for I had kept my place on the inside.

"Mr. Griggs?" said Mr. Currie Ghyrkins. "Mr.
Griggs of Allahabad? *Daily Howler?* Yes, yes,
corresponded; glad to see you in the flesh."

I did not think he looked particularly glad. He
was a Revenue Commissioner residing in Mudnugger; a rank Conservative; a regular old "John Company" man, with whom I had had more than one tiff
in the columns of the *Howler*, leading to considerable
correspondence.

"I trust that our collision in the flesh has had no
worse results than our tilts in print, Mr. Ghyrkins?"

"Not at all. Oh don't mention it. Bad enough,
though, but no harm done, none whatever," pulling
up and looking at me as he pronounced the last two
words with a peculiarly English slowness after a
very quick sentence.

While he was speaking, I was aware of a pair of

riders walking their horses toward us, and apparently struggling to suppress their amusement at the mishap to the old gentleman, which they must have witnessed. In truth, Mr. Ghyrkins, who was stout and rode a broad-backed obese "tat," can have presented no very dignified appearance, for he was jerked half out of the saddle by the concussion, and his near leg, returning to its place, had driven his nether garment half way to his knee, while the large felt hat was settling back on to his head at a rakish angle, and his coat collar had gone well up the back of his neck.

"Dear uncle," said the lady as she rode up, "I hope you are not hurt?" She was very handsome as she sat there trying not to laugh. A lithe figure in a gray habit and a broad-brimmed hat, fair as a Swede, but with dark eyes and heavy lashes. Just then she was showing her brilliant teeth, ostensibly in delight at her dear uncle's escape, and her whole expression was animated and amused. Her companion was a soldierly looking young Englishman, with a heavy moustache and a large nose. A certain devil-may-care look about his face was attractive as he sat carelessly watching us. I noticed his long stirrups and the curb rein hanging loose, while he held the snaffle, and concluded he was a cavalry officer. Isaacs bowed low to the lady and wheeled his horse. She replied by a nod, indifferent enough; but as he turned, her eyes instantly went back to him, and a pleasant thoughtful look passed over her face, which betrayed at least a trifling interest in the stranger, if stranger he were.

All this time Mr. Ghyrkins was talking and asking questions of me. When had I come? what brought me here? how long would I stay? and so on, showing that whether friendly or not he had an interest in my movements. In answering his questions I found an opportunity of calling the Queen the "Empress," of lauding Lord Beaconsfield's policy in India, and of congratulating Mr. Ghyrkins upon the state of his district, with which he had nothing to do, of course; but he swallowed the bait, all in a breath, as he seemed to do everything. Then he introduced us.

"Katharine, you know Mr. Isaacs; Mr. Griggs, Miss Westonhaugh, Lord Steepleton Kildare, Mr. Isaacs."

We bowed and rode back together over the straight piece we passed before the encounter. Isaacs and the Englishman walked their horses on each side of Miss Westonhaugh, and Ghyrkins and I brought up the rear. I tried to turn the conversation to Isaacs, but with little result.

"Yes, yes, good fellow Isaacs, for a fire-worshipper, or whatever he is. Good judge of a horse. Lots of rupees too. Queer fish. By-the-bye, Mr. Griggs, this new expedition is going to cost us something handsome, eh?"

"Why, yes. I doubt whether you will get off under ten millions sterling. And where is it to come from? You will have a nice time making your assessments in Bengal, Mr. Ghyrkins, and we shall have an income-tax and all sorts of agreeable things."

"Income-tax? Well, I think not. You see, Mr. Griggs, it would hit the members of the council, so they won't do it, for their own sakes, and the Viceroy too. Ha, ha, how do you think Lord Lytton would like an income-tax, eh?" And the old fellow chuckled.

We reached the end of the straight, and Isaacs reined in and bid Miss Westonhaugh and her companion good evening. I bowed from where I was, and took Mr. Ghyrkins' outstretched hand. He was in a good humour again, and called out to us to come and see him, as we rode away. I thought to myself I certainly would; and we paced back, crossing the open stretch for the third time.

It was almost dark under the trees as we re-entered the woods; I pulled out a cheroot and lit it. Isaacs did the same, and we walked our horses along in silence. I was thinking of the little picture I had just seen. The splendid English girl on her thoroughbred beside the beautiful Arab steed and his graceful rider. What a couple, I thought: what noble specimens of great races. Why did not this fiery young Persian, with his wealth, his beauty, and his talents, wed some such wife as that, some high-bred Englishwoman, who should love him and give him home and children — and, I was forced to add, commonplace happiness? How often does it happen that some train of thought, unacknowledged almost to ourselves, runs abruptly into a blind alley; especially when we try to plan out the future life of some one else, or to sketch for him what we should call happiness. The accidental confronting of two individuals pleases the eye, we unite them in our imagination, carrying on the picture before us, and suddenly we find ourselves in a quagmire of absurd incongruities. Now what could be more laughable than to suppose the untamed, and probably untameable young man at my side, with his three wives, his notions about the stars and his Mussulman faith, bound for life to a girl like Miss Westonhaugh? A wise man of the East trying to live the life of an English country gentleman, hunting in pink and making speeches on the local hustings! I smiled to myself in the dark and puffed at my cigar.

Meanwhile Isaacs was palpably uneasy. First he kicked his feet free of the stirrups, and put them back again. Then he hummed a few words of a Persian song and let his cigar go out, after which he swore loudly in Arabic at the eternal matches that never would light. Finally he put his horse into a hand gallop, which could not last on such a road in the dark, and at last he broke down completely in his efforts to do impossible things, and began talking to me.

"You know Mr. Ghyrkins by correspondence, then?"

"Yes, and by controversy. And you, I see, know Miss Westonhaugh?"

"Yes; what do you think of her?"

"A charming creature of her type. Fair and

English, she will be fat at thirty-five, and will probably paint at forty, but at present she is perfection —of her kind of course," I added, not wishing to engage my friend in the defence of his three wives on the score of beauty.

"I see very little of Englishwomen," said Isaacs. "My position is peculiar, and though the men, many of whom I know quite intimately, often ask me to their houses, I fancy when I meet their women I can detect a certain scorn of my nationality, a certain undefinable manner toward me, by which I suppose they mean to convey to my obtuse comprehension that I am but a step better than a 'native'—a 'nigger' in fact, to use the term they love so well. So I simply avoid them, as a rule, for my temper is hasty. Of course I understand it well enough; they are brought up or trained by their fathers and husbands to regard the native Indian as an inferior being, an opinion in which, on the whole, I heartily concur. But they go a step farther and include all Asiatics in the same category. I do not choose to be confounded with a race I consider worn out and effete. As for the men, it is different. They know I am rich and influential in many ways that are useful to them now, and they hope that the fortunes of war or revolution may give them a chance of robbing me hereafter, in which they are mistaken. Now there is our stout friend, whom we nearly brought to grief a few minutes ago; he is always extremely civil, and never meets me that he does not renew his invitation to visit him."

"I should like to see something more of Mr. Currie Ghyrkins myself. I do not believe he is half as bad as I thought. Do you ever go there?"

"Sometimes. Yes, on second thoughts I believe I call on Mr. Currie Ghyrkins pretty often." Then after a pause he added, "I like her."

I pointed out the confusion of genders. Isaacs must have smiled to himself in the gloom, but he answered quietly —

"I mean Miss Westonhaugh. I like her — yes, I am quite sure I do. She is beautiful and sensible, though if she stays here much longer she will be like all the rest. We will go and see them to-morrow. Here we are; just in time for dinner. Come and smoke afterwards."

CHAPTER III.

A LOOSE robe of light material from Kashmir thrown around him, Isaacs half sat, half lay, on the soft dark cushions in the corner of his outer room. His feet were slipperless, Eastern fashion, and his head covered with an embroidered cap of curious make. By the yellow light of the hanging lamps he was reading an Arabic book, and his face wore a puzzled look that sat strangely on the bold features. As I entered the book fell back on the cushion, sinking deep into the down by its weight, and one of the heavy gold clasps clanged sharply as it turned. He looked up, but did not rise, and greeted me, smiling, with the Arabic salutation —

"Peace be with you!"

"And with you, peace," I answered in the same tongue. He smiled again at my unfamiliar pronunciation. I established myself on the divan near him, and inquired whether he had arrived at any satisfactory solution of his domestic difficulties.

"My father," he said, "upon whom be peace, had but one wife, my mother. You know Mussulmans are allowed four lawful wives. Here is the passage in the beginning of the fourth chapter, 'If ye fear

that ye shall not act with equity towards orphans of
the female sex, take in marriage of such other women
as please you, two, or three, or four, and not more.
But, if ye fear that ye cannot act equitably towards
so many, marry one only, or the slaves which ye shall
have acquired.'

"The first part of this passage," continued Isaacs,
"is disputed; I mean the words referring to orphans.
But the latter portion is plain enough. When the
apostle warns those who fear they ' cannot act equitably towards so many,' I am sure that in his wisdom
he meant something more by 'equitable' treatment
than the mere supplying of bodily wants. He meant
us to so order our households that there should be no
jealousies, no heart-burnings, no unnecessary troub-
ling of the peace. Now woman is a thing of the
devil, jealous; and to manage a number of such creatures so that they shall be even passably harmonious
among themselves is a fearful task, soul-wearying,
heart-hardening, never-ending, leading to no result."

"Just what I told you; a man is better with no
wife at all than with three. But why do you talk
about such matters with me, an unbeliever, a Christian, who, in the words of your prophet, ' shall
swallow down nothing but fire into my belly, and
shall broil in raging flames ' when I die? Surely it
is contrary to the custom of your co-religionists; and
how can you expect an infidel Frank to give you
advice?"

"I don't," laconically replied my host.

"Besides, with your views of women in general, their vocation, their aims, and their future state, is it at all likely that we should ever arrive at even a fair discussion of marriage and marriage laws? With us, women have souls, and, what is a great deal more, seem likely to have votes. They certainly have the respectful and courteous service of a large proportion of the male sex. You call a woman a thing of the devil; we call her an angel from heaven; and though some eccentric persons like myself refuse to ally themselves for life with any woman, I confess, as far as I am concerned, that it is because I cannot contemplate the constant society of an angel with the degree of appreciation such a privilege justly deserves; and I suspect that most confirmed bachelors, knowingly or unconsciously, think as I do. The Buddhists are not singular in their theory that permanent happiness should be the object."

"They say," said Isaacs, quickly interrupting, "that the aim of the ignorant is pleasure; the pursuit of the wise, happiness. Pray, under which category would you class marriage? I suppose it comes under one or the other."

"I cannot say I see the force of that. Look at your own case, since you have introduced it."

"Never mind my own case. I mean with your ideas of one wife, and heavenly woman, and voting, and domestic joy, and all the rest of it. Take the ideal creature you rave about —— "

"I never rave about anything."

"Take the fascinating female you describe, and for the sake of argument imagine yourself very poor or very rich, since you would not enter wedlock in your present circumstances. Suppose you married your object of 'courteous service and respectful adoration;' which should you say you would attain thereby, pleasure or happiness?"

"Pleasure is but the refreshment that cheers us in the pursuit of true happiness," I answered, hoping to evade the direct question by a sententious phrase.

"I will not let you off so easily. You shall answer my question," he said. He looked full at me with a deep searching gaze that seemed hardly warranted by the lightness of the argument. I hesitated, and he impatiently leaned forward, uncrossing his legs and clasping his hands over one knee to bring himself nearer to me.

"Pleasure or happiness?" he repeated, "which is it to be?"

A sudden light flashed over my obscured intellect.

"Both," I answered. "Could you see the ideal woman as I would fain paint her to you, you would understand me better. The pleasure you enjoy in the society of a noble and beautiful woman should be but the refreshment by the wayside as you journey through life together. The day will come when she will be beautiful no longer, only noble and good, and true to you as to herself; and then, if pleasure has been to you what it should be, you will find that in the happiness attained it is no longer counted, or needed, or thought of. It will have served its end, as the crib holds the ship in her place while she is building; and when your white-winged vessel has smoothly glided off into the great ocean of happiness, the crib and the stocks and the artificial supports will fall to pieces and be forgotten for ever. Yet have they had a purpose, and have borne a very important part in the life of your ship."

Having heard me attentively till I had finished, Isaacs relaxed his hold on his knee and threw himself back on the cushions, as if to entrench himself for a better fight. I had made an impression on him, but he was not the man to own it easily. Presumably to gain time, he called for hookahs and sherbet, and though the servants moved noiselessly in preparing them, their presence was an interruption.

When we were settled again he had taken a nearly upright position on the couch, and as he pulled at the long tube his face assumed that stolid look of Oriental indifference which is the most discouraging shower-bath to the persuasive powers. I had really no interest in converting him to my own point of view about women. Honestly, was it my own point of view at all? Would anything under heaven induce me, Paul Griggs, rich, or poor, or comfortably off, to marry any one — Miss Westonhaugh, for instance? Probably not. But then my preference for single blessedness did not prevent me from believing that women have souls. That morning the question of the marriage of the whole universe had been a matter of the utmost indifference, and now I, a confirmed and hopelessly contented bachelor, was trying to convince a man with three wives that matrimony was a most excellent thing in its way, and that the pleasure of the honeymoon was but the faint introduction to the bliss of the silver wedding. It certainly must be Isaacs' own doing. He had launched on a voyage of discovery and had taken me in tow. I had a strong suspicion that he wanted to be convinced, and was playing indifference to soothe his conscience.

"Well," said I at last, "have you any fault to find with my reasoning or my simile?"

"With your simile — none. It is faultlessly perfect. You have not mixed up your metaphors in the least. Crib, stocks, ocean, ship — all correct, and very nautical. As for your reasoning, I do not believe there is anything in it. I do not believe that pleasure leads to happiness; I do not believe that a woman has a soul, and I deny the whole argument from beginning to end. There," he added with a smile that belied the brusqueness of his words, "that is my position. Talk me out of it if you can; the night is long, and my patience as that of the ass."

"I do not think this is a case for rigid application of logic. When the feelings are concerned — and where can they be more concerned than in our intercourse with women? — the only way to arrive at any conclusion is by a sort of trying-on process, imagining ourselves in the position indicated, and striving

to fancy how it would suit us.   Let us begin in that
way.   Suppose yourself unmarried, your three wives
and their children removed —— "

"Allah in his mercy grant it!" ejaculated Isaacs
with great fervour

" —— removed from the question altogether.   Then
imagine yourself thrown into daily conversation with
some beautiful woman who has read what you have
read, thought what you have thought, and dreamed
the dreams of a nobler destiny that have visited you
in waking and sleeping hours.   A woman who, as
she learned your strange story, should weep for the
pains you suffered and rejoice for the difficulties
overcome, who should understand your half spoken
thoughts and proudly sympathise in your unuttered
aspirations; in whom you might see the twin nature
to your own, and detect the strong spirit and the
brave soul, half revealed through the feminine gentleness and modesty that clothe her as with a garment.
Imagine all this, and then suppose it lay in your
power, was a question of choice, for you to take her
hand in yours and go through life and death together,
till death seem life for the joy of being united for
ever.   Suppose you married her — not to lock her up
in an indolent atmosphere of rosewater, narghyles,
and sweetmeats, to die of inanition or to pester you
to death with complaints and jealousies and inoppor-
tune caresses; but to be with you and help your life
when you most need help, by word and thought and
deed, to grow more and more a part of you, an essen-

tial element of you in action or repose, to part from which would be to destroy at a blow the whole fabric of your existence. Would you not say that with such a woman the transitory pleasure of early conversation and intercourse had been the stepping-stone to the lasting happiness of such a friendship as you could never hope for in your old age among your sex? Would not her faithful love and abounding sympathy be dearer to you every day, though the roses in her cheek should fade and the bright hair whiten with the dust of life's journey? Would you not feel that when you died your dearest wish must be to join her where there should be no parting—her from whom there could be no parting here, short of death itself? Would you not believe she had a soul?"

"There is no end of your 'supposing,' but it is quite pretty. I am half inclined to 'suppose' too." He took a sip of sherbet from the tall crystal goblet the servant had placed on a little three-legged stool beside him, and as he drank the cool liquid slowly, looked over the glass into my eyes, with a curious, half earnest, half smiling glance. I could not tell whether my enthusiastic picture of conjugal bliss amused him or attracted him, so I waited for him to speak again.

"Now that you have had your cruise in your ship of happiness on the waters of your cerulean imagination, permit me, who am land-born and a lover of the chase, to put my steed at a few fences in the difficult country of unadorned facts over which I propose to hunt the wily fox, matrimony. I have never hunted a fox, but I can quite well imagine what it is like.

"In the first place, it is all very well to suppose that it had pleased Allah in his goodness to relieve me of my three incumbrances — meanwhile, there they are, and they are very real difficulties I assure you. Nevertheless are there means provided us by the foresight of the apostle, by which we may ease ourselves of domestic burdens when they are too heavy for us to bear. It would be quite within the bounds of possibility for me to divorce them all three, without making any special scandal. But if I did this thing, do you not think that my experience of married life has given me the most ineradicable prejudices against women as daily companions? Am I not persuaded that they all bicker and chatter and nibble sweetmeats alike — absolutely alike? Or if I looked abroad —— "

"Stop," I said, "I am not reasoner enough to persuade you that all women have souls. Very likely in Persia and India they have not. I only want you to believe that there may be women so fortunate as to possess a modicum of immortality. Well, pardon my interruption, 'if you looked abroad,' as you were saying? —— "

"If I looked abroad, I should probably discover little petty traits of the same class, if not exactly identical. I know little of Englishmen, and might be the more readily deceived. Supposing, if you will, that, after freeing myself from all my present

ties, in order to start afresh, I were to find myself
attracted by some English girl here "— there must
have been something wrong with the mouthpiece of
his pipe, for he examined it very attentively —
"attracted," he continued, "by some one, for instance, by Miss Westonhaugh ——" he stopped short

So my inspiration was right. My little picture,
framed as we rode homeward, and indignantly scoffed
at by my calmer reason, had visited his brain too.
He had looked on the fair northern woman and fancied
himself at her side, her lover, her husband. All this
conversation and argument had been only a set plan
to give himself the pleasure of contemplating and
discussing such a union, without exciting surprise
or comment. I had been suspecting it for some time,
and now his sudden interest in his mouthpiece, to
conceal a very real embarrassment, put the matter
beyond all doubt.

He was probably in love, my acquaintance of two
days. He saw in me a plain person, who could not
possibly be a rival, having some knowledge of the
world, and he was in need of a confidant, like a
schoolgirl. I reflected that he was probably a victim
for the first time. There is very little romance in
India, and he had, of course, married for convenience
and respectability rather than for any real affection.
His first passion! This man who had been tossed
about like a bit of driftwood, who had by his own determination and intelligence carved his way to wealth
and power in the teeth of every difficulty. Just

now, in his embarrassment, he looked **very boyish.**
His troubles had left no wrinkles on his smooth **forehead,** his bright black hair was untinged by a single
thread of gray, and as he looked up, after the pause
that followed when **he** mentioned the name of the
woman he loved, **there** was a very really youthful
look of mingled passion and distress in his beautiful
eyes.

"I think, **Mr. Isaacs, that you have** used a stronger
argument against the opinions you profess to hold
than I could have found in my whole armoury of
logic."

As he looked at me, the whole field of possibilities
seemed opened. **I must** have **been** mistaken in
thinking this marriage impossible and incongruous.
What incongruity could there be in Isaacs marrying
Miss Westonhaugh? My conclusions were false.
Why must he necessarily return with her to England,
and wear a red coat, and make himself ridiculous at
the borough **elections?** Why **should not this ideal
couple choose some happy spot, as far from** the cor-
rosive influence of Anglo-Saxon prejudice as from the
wretched sensualism of prosperous life east of the
Mediterranean? I was carried away by the idea,
returning with redoubled strength as a sequel to
what I had argued and to what I had guessed.
"Why not?" was the question I repeated to myself
over and over again in the half minute's pause after
Isaacs finished speaking.

"You are right," he said slowly, his half-closed

eyes fixed on his feet. "Yes, you are right. Why not? Indeed, indeed, why not?"

It must have been pure guess-work, this reading of my thoughts. When he was last speaking his manner was all indifference, scorn of my ideas, and defiance of every western mode of reasoning. And now, apparently by pure intuition, he gave a direct answer to the direct question I had mentally asked, and, what is more, his answer came with a quiet, far-away tone of conviction that had not a shade of unbelief in it. It was delivered as monotonously and naturally as a Christian says "Credo in unum Deum," as if it were not worth disputing; or as the devout Mussulman says "La Illah illallah," not stooping to consider the existence of any one bold enough to deny the dogma. No argument, not hours of patient reasoning, or weeks of well directed persuasion, could have wrought the change in the man's tone that came over it at the mere mention of the woman he loved. I had no share in his conversion. My arguments had been the excuse by which he had converted himself. Was he converted? was it real?

"Yes — I think I am," he replied in the same mechanical monotonous accent.

I shook myself, drank some sherbet, and kicked off one shoe impatiently. Was I dreaming? or had I been speaking aloud, really putting the questions he answered so quickly and appositively? Pshaw! a coincidence. I called the servant and ordered my hookah to be refilled. Isaacs sat still, immovable, lost in thought, looking at his toes; an **expression,** almost stupid in its vacancy, was on his face, **and the** smoke curled slowly **up in** lazy wreaths **from his** neglected narghyle.

"You are converted then at last?" I said aloud. No answer followed my question; I watched him attentively.

"Mr. Isaacs!" still silence, was it possible that he **had** fallen **asleep? his eyes** were open, but I thought **he** was very pale. His upright position, however, belied any symptoms of unconsciousness.

"Isaacs! Abdul Hafiz! what is the matter!" He did not move. I rose to **my** feet and knelt beside him where **he** sat rigid, **immovable,** like **a** statue. Kiramat Ali, who had been watching, clapped his hands wildly and cried, "Wah! wah! Sahib margyâ!" — "The lord is dead." I motioned him away with a gesture and he **held** his peace, cowering in the corner, **his eyes** fixed **on** us. Then I bent low as **I** knelt and looked under my friend's brows, into his eyes. It was clear he did not see me, though he was looking straight at **his** feet. I felt for his pulse. It was **very** low, almost imperceptible, and certainly **below** forty beats to the minute. I took his right arm and tried to put it on my shoulder. It was perfectly rigid. There was no doubt about it — the man was in a cataleptic trance. I felt for the pulse again; it was lost.

I was no stranger to this curious phenomenon, where the **mind is** perfectly awake, but every **bodily** faculty is lulled to sleep beyond possible excitation, unless the right means be employed. I went out and breathed the cool night air, bidding the servants be quiet, as the sahib was asleep. When sufficiently refreshed I re-entered the room, cast off my slippers, and stood a moment by my friend, who was as rigid as ever.

Nature, in her bountiful wisdom, has compensated me for a singular absence of beauty by endowing me with great strength, and with one of those exceptional constitutions which seem constantly charged with electricity. Without being what is called a mesmerist, I am possessed of considerable magnetic power, which I have endeavoured to develop as far as possible. In many a long conversation with old Manu Lal, my Brahmin instructor in languages and philosophy while in the plains, we had discussed the trance state in all its bearings. This old pundit was himself a distinguished mesmerist, and though generally unwilling to talk about what is termed occultism, on finding in me a man naturally endowed with the physical characteristics necessary to those pursuits, he had given me several valuable hints as to the application of my powers. Here was a worthy opportunity.

I rubbed my feet on the soft carpet, and summoning all my strength, began to make the prescribed passes over my friend's head and body. Very gradually the look of life returned to his face, the generous blood welled up under the clear olive skin, the lips parted, and he sighed softly. Animation, as always happens in such cases, began at the precise point at which it had been suspended, and his first movement was to continue his examination of the mouthpiece in his hand. Then he looked up suddenly, and seeing me standing over him, gave a little shake, half turning his shoulders forward and back, and speaking once more in his natural voice, said —

"I must have been asleep! Have I? What has happened? Why are you standing there looking at me in that way?" Then, after a short interrogatory silence, his face changed and a look of annoyance shaded his features as he added in a low tone, "Oh! I see. It has happened to me once before. Sit down. I am all right now." He sipped a little sherbet and leaned back in his old position. I begged him to go to bed, and prepared to withdraw, but he would not let me, and he seemed so anxious that I should stay, that I resumed my place. The whole incident had passed in ten minutes.

"Stay with me a little longer," he repeated. "I need your company, perhaps your advice. I have had a vision, and you must hear about it."

"I thought as I sat here that my spirit left my body and passed out through the night air and hovered over Simla. I could see into every bungalow, and was conscious of what passed in each, but there was only one where my gaze rested, for I saw upon a couch in a spacious chamber the sleeping form of one I knew. The masses of fair hair were heaped as they fell upon the pillow, as if she had lain down weary of bearing the burden of such wealth of gold. The long dark lashes threw little shadows on her cheeks, and the parted lips seemed to smile at the sweetness of the gently heaving breath that fanned them as it came and went. And while I looked, the breath of her body became condensed, as it were, and took shape and form and colour, so that the image of herself floated up between her body and my watching spirit. Nearer and nearer to me came the exquisite vision of beauty, till we were face to face, my soul and hers, high up in the night. And there came from her eyes, as the long lids lifted, a look of perfect trust, and of love, and of infinite joy. Then she turned her face southward and pointed to my life star burning bright among his lesser fellows; and with a long sweet glance that bid me follow where she led, her maiden soul floated away, half lingering at first, as I watched her; then, with dizzy speed, vanishing in the firmament as a falling star, and leaving no trace behind, save an infinitely sad regret, and a longing to enter with her into that boundless empire of peace. But I could not, for my spirit was called back to this body. And I bless Allah that he has given me to see her once so, and to know that she has a soul, even as I have, for I have looked upon her spirit and I know it."

Isaacs rose slowly to his feet and moved towards the open door. I followed him, and for a few moments we stood looking out at the scene below us.

It was near midnight, and the ever-decreasing moon was dragging herself up, as if ashamed of her waning beauty and tearful look.

"Griggs," said my friend, dropping the formal prefix for the first time, "all this is very strange.　I believe I am in love!"

"I have not a doubt of it," I replied.　"Peace be with you!"

"And with you peace."

So we parted.

CHAPTER IV.

In Simla people make morning calls in the morning instead of after dark, as in more civilised countries. Soon after **dawn** I received a note from Isaacs, saying that he had business with the Maharajah of Baithopoor about some precious stones, but that he would be ready to go with me to call on **Mr.** Currie Ghyrkins at ten o'clock, or soon after. I had been thinking a great deal about the events of the previous evening, and I was looking forward to my next meeting with Isaacs with intense interest. After what had passed, nothing could be such a test of his true feelings as the visit to Miss Westonhaugh, which we proposed to make together, and I promised myself to lose no gesture, no word, no expression, which might throw light on the question that interested me — whether such a union were practical, possible, and wise.

At the appointed time, therefore, I was ready, and we mounted and sallied forth into the bright autumn day. All visits are made on horseback in Simla, as the distances are often considerable. You ride quietly along, and the saice follows you, walking or keeping pace with your gentle trot, as the case may

be. We rode along the bustling mall, crowded with
men and women on horseback, with numbers of
gorgeously arrayed native servants and *chuprassies* of
the Government offices hurrying on their respective
errands, or dawdling for a chat with some shabby-
looking acquaintance in private life; we passed by
the crowded little shops on the hill below the church,
and glanced at the conglomeration of grain-sellers,
jewellers, confectioners, and dealers in metal or
earthen vessels, every man sitting knee-deep in his
wares, smoking the eternal "hubble-bubble;" we
noted the keen eyes of the buyers and the hawk's
glance of the sellers, the long snake-like fingers
eagerly grasping the passing coin, and seemingly con-
vulsed into serpentine contortion when they relin-
quished their clutch on a single "pi;" we marked
this busy scene, set down, like a Punch and Judy
show, in the midst of the trackless waste of the Himalayas, as if for the delectation and pastime of some
merry *genius loci* weary of the solemn silence in his
awful mountains, and we chatted carelessly of the
sights animate and inanimate before us, laughing at
the asseverations of the salesmen, and at the hardened
scepticism of the customer, at the portentous dignity
of the superb old messenger, white-bearded and clad
in scarlet and gold, as he bombastically described
to the knot of poor relations and admirers that
elbowed him the splendours of the last entertainment
at "Peterhof," where Lord Lytton still reigned. I
smiled, and Isaacs frowned at the ancient and hairy

ascetic believer, who suddenly rose from his lair in a corner, and bustled through the crowd of Hindoos, shouting at the top of his voice the confession of his faith — "Beside God there is no God, and Muhammad is his apostle!" The universality of the Oriental spirit is something amazing. Customs, dress, thought, and language, are wonderfully alike among all Asiatics west of Thibet and south of Turkistan. The greatest difference is in language, and yet no one unacquainted with the dialects could distinguish by the ear between Hindustani, Persian, Arabic, and Turkish.

So we moved along, and presently found ourselves on the road we had traversed the previous evening, leading round Jako. On the slope of the hill, hidden by a dense growth of rhododendrons, lay the bungalow of Mr. Currie Ghyrkins, and a board at the entrance of the ride — drive there was none — informed us that the estate bore the high-sounding title of "Carisbrooke Castle," in accordance with the Simla custom of calling little things by big names.

Having reached the lawn near the house, we left our horses in charge of the saice and strolled up the short walk to the verandah. A charming picture it was, prepared as if on purpose for our especial delectation. The bungalow was a large one for Simla, and the verandah was deep and shady; many chairs of all sorts and conditions stood about in natural positions, as if they had just been sat in, instead of being ranged in stiff rows against the wall, and across one angle hung a capacious hammock. Therein, swinging her feet to the ground, and holding on by the edge rope, sat the beautiful Miss Westonhaugh, clad in one of those close-fitting unadorned costumes of plain dark-blue serge, which only suit one woman in ten thousand, though, when they clothe a really beautiful young figure, I know of no garment better calculated to display grace of form and motion. She was kicking a ball of worsted with her dainty toes, for the amusement and instruction of a small tame jackal — the only one I ever saw thoroughly domesticated. A charming little beast it was, with long gray fur and bright twinkling eyes, mischievous and merry as a gnome's. From a broad blue ribbon round its neck was suspended a small silver bell that tinkled spasmodically, as the lively little thing sprang from side to side in pursuit of the ball, alighting with apparent indifference on its head or its heels.

So busy was the girl with her live plaything that she had not seen us dismount and approach her, and it was not till our feet sounded on the boards of the verandah that she looked up with a little start, and tried to rise to her feet. Now any one who has sat sideways in a netted hammock, with feet swinging to the ground, and all the weight in the middle of the thing, knows how difficult it is to get out with grace, or indeed in any way short of rolling out and running for luck. You may break all your bones in the feat, and you both look and feel as if you were going to. Though we both sprang forward to her assistance, Miss Westonhaugh had recognised the inexpediency of moving after the first essay, and, with a smile of greeting, and the faintest tinge of embarrassment on her fair cheek, abandoned the attempt; the quaint little jackal sat up, backing against the side of the house, and, eyeing us critically, growled a little.

"I'm so glad to see you, Mr. Isaacs. How do you do, Mr. —— "

"Griggs," murmured Isaacs, as he straightened a rope of the hammock by her side.

"Mr. Griggs?" she continued. "We met last night, briefly, but to the point, or at least you and my uncle did. I am alone; my uncle is gone down towards Kalka to meet my brother, who is coming up for a fortnight at the end of the season to get rid of the Bombay mould. Bring up some of those chairs and sit down. I cannot tell what has become of the 'bearer' and the 'boy,' and the rest of the servants, and I could not make them understand me if they were here. So you must wait on yourselves."

I was the first to lay hands on a chair, and as I turned to bring it I noticed she was following Isaacs with the same expression I had seen on her face the previous evening; but I could see it better now. A pleasant friendly look, not tender so much as kind, while the slightest possible contraction of the eyes showed a feeling of curiosity. She was evidently going to speak to him as soon as he turned his face.

"You see I have been giving him lessons," she said, as he brought back the seat he had chosen.

Isaacs looked at the queer small beast sitting up against the boards under the window, his brush tail curled round him, and his head turned inquiringly on one side.

"He seems to be learning manners, at all events," said my friend.

"Yes; I think I may say now, with safety, that his bark is worse than his bite."

"I am sure you could not have said so the last time I came. Do you remember what fearful havoc he made among my nether garments? And yet he is my god-child, so to speak, for I gave him into your care, and named him into the bargain."

"Don't suppose I am ungrateful for the gift," answered Miss Westonhaugh. "Snap! Snap! here! come here, darling, to your mistress, and be petted!" In spite of this eloquent appeal Snap, the baby jackal, only growled pleasantly and whisked his brush right and left. "You see," she went on, "your sponsorship has had no very good results. He will not obey any more than you yourself." Her glance, turning towards Isaacs, did not reach him, and, in fact, she could not have seen anything beyond the side of his chair. Isaacs, on the contrary, seemed to be counting her eyelashes, and taking a mental photograph of her brows.

"Snap!" said he. The jackal instantly rose and trotted to him, fawning on his outstretched hand.

"You malign me, Miss Westonhaugh. Snap is no less obedient than I."

"Then why did you insist on playing tennis left-handed the other day, though you know very well how it puzzles me?"

"My dear Miss Westonhaugh," he answered, "I am not a tennis-player at all, to begin with, and as I do not understand the *finesse* of the game, to use a word I do not understand either, you must pardon my clumsiness in employing the hand most convenient and ready."

"Some people," I began, "are what is called ambi-dexter, and can use either hand with equal ease. Now the ancient Persians, who invented the game of polo ——"

"I do not quarrel so much with you, Mr. Isaacs —" as she said this, she looked at me, though entirely disregarding and interrupting my instructive sentence —"I don't quarrel with you so much for using your left hand at tennis as for employing left-handed weapons when you speak of other things, or beings, for you are never so left-handed and so adroit as when you are indulging in some elaborate abuse of our sex."

"How can you say that?" protested Isaacs. "You know with what respectful and almost devotional reverence I look upon all women, and," his eyes brightening perceptibly, "upon you in particular."

English women, especially in their youth, are not used to pretty speeches. They are so much accus-

tomed to the men of their own nationality that they
regard the least approach to a compliment as the
inevitable introduction to the worst kind of insult.
Miss Westonhaugh was no exception to this rule,
and she drew herself up proudly.

There was a moment's pause, during which Isaacs
seemed penitent, and she appeared to be revolving
the bearings of the affront conveyed in his last words.
She looked along the floor, slowly, till she might
have seen his toes; then her eyes opened a moment
and met his, falling again instantly with a change of
colour.

"And pray, Mr. Isaacs, would you mind giving us
a list of the ladies you look upon with 'respectful
and devotional reverence?'" One of the horses
held by the saice at the corner of the lawn neighed
lowly, and gave Isaacs an opportunity of looking
away.

"Miss Westonhaugh," he said quietly, "you know
I am a Mussulman, and that I am married. It may
be that I have borrowed a phrase from your language which expresses more than I would convey,
though it would ill become me to withdraw my last
words, since they are true."

It was my turn to be curious now. I wondered
where his boldness would carry him. Among his
other accomplishments, this man was capable of
speaking the truth even to a woman, not as a luxury
and a *bonne bouche*, but as a matter of habit. As
I looked, the hot blood mantled up to his brows.

She was watching him, and womanlike, seeing he was in earnest and embarrassed, she regained her perfect natural composure.

"Oh, I had forgotten!" she said. "I forgot about your wife in Delhi." She half turned in the hammock, and after some searching, during which we were silent, succeeded in finding a truant piece of worsted work behind her. The wool was pulled out of the needle, and she held the steel instrument up against the light, as she doubled the worsted round the eye and pushed it back through the little slit. I observed that Isaacs was apparently in a line with the light, and that the threading took some time.

"Mr. Griggs," she said slowly, and by the very slowness of the address I knew she was going to talk to me, and at my friend, as women will; "Mr. Griggs, do you know anything about Mohammedans?"

"That is a very broad question," I answered; "almost as broad as the Mussulman creed." She began making stitches in the work she held, and with a little side shake settled herself to listen, anticipating a discourse. The little jackal sidled up and fawned on her feet. I had no intention, however, of delivering a lecture on the faith of the prophet. I saw my friend was embarrassed in the conversation, and I resolved, if possible, to interest her.

"Among primitive people and very young persons," I continued, "marriage is an article of faith, a moral precept, and a social law."

"I suppose you are married, Mr. Griggs," she said, with an air of childlike simplicity.

"Pardon me, Miss Westonhaugh, I neither condescend to call myself primitive, nor aspire to call myself young."

She laughed. I had put a wedge into my end of the conversation.

"I thought," said she, "from the way in which you spoke of 'primitive and young persons' that you considered their opinion in regard to — to this question, as being the natural and proper opinion of the original and civilised young man."

"I repeat that I do not claim to be very civilised, or very young — certainly not to be very original, and my renunciation of all these qualifications is my excuse for the confirmed bachelorhood to which I adhere. Many Mohammedans are young and original; some of them are civilised, as you see, and all of them are married. 'There is no God but God, Muhammad is his prophet, and if you refuse to marry you are not respectable,' is their full creed."

Isaacs frowned at my profanity, but I continued — "I do not mean to say anything disrespectful to a creed so noble and social. I think you have small chance of converting Mr. Isaacs."

"I would not attempt it," she said, laying down her work in her lap, and looking at me for a moment. "But since you speak of creeds, to what confession do you yourself belong, if I may ask?"

"I am a Roman Catholic," I answered; adding

presently — "Really, though, I do not see how my belief in the papal infallibility affects my opinion of Mohammedan marriages."

"And what *do* you think of them?" she inquired, resuming her work and applying herself thereto with great attention.

"I think that, though justified in principle by the ordinary circumstances of Eastern life, there are cases in which the system acts very badly. I think that young men are often led by sheer force of example into marrying several wives before they have sufficiently reflected on the importance of what they are doing. I think that both marriage and divorce are too easily managed in consideration of their importance to a man's life, and I am convinced that no civilised man of Western education, if he were to adopt Islam, would take advantage of his change of faith to marry four wives. It is a case of theory *versus* practice, which I will not attempt to explain. It may often be good in logic, but it seems to me it is very often bad in real life."

"Yes," said Isaacs; "there are cases ——" He stopped, and Miss Westonhaugh, who had been very busy over her work, looked quietly up, only to find that he was profoundly interested in the horses cropping the short grass, as far as the saice would let them stretch their necks, on the other side of the lawn.

"I confess," said Miss Westonhaugh, "that my ideas about Mohammedans are chiefly the result of reading the Arabian Nights, ever so long ago. It seems to me that they treat women as if they had no souls and no minds, and were incapable of doing anything rational if left to themselves. It is a man's religion. My uncle says so too, and he ought to know."

The conversation was meandering in a kind of vicious circle. Both Isaacs and I were far too deeply interested in the question to care for such idle discussion. How could this beautiful but not very intellectual English girl, with her prejudices and her clumsiness at repartee or argument, ever comprehend or handle delicately so difficult a subject? I was disappointed in her. Perhaps this was natural enough, considering that with two such men as we she must be entirely out of her element. She was of the type of brilliant, healthy, northern girls, who depend more on their animal spirits and enjoyment of living for their happiness than upon any natural or acquired mental powers. With a horse, or a tennis court, or even a ball to amuse her, she would appear at her very best; would be at ease and do the right thing. But when called upon to sustain a conversation, such as that into which her curiosity about Isaacs had plunged her, she did not know what to do. She was constrained, and even some of her native grace of manner forsook her. Why did she avoid his eyes and resort to such a petty little trick as threading a needle in order to get a look at him? An American girl, or a French woman, would have seen that her strength lay in perfect frankness; that Isaacs' straightforward nature would make him tell her unhesitatingly anything she wanted to know about himself, and that her position was strong enough for her to look him in the face and ask him what she pleased. But she allowed herself to be embarrassed, and though she had been really glad to see him, and liked him and thought him handsome, she was beginning to wish he would go, merely because she did not know what to talk about, and would not give him a chance to choose his own subject. As neither of us were inclined to carry the analysis of matrimony any farther, nor to dispute the opinions of Mr. Currie Ghyrkins as quoted by his niece, there was a pause. I struck in and boldly changed the subject.

"Are you going to see the polo this afternoon, Miss Westonhaugh? I heard at the hotel that there was to be a match to-day of some interest."

"Oh yes, of course. I would not miss it for anything. Lord Steepleton is coming to tiffin, and we shall ride down together to Annandale. Of course you are going too; it will be a splendid thing. Do you play polo, Mr. Griggs? Mr. Isaacs is a great player, when he can be induced to take the trouble. He knows more about it than he does about tennis."

"I am very fond of the game," I answered, "but I have no horses here, and with my weight it is not easy to get a mount for such rough work."

"Do not disturb yourself on that score," said

Isaacs; "you know my stable is always at your disposal, and I have a couple of ponies that would carry
you well enough. Let us have a game one of those
days, whenever we can get the ground. We will
play on opposite sides and match the far west against
the far east."

"What fun!" cried Miss Westonhaugh, her face
brightening at the idea, "and I will hold the stakes
and bestow the crown on the victor."

"What is to be the prize?" asked Isaacs, with a
smile of pleasure. He was very literal and boyish
sometimes.

"That depends on which is the winner," she
answered.

There was a noise among the trees of horses' hoofs
on the hard path, and presently we heard a voice calling loudly for a saice who seemed to be lagging far
behind. It was a clear strong voice, and the speaker
abused the groom's female relations to the fourth
and fifth generations with considerable command of
the Hindustani language. Miss Westonhaugh, who
had not been in the country long, did not understand
a word of the very free swearing that was going on
in the woods, but Isaacs looked annoyed, and I regis-
tered a black mark against the name of the new-comer,
whoever he might be.

"Oh! it is Lord Steepleton," said the young girl.
"He seems to be always having a row with his servants. Don't go," she went on as I took up my hat;
"he is such a good fellow, you ought to know him."

Lord Steepleton Kildare now appeared at the corner
of the lawn, hotly pursued by his breathless groom,
who had been loitering on the way, and had thus
roused his master's indignation. He was, as I have
said, a fine specimen of a young Englishman, though
being Irish by descent he would have indignantly
denied any such nationality. I saw when he had dismounted that he was tall and straight, though not a
very heavily built man. He carried his head high,
and looked every inch a soldier as he strode across
the grass, carefully avoiding the pegs of the tennis
net. He wore a large gray felt hat, like every one
else, and he shook hands all round before he took it
off, and settled himself in an easy chair as near as
he could get to Miss Westonhaugh's hammock.

"How are ye? Ah — yes, Mr. Isaacs, Mr. Griggs
of Allahabad. Jolly day, isn't it?" and he looked
vaguely at the grass. "Really, Miss Westonhaugh,
I got in such a rage with my rascal of a saice that I
did not remember I was so near the house. I am
really very sorry I talked like that. I hope you did
not think I was murdering him?"

Isaacs looked annoyed.

"Yes," said he, "we thought Mahmoud was going
to have a bad time of it. I believe Miss Westonhaugh does not understand Hindustani."

A look of genuine distress came into the Englishman's face.

"Really," said he, very simply. "You don't know
how sorry I am that any one should have heard me.

I am so hasty.   But let me apologise to you all most sincerely for disturbing you with my brutal temper."

His misdeed had not been a very serious crime after all, and there was something so frank and honest about his awkward little apology that I was charmed.   The man was a gentleman.   Isaacs bowed in silence, and Miss Westonhaugh had evidently never thought much about it.

"We were talking about polo when you came, Lord Steepleton; Mr. Isaacs and Mr. Griggs are going to play a match, and I am to hold the stakes. Do you not want to make one in the game?"

"May I?" said the young man, grateful to her for having helped him out.   "May I? I should like it awfully.   I so rarely get a chance of playing with any except the regular set here."   And he looked inquiringly at us.

"We should be delighted, of course," said Isaacs. "By the way, can you help us to make up the number?   And when shall it be?"   He seemed suddenly very much interested in this projected contest.

"Oh yes," said Kildare, "I will manage to fill up the game, and we can play next Monday.   I know the ground is free then."

"Very good; on Monday.   We are at Laurie's on the hill."

"I am staying with Jack Tygerbeigh, near Peter-hof.   Come and see us.   I will let you know before Monday.   Oh, Mr. Griggs, I saw such a nice thing about me in the *Howler* the other day — so many thanks. No, really, greatly obliged, you know; people say horrid things about me sometimes. Good-bye, good-bye, delighted to have seen you."

"Good morning, Miss Westonhaugh."

"Good morning; so good of you to take pity on my solitude." She smiled kindly at Isaacs and civilly at me. And we went our way. As we looked back after mounting to lift our hats once more, I saw that Miss Westonhaugh had succeeded in getting out of the hammock and was tying on a pith hat, while Lord Steepleton had armed himself with balls and rackets from a box on the verandah. As we bowed they came down the steps, looking the very incarnation of animal life and spirits in the anticipation of the game they loved best. The bright autumn sun threw their figures into bold relief against the dark shadow of the verandah, and I thought to myself they made a very pretty picture. I seemed to be always seeing pictures, and my imagination was roused in a new direction.

We rode away under the trees. My impression of the whole visit was unsatisfactory. I had thought Mr. Currie Ghyrkins would be there, and that I would be able to engage him in a political discussion. We could have talked income-tax, and cotton duties, and Kabul by the hour, and Miss Weston-haugh and Isaacs would have had a pleasant tête-à-tête. Instead of this I had been decidedly the unlucky third who destroys the balance of so much pleasure in life, for I felt that Isaacs was not a man

to be embarrassed if left alone with a woman, **or to**
embarrass her.   He was too full of tact, and his
sensibilities were so fine that, with his easy command of language, he must be agreeable *quand même;*
and such an opportunity would have given him an
easy lead away from the athletic Kildare, whom **I**
suspected strongly of being a rival for Miss Westonhaugh's favour.   There **is** an easy air of familiar pro-
prietorship **about an** Englishman in love that is not
to be mistaken.   It is a subtle thing, and expresses
itself neither in word nor deed in its earlier stages
of development; but it is there all the same, and the
combination of this **possessive mood**, with a certain
shyness which often goes with it, **is amusing.**

"Griggs," said Isaacs, "**have you ever seen the**
Rajah of Baithopoor?"

"No; you had some business with him this morning, had you not?"

"Yes — some — business — if you call it so.   If
you would like to see him I can take you there, and
I think you would be interested in the — the business.   It is not often such gems are bought and sold
in such a way, and besides, he is very amusing.   He
is at least two thousand years old, and will go to
Saturn when he dies. His fingers are long and
crooked, and that which he putteth into his pockets,
verily he shall not take it out."

"A pleasing picture; a good contrast to the one
we have left behind us.   I like contrasts, and I
should like to see him."

"You shall."   And we lit our cheroots.

CHAPTER V.

"WE will go there at four," said Isaacs, coming into my rooms after tiffin, a meal of which I found he rarely partook. "I said three, this morning, but it is not a bad plan to keep natives waiting. It makes them impatient, and then they commit themselves."

"You are Machiavellian. It is pretty clear which of you is asking the favour."

"Yes, it is pretty clear." He sat down and took up the last number of the *Howler* which lay on the table. Presently he looked up. "Griggs, why do you not come to Delhi? We might start a newspaper there, you know, in the Conservative interest."

"In the interest of Mr. Algernon Currie Ghyrkins?" I inquired.

"Precisely. You anticipate my thoughts with a true sympathy. I suppose you have no conscience?"

"Political conscience? No, certainly not, out of my own country, which is the only one where that sort of thing commands a high salary. No, I have no conscience."

"You would really write as willingly for the Conservatives as you do for the Liberals?"

"Oh yes. I could not write so well on the Conservative side just now, because they are ' in,' and it is more blessed to abuse than to be abused, and ever so much easier. But as far as any prejudice on the subject is concerned, I have none. I had as lief defend a party that robs India ' for her own good,' as support those who would rob her with a more cynical frankness and unblushingly transfer the proceeds to their own pockets. I do not care a rush whether they rob Peter to pay Paul, or fraudulently deprive Paul of his goods for the benefit of Peter."

"That is the way to look at it. I could tell you some very pretty stories about that kind of thing. As for the journalistic enterprise, it is only a possible card to be played if the old gentleman is obdurate."

"Isaacs," said I, "I have only known you three days, but you have taken me into your confidence to some extent; probably because I am not English. I may be of use to you, and I am sure I sincerely hope so. Meanwhile I want to ask you a question, if you will allow me to." I paused for an answer. We were standing by the open door, and Isaacs leaned back against the door-post, his eyes fixed on me, half closed, as he threw his head back. He looked at me somewhat curiously, and I thought a smile flickered round his mouth, as if he anticipated what the question would be.

"Certainly," he said slowly. "Ask me anything you like. I have nothing to conceal."

"Do you seriously think of marrying, or proposing to marry, Miss Katharine Westonhaugh?"

"I do seriously think of proposing to marry, and of marrying, Miss Westonhaugh." He looked very determined as he thus categorically affirmed his intention. I knew he meant it, and I knew enough of Oriental character to understand that a man like Abdul Hafizben-Isâk, of strong passions, infinite wit, and immense wealth, was not likely to fail in anything he undertook to do. When Asiatic indifference gives way under the strong pressure of some master passion, there is no length to which the hot and impetuous temper beneath may not carry the man. Isaacs had evidently made up his mind. I did not think he could know much about the usual methods of wooing English girls, but as I glanced at his graceful figure, his matchless eyes, and noted for the hundredth time the commanding, high-bred air that was the breath of his character, I felt that his rival would have but a poor chance of success. He guessed my thoughts.

"What do you think of me?" he asked, smiling. "Will you back me for a place? I have advantages, you must allow — and worldly advantages too. They are not rich people at all."

"My dear Isaacs, I will back you to win. But as far as 'worldly advantages' are concerned, do not trust to wealth for a moment. Do not flatter yourself that there will be any kind of a bargain, as if you were marrying a Persian girl. There is nothing venal in that young lady's veins, I am sure."

"Allah forbid! But there is something very venal

in the veins of Mr. Currie Ghyrkins. I propose to carry the outworks one by one. He is her uncle, her guardian, her only relation, save her brother. I do not think either of those men would be sorry to see her married to a man of stainless name and considerable fortune."

"You forget your three incumbrances, as you called them last night."

"No — I do not forget them. It is allowed me by my religion to marry a fourth, and I need not tell you that she would be thenceforth my only wife."

"But would her guardian and brother ever think of allowing her to take such a position?"

"Why not? You know very well that the English in general hardly consider our marriages to be marriages at all — knowing the looseness of the bond. That is the prevailing impression."

"Yes, I know. But then they would consider your marriage with Miss Westonhaugh in the same light, which would not make matters any easier, as far as I can see."

"Pardon me. I should marry Miss Westonhaugh by the English marriage service and under English law. I should be as much bound to her, and to her alone, as if I were an Englishman myself."

"Well, you have evidently thought it out and taken legal advice; and really, as far as the technical part of it goes, I suppose you have as good a chance as Lord Steepleton Kildare."

Isaacs frowned, and his eyes flashed. I saw at

once that he considered the Irish officer a rival, and a dangerous one. I did not think that if Isaacs had fair play and the same opportunities Kildare had much chance. Besides there was a difficulty in the way.

"As far as religion is concerned, Lord Steepleton is not much better off than you, if he wants to marry Miss Westonhaugh. The Kildares have been Roman Catholics since the memory of man, and they are very proud of it. Theoretically, it is as hard for a Roman Catholic man to marry a Protestant woman, as for a Mussulman to wed a Christian of any denomination. Harder, in fact, for your marriage depends upon the consent of the lady, and his upon the consent of the Church. He has all sorts of difficulties to surmount, while you have only to get your personality accepted — which, when I look at you, I think might be done," I added, laughing.

"*Jo hoga, so hoga* — what will be, will be," he said; "but religion or no religion, I mean to do it." Then he lighted a cigarette and said, "Come, it is time to go and see his Saturnine majesty, the Maharajah of Baithopoor."

I called for my hat and gloves.

"By-the-bye, Griggs, you may as well put on a black coat. You know the old fellow is a king, after all, and you had better produce a favourable impression." I retired to comply with his request, and as I came back he turned quickly and came towards me, holding out both hands, with a very earnest look in his face.

"Griggs, I care for that lady more than I can tell you," he said, taking my hands in his.

"My dear fellow, I am sure you do. People do not go suddenly into trances at a name that is indifferent to them. I am sure you love her very honestly and dearly."

"You and she have come into my life almost together, for it was not until I talked with you last night that I made up my mind. Will you help me? I have not a friend in the world." The simple, boyish look was in his eyes, and he stood holding my hands and waiting for my answer. I was so fascinated that I would have then and there gone through fire and water for him, as I would now.

"Yes. I will help you. I will be a friend to you."

"Thank you. I believe you." He dropped my hands, and we turned and went out, silent.

In all my wanderings I had never promised any man my friendship and unconditional support before. There was something about Isaacs that overcame and utterly swept away preconceived ideas, rules, and prejudices. It was but the third day of our acquaintance, and here was I swearing eternal friendship like a school-girl; promising to help a man, of whose very existence I knew nothing three days ago, to marry a woman whom I had seen for the first time yesterday. But I resolved that, having pledged myself, I would do my part with my might, whatever that part might be. Meanwhile we rode along, and

Isaacs began to talk about the visit we were going
to make.

"I think," he said, "that you had better know
something about this matter beforehand. The way
is long, and we cannot ride fast over the steep roads,
so there is plenty of time. Do not imagine that I
have idly asked you to go with me because I supposed it would amuse you. Dismiss also from your
mind the impression that it is a question of buying
and selling jewels. It is a very serious matter, and
if you would prefer to have nothing to do with it, do
not hesitate to say so. I promised the maharajah
this morning that I would bring, this afternoon, a
reliable person of experience, who could give advice,
and who might be induced to give his assistance as
well as his counsel. I have not known you long, but
I know you by reputation, and I decided to bring
you, if you would come. From the very nature of
the case I can tell you nothing more, unless you consent to go with me."

"I will go," I said.

"In that case I will try and explain the situation
in as few words as possible. The maharajah is in
a tight place. You will readily understand that
the present difficulties in Kabul cause him endless
anxiety, considering the position of his dominions.
The unexpected turn of events, following now so
rapidly on each other since the English wantonly
sacrificed Cavagnari and his friends to a vainglorious
love of bravado, has shaken the confidence of the

native princes in the stability of English rule.　They
are frightened out of their senses, having the fear
of the tribes before them if the English should be
worsted; and they dread, on the other hand, lest the
English, finding themselves in great straits, should
levy heavy contributions on them — the native princes
— for the consolidation of what they term the
'Empire.'　They have not much sense, these poor
old kings and boy princes, or they would see that the
English do not dare to try any of those old-fashioned
Clive tactics now.　But old Baithopoor has heard
all about the King of Oude, and thinks he may share
the same fate."

"I think he may make his mind easy on that score.
The kingdom of Baithopoor is too inconveniently
situated and too full of mosquitoes to attract the
English.　Besides, there are more roses than rubies
there just now."

"True, and that question interests me closely, for
the old man owes me a great deal of money.　It was
I who pulled him through the last famine."

"Not a very profitable investment, I should think.
Shall you ever see a rupee of that money again?"

"Yes; he will pay me; though I did not think so
a week ago, or indeed yesterday.　I lent him the
means of feeding his people and saving many of them
from actual death by starvation, because there are so
many Mussulmans among them, though the maharajah is a Hindoo.　As for him, he might starve to-
morrow, the infidel hound; I would not give him a

chowpatti or a mouthful of *dal* to keep his wretched old body alive."

"Do I understand that this interview relates to the repayment of the moneys you have advanced?"

"Yes; though that is not the most interesting part of it. He wanted to pay me in flesh — human flesh, and he offered to make me a king into the bargain, if I would forgive him the debt. The latter part of the proposal was purely visionary. The promise to pay in so much humanity he is able to perform. I have not made up my mind."

I looked at Isaacs in utter astonishment. What in the world could he mean? Had the maharajah offered him some more wives — creatures of peerless beauty and immense value? No; I knew he would not hesitate now to refuse such a proposition.

"Will you please to explain what you mean by his paying you in man?" I asked.

"In two words. The Maharajah of Baithopoor has in his possession a man. Safely stowed away under a triple watch and carefully tended, this man awaits his fate as the maharajah may decide. The English Government would pay an enormous sum for this man, but Baithopoor fears that they would ask awkward questions, and perhaps not believe the answers he would give them. So, as he owes me a good deal, he thinks I might be induced to take his prisoner and realise him, so to speak; thus cancelling the debt, and saving him from the alternative of putting the man to death privately, or of going through dangerous negotiations with the Government. Now this thing is perfectly feasible, and it depends upon me to say 'yes' or 'no' to the proposition. Do you see now? It is a serious matter enough."

"But the man — who is he? Why do the English want him so much?"

Isaacs pressed his horse close to mine, and looking round to see that the saice was a long way behind, he put his hand on my shoulder, and, leaning out of the saddle till his mouth almost touched my ear, he whispered quickly —

"Shere Ali."

"The devil, you say!" I ejaculated, surprised out of grammar and decorum by the startling news. Persons who were in India in 1879 will not have forgotten the endless speculation caused by the disappearance of the Emir of Afghanistan, Shere Ali, in the spring of that year. Defeated by the English at Ali Musjid and Peiwar, and believing his cause lost, he fled, no one knew whither; though there is reason to think that he might have returned to power and popularity among the Afghan tribes if he had presented himself after the murder of Cavagnari.

"Yes," continued Isaacs, "he has been a prisoner in the palace of Baithopoor for six weeks, and not a soul save the maharajah and you and I know it. He came to Baithopoor, humbly disguised as a Yogi from the hills, though he is a Mussulman, and having obtained a private hearing, disclosed his real name, proposing to the sovereign a joint movement on

Kabul, then just pacified by the British, and promising all manner of things for the assistance. Old
Baitho, who is no fool, clapped him into prison
under a guard of Punjabi soldiers who could not
speak a word of Afghan, and after due consideration
packed up his traps and betook himself to Simla by
short stages, for the journey is not an easy one for a
man of his years. He arrived the day before yesterday, and has ostensibly come to congratulate the
Viceroy on the success of the British arms. He has
had to modify the enthusiasm of his proposed
address, in consequence of the bad news from Kabul.
Of course, his first move was to send for me, and I
had a long interview this morning, in which he
explained everything. I told him that I would not
move in the matter without a third person — necessary as a witness when dealing with such people —
and I have brought you."

"But what was his proposal to invest you with a
crown? Did he think you were a likely person for
a new Emir of Kabul?"

"Exactly. My faith, and above all, my wealth,
suggested to him that I, as a born Persian, might be
the very man for the vacant throne. No doubt, the
English would be delighted to have me there. But
the whole thing is visionary and ridiculous. I think
I shall accept the other proposition, and take the
prisoner. It is a good bargain."

I was silent. The intimate way in which I had
seen Isaacs hitherto had made me forget his immense

wealth and his power. I had not realised that he could be so closely connected with intrigues of such importance as this, or that independant native princes were likely to look upon him as a possible Emir of Afghanistan. I had nothing to say, and I determined to keep to the part I was brought to perform, which was that of a witness, and nothing more. If my advice were asked, I would speak boldly for Shere Ali's liberation and protest against the poor man being bought and sold in this way. This train of thought reminded me of Isaacs' words when we left Miss Westonhaugh that morning. "It is not often," he had said, "that you see such jewels bought and sold." No, indeed!

"You see," said Isaacs, as we neared our destination, "Baithopoor is in my power, body and soul, for a word from me would expose him to the British Government as 'harbouring traitors,' as they would express it. On the other hand, the fact that you, the third party, are a journalist, and could at a moment's notice give publicity to the whole thing, will be an additional safeguard. I have him as in a vice. And now put on your most formal manners and look as if you were impenetrable as the rock and unbending as cast iron, for we have reached his bungalow."

I could not but admire the perfect calm and caution with which he was conducting an affair involving millions of money, a possible indictment for high treason, and the key-note of the Afghan question, while I knew that his whole soul was absorbed in the contemplation of a beautiful picture ever before him, sleeping or waking. Whatever I might think of his bargaining for the possession of Shere Ali, he had a great, even untiring, intellect. He had the elements of a leader of men, and I fondly hoped he might be a ruler some day.

The bungalow in which the Maharajah of Baithopoor had taken up his residence during his visit was very much like all the rest of the houses I saw in Simla. The verandah, however, was crowded with servants and sowars in gorgeous but rather tawdry liveries, not all of them as clean as they should have been. Horses with elaborate high saddles and embroidered trappings rather the worse for wear were being led up and down the walk. As we neared the door there was a strong smell of rosewater and native perfumes and hookah tobacco — the indescribable odour of Eastern high life. There was also a general air of wasteful and tawdry dowdiness, if I may coin such a word, which one constantly sees in the retinues of native princes and rich native merchants, ill contrasting with the great intrinsic value of some of the ornaments worn by the chief officers of the train.

Isaacs spoke a few words in a low voice to the jemadar at the door, and we were admitted into a small room in the side of the house, opening, as all rooms do in India, on to the verandah. There were low wooden charpoys around the walls, and we sat

down, waiting till the maharajah should be advised
of our arrival. Very soon a jemadar came in and
informed us that "if the *sahib log*, who were the protectors of the poor, would deign to be led by him,"
we should be shown into the royal presence. So we
rose and followed the obsequious official into another
apartment.

The room where the maharajah awaited us was
even smaller than the one into which we had been
first shown. It was on the back of the house, and
only half lighted by the few rays of afternoon sun
that struggled through the dense foliage outside.
I suppose this apartment had been chosen as the
scene of the interview on account of its seclusion.
Outside the window, which was closed, a sowar
paced slowly up and down to keep away any curious
listeners. A heavy curtain hung before the door
through which we had entered. I thought that on the
whole the place seemed pretty safe.

The old maharajah sat cross-legged upon a great
pile of dark-red cushions, his slippers by his side,
and a huge hookah before him. He wore a plain
white pugree with a large jewel set on one side,
and his body was swathed and wrapped in dark thick
stuffs, as if he felt keenly the cold autumn air. His
face was long, of an ashy yellowish colour, and an
immense white moustache hung curling down over
his sombre robe. One hand protruded from the folds
and held the richly-jewelled mouthpiece of the pipe
to his lips, and I noticed that the fingers were long

and crooked, winding themselves curiously round the gold stem, as if revelling in the touch of the precious metal and the gems. As we came within his range of vision, his dark eyes shot a quick glance of scrutiny at me and then dropped again. Not a movement of the head or body betrayed a consciousness of our presence. Isaacs made a long salutation in Hindustani, and I followed his example, but he did not take off his shoes or make anything more than an ordinary bow. It was quite evident that he was master of the situation. The old man took the pipe from his mouth and replied in a deep hollow voice that he was glad to see us, and that, in consideration of our wealth, fame, and renowned wisdom, he would waive all ceremony and beg us to be seated. We sat down cross-legged on cushions before him, and as near as we could get, so that it seemed as if we three were performing some sacred rite of which the object was the tall hookah that stood in the centre of our triangle.

Being seated, Isaacs addressed the prince, still in Hindustani, and said that the splendour of his sublime majesty, which was like the sun dispelling the clouds, so overcame him with fear and trembling, that he humbly implored permission to make use of the Persian tongue, which, he was aware, the lord of boundless wisdom spoke with even greater ease than himself.

Without waiting for an answer, and with no perceptible manifestation of any such "fear and trem-

bling " as he professed, Isaacs at once began to speak
in his native tongue, and dropping all forms of ceremony or circumlocution plunged boldly into business.
He did not hesitate to explain to the maharajah the
strength of his position, dwelling on the fact that,
by a word to the English of the whereabouts of Shere
Ali, he could plunge Baithopoor into hopeless and
endless entanglements, to which there could be but
one issue — absorption into the British Rāj. He
dwelt on the large sums the maharajah owed him for
assistance lent during the late famine, and he skil-
fully produced the impression that he wanted the
money down, then and there.

"If your majesty should refuse to satisfy my just
claims, I have ample weapons by which to satisfy
them for myself, and no considerations of mercy or
pity for your majesty will tempt me to abate one
rupee in the account of your indebtedness, which, as
you well know, is not swelled by any usurious interest. You could not have borrowed the money on such
easy terms from any bank in India or England, and if
I have been merciful hitherto, I will be so no longer.
What saith the Apostle of Allah? 'Verily, life for
life, and eye for eye, and nose for nose, and ear for
ear, and tooth for tooth, and for wounding retaliation.' And the time of your promise is expired and
you shall pay me. And is not the wise Frank, who
sitteth at my right hand, the ready writer, who giveth
to the public every day a new book to read, the paper
of news, *Khabar-i-Khagaz* wherein are written the

misdeeds of the wicked, and the dealings of the
fraudulent and the unwary receive their just reward?
And think you he will not make a great writing,
several columns in length, and deliver it to the
devils that perform his bidding, and shall they not
multiply what he hath written, and sow it broadcast
over the British Rāj for the minor consideration of
one anna a copy, that all shall see how the Maharajah
of Baithopoor doth scandalously repudiate his debts,
and harbour traitors to the Rāj in his palace?"

Isaacs said all this in a solemn and impressive manner, calculated to inspire awe and terror in the soul
of the unhappy debtor. As for the maharajah, the
cold sweat stood on his face, and at the last words
his anxiety was so great that the long fingers uncurled
spasmodically and the jewelled mouthpiece fell back,
as the head of a snake, among the silken coils of the
tube at his feet. Instantly, on feeling the grasping
hand empty, his majesty, with more alacrity than I
would have expected, darted forward with outstretched claws, as a hawk on his prey, and seizing
the glittering thing returned it to his lips with a
look of evident relief. It was habit, of course, for
we were not exactly the men to plunder him of his
toy, but there was a fierceness about the whole action
that spoke of the real miser. Then there was silence
for a moment. The old man was evidently greatly
impressed by the perils of his situation. Isaacs
continued.

"Your majesty well perceives that you have surrounded yourself with dangers on all sides. No danger threatens me. I could buy you and Baithopoor to-morrow if I chose. But I am a just man. When the prophet, whose name be blessed, saith that we shall have eye for eye, and nose for nose, and for wounding retaliation, he saith also that 'he that remitteth the same as alms it shall be an atonement unto him.' Now your majesty is a hard man, and I well know that if I force you to pay me now you will cruelly tax and oppress your subjects to refill your coffers. And many of your subjects are true believers, following the prophet, upon whom be peace; and it is also written 'Thou shalt rob a stranger, but thou shalt not rob a brother,'—and if I cause you to rob my brethren is not the sin mine, and the atonement thereof? Now also has the lawful interest on your bond mounted up to several lakhs of rupees. But for the sake of my brethren who are in bondage to you, who are an unbeliever and shall broil everlastingly in raging flames, I will yet make a covenant with you, and the agreement thereof shall be this:

"You shall deliver into my hand, before the dark half of the next moon, the man"—Isaacs lowered his voice to a whisper, barely audible in the still room, where the only sound heard as he paused was the tread of the sowar on the verandah outside— "the man Shere Ali, formerly Emir of Afghanistan, now hidden in your palace of Baithopoor. Him you shall give to me safe and untouched at the place which I shall choose, northwards from here, in the pass towards Keitung. And there shall not be an hair of his head touched, and if it is good in my eyes I will give him up to the British; and if it is good in my eyes, I will slay him, and you shall ask no questions. And if you refuse to do this I will go to the great lord sahib and tell him of your doings, and you will be arrested before this night and shall not escape. But if you consent and put your hand to this agreement, I will speak no word, and you shall depart in peace; and moreover, for the sake of the true believers in your kingdom I will remit to you the whole of the interest on your debt; and the bond you shall pay at your convenience. I have spoken, do you answer me." Isaacs calmly took from his pocket two rolls covered with Persian writing, and lighting a cigarette, proceeded to peruse them carefully, to detect any flaw or error in their composition. The face of the old maharajah betrayed great emotion, but he bravely pulled away at his hookah and tried to think over the situation. In the hope of delivering himself from his whole debt he had rashly given himself into the hands of a man who hated him, though he had discovered that hatred too late. He had flattered himself that the loan had been made out of friendly feeling and a desire for his interest and support; he found that Isaacs had lent the money, for real or imaginary religious motives, in the interest of his co-religionists. I sat silently watching the varying passions as they swept over the repulsive face of the old man. The silence must have lasted a quarter of an hour.

"Give me the covenant," he said at last, "for I am in the tiger's clutches. I will sign it, since I must. But it shall be requited to you, Abdul Hafiz; and when your body has been eaten of jackals and wild pigs in the forest, your soul shall enter into the shape of a despised sweeper, and you and your offspring shall scavenge the streets of the cities of my kingdom and of the kingdom of my son, and son's son, to ten thousand generations." A Hindoo cannot express scorn more deadly or hate more lasting than this. Isaacs smiled, but there was a concentrated look in his face, relentless and hard, as he answered the insult.

"I am not going to bandy words with you. But if you are not quick about signing that paper I may change my mind, and send for the Angrezi sowars from Peterhof. So you had better hurry yourself." Isaacs produced a small inkhorn and a reed pen from his pocket. "Sign," he said, rising to his feet "before that soldier outside passes the window three times, or I will deliver you to the British."

Trembling in every joint, and the perspiration standing on his face like beads, the old man seized the pen and traced his name and titles at the foot, first of one copy, and then of the other. Isaacs followed, writing his full name in the Persian character, and I signed my name last, "Paul Griggs," in large letters at the bottom of each roll, adding the word "witness," in case of the transaction becoming known.

"And now," said Isaacs to the maharajah, "despatch at once a messenger, and let the man here mentioned be brought under a strong guard and by circuitous roads to the pass of Keitung, and let them there encamp before the third week from to-day, when the moon is at the full. And I will be there and will receive the man. And woe to you if he come not; and woe to you if you oppress the true believers in your realm." He turned on his heel, and I followed him out of the room after making a brief salutation to the old man, cowering among his cushions, a ceremony which Isaacs omitted, whether intentionally or from forgetfulness, I could not say. We passed through the house out into the air, and mounting our horses rode away, leaving the double row of servants salaaming to the ground. The duration of our private interview with the maharajah had given them an immense idea of our importance. We had come at four and it was now nearly five. The long pauses and the Persian circumlocutions had occupied a good deal of time.

"You do not seem to have needed my counsel or assistance much," I said. "With such an armoury of weapons you could manage half-a-dozen maharajahs."

"Yes—perhaps so. But I have strong reasons for wishing this affair quickly over, and the editor of a daily paper is a thing of terror to a native prince; you must have seen that."

"What do you mean to do with your man when he is safely in your hands, if it is not an indiscreet question?"

"Do with him?" asked Isaacs with some astonishment. "Is it possible you have not guessed? He is a brave man, and a true believer. I will give him money and letters, that he may make his way to Baghdad, or wherever he will be safe. He shall depart in peace, and be as free as air."

I had half suspected my friend of some such generous intention, but he had played his part of unrelenting hardness so well in our late interview with the Hindoo prince that it seemed incomprehensible that a man should be so pitiless and so kind on the same day. There was not a trace of hardness on his beautiful features now, and as we rounded the hill and caught the last beams of the sun, now sinking behind the mountains, his face seemed transfigured as with a glory, and I could hardly bear to look at him. He held his hat in his hand and faced the west for an instant, as though thanking the declining day for its freshness and beauty; and I thought to myself that the sun was lucky to see such an exquisite picture before he bid Simla good-night, and that he should shine the brighter for it the next day, since he would look on nothing fairer in his twelve hours' wandering over the other half of creation.

"And now," said he, "it is late, but if we ride towards Annandale we may meet them coming back

from the polo match we have missed." His eyes
glowed at the thought. Shere Ali, the maharajah,
bonds, principal, and interest, were all forgotten in
the anticipation of a brief meeting with the woman
he loved.

CHAPTER VI.

"Why did you not come and see the game? After
all your enthusiasm about polo this morning, I did
not think you would miss anything so good," were
the first words of Miss Westonhaugh as we met her
and Kildare in the narrow path that leads down to
Annandale. Two men were riding behind them,
who proved to be Mr. Currie Ghyrkins and Mr. John
Westonhaugh. The latter was duly introduced to
us; a quiet, spare man, with his sister's features,
but without a trace of her superb colour and animal
spirits. He had the real Bombay paleness, and had
been steamed to the bone through the rains. As we
were introduced, Isaacs started and said quickly that
he believed he had met Mr. Westonhaugh before.

"It is possible, quite possible," said that gentleman affably, "especially if you ever go to Bombay."

"Yes — it was in Bombay — some twelve years ago.
You have probably forgotten me."

"Ah, yes. I was young and green then. I wonder you remember me." He did not show any very
lively interest in the matter, though he smiled
pleasantly.

Miss Westonhaugh must have been teasing Lord

Steepleton, for he looked flushed and annoyed, and
she was in capital spirits. We turned to go back
with the party, and by a turn of the wrist Isaacs
wheeled his horse to the side of Miss Westonhaugh's,
a position he did not again abandon. They were
leading, and I resolved they should have a chance,
as the path was not broad enough for more than two
to ride abreast. So I furtively excited my horse by
a touch of the heel and a quick strain on the curb,
throwing him across the road, and thus producing a
momentary delay, of which the two riders in front
took advantage to increase their distance. Then we
fell in, Mr. Ghyrkins and I in front, while the
dejected Kildare rode behind with Mr. John Westonhaugh. Ghyrkins and I, being heavy men, heavily
mounted, controlled the situation, and before long
Isaacs and Miss Westonhaugh were a couple of hundred yards ahead, and we only caught occasional
glimpses of them through the trees as they wound in
and out along the path.

"What are those youngsters talking about, back
there? Tigers, I'll be bound," said Mr. Ghyrkins
to me. Sure enough, they were.

"What do you suppose I found when we got back
this afternoon, Mr. Griggs? Why, this hairbrained
young Kildare has been proposing to my niece ——"
his horse stumbled, but recovered himself in a
moment.

"You don't mean it," said I, rather startled.

"Oh no, no, no. I don't mean that at all. Ha!

ha! ha! very good, very good. No, no. Lord
Steepleton wants us all to go on a tiger-hunt to
amuse John, and he proposes — ha! ha! — really too
funny of me — that Miss Westonhaugh should go
with us."

"I suppose you have no objection, Mr. Ghyrkins?
Ladies constantly go on such expeditions, and they
do not appear to be the least in the way."

"Objections? Of course I have objections. Do
you suppose I want to drag my niece to a premature
grave? Think of the fever and the rough living and
all, and she only just out from England."

"She looks as if she could stand anything," I said,
as just then an open space in the trees gave us a
glimpse of Miss Westonhaugh and Isaacs ambling
along and apparently in earnest conversation. She
certainly looked strong enough to go tiger-hunting
that minute, as she sat erect but half turned to the
off side, listening to what Isaacs seemed to be saying.

"I hope you will not go and tell her so," said
Ghyrkins. "If she gets an idea that the thing is
possible, there will be no holding her. You don't
know her. I hardly know her myself. Never saw
her since she was a baby till the other day. Now
you are the sort of person to go after tigers. Why
do you not go off with my nephew and Mr. Isaacs
and Kildare, and kill as many of them as you like?"

"I have no objection, I am sure. I suppose the
Howler could spare me for a fortnight, now that I
have converted the Press Commissioner, your new

deus ex machinâ for the obstruction of news. What a motley party we should be. Let me see — a Bombay Civil Servant, an Irish nobleman, a Persian millionaire, and a Yankee newspaper man. By Jove! add to that a famous Revenue Commissioner and a reigning beauty, and the sextett is complete." Mr. Ghyrkins looked pleased at the gross flattery of himself. I recollected suddenly that, though he was far from famous as a revenue commissioner, I had read of some good shooting he had done in his younger days. Here was a chance.

"Besides, Mr. Ghyrkins, a tiger-hunting party would not be the thing without some seasoned Nimrod to advise and direct us. Who so fitted for the post as the man of many a chase, the companion of Maori, the slayer of the twelve foot tiger in the Nepaul hills in 1861?"

"You have a good memory, Mr. Griggs," said the old fellow, perfectly delighted, and now fairly launched on his favourite topic. "By Gad, sir, if I thought I should get such another chance I would go with you to-morrow!"

"Why not? there are lots of big man-eaters about," and I incontinently reeled off half a page of statistics, more or less accurate, about the number of persons destroyed by snakes and wild beasts in the last year. "Of course most of those deaths were from tigers, and it is a really good action to kill a few. Many people can see tigers but cannot shoot them, whereas your deeds of death amongst them are a matter of history. You really ought to be philanthropic, Mr. Ghyrkins, and go with us. We might stand a chance of seeing some real sport then."

"Why, really, now that you make me think of it, I believe I should like it amazingly, and I could leave my niece with Lady — Lady — Stick-in-the-mud; what the deuce is her name? The wife of the Chief Justice, you know. You ought to know, really — I never remember names much;" he jerked out his sentences irately.

"Certainly, Lady Smith-Tompkins, you mean. Yes, you might do that — that is, if Miss Westonhaugh has had the measles, and is not afraid of them. I heard this morning that three of the little Smith-Tompkinses had them quite badly."

"You don't say so! Well, well, we shall find some one else, no doubt."

I was certain that at that very moment Isaacs and Miss Westonhaugh were planning the whole expedition, and so I returned to the question of sport and inquired where we should go. This led to considerable discussion, and before we arrived at Mr. Ghyrkins' bungalow — still in the same order — it was very clear that the old sportsman had made up his mind to kill one more tiger at all events; and that, rather than forego the enjoyment of the chase, he would be willing to take his niece with him. As for the direction of the expedition, that could be decided in a day or two. It was not the best season for tigers — the early spring is better — but they are always to be found in the forests of the Terai, the country along the base of the hills, north of Oude.

When we reached the house it was quite dark, for we had ridden slowly. The light from the open door, falling across the verandah, showed us Miss Westonhaugh seated in a huge chair, and Isaacs standing by her side slightly bending, and holding his hat in his hand. They were still talking, but as we rode up to the lawn and shouted for the saices, Isaacs stood up and looked across towards us, and their voices ceased. It was evident that he had succeeded in thoroughly interesting her, for I thought — though it was some distance, and the light on them was not strong — that as he straightened himself and stopped speaking, she looked up to his face as if regretting that he did not go on. I dismounted with the rest and walked up to bid Miss Westonhaugh good-night.

"You must come and dine to-morrow night," said Mr. Ghyrkins, "and we will arrange all about it. Sharp seven. To-morrow is Sunday, you know. Kildare, you must come too, if you mean business. Seven. We must look sharp and start, if we mean to come back here before the Viceroy goes."

"Oh in that case," said Kildare, turning to me, "we can settle all about the polo match for Monday, can't we?"

"Of course, very good of you to take the trouble."

"Not a bit of it. Good-night." We bowed and went back to find our horses in the gloom. After

some fumbling, for it was intensely dark after facing
the light in the doorway of the bungalow, we got
into the saddle and turned homeward through the
trees.

"Thank you, Griggs," said Isaacs. "May your
feet never weary, and your shadow never be less."

"Don't mention it, and thanks about the shadow.
Only it is never likely to be less than at the present
moment. How dark it is, to be sure!" I knew well
enough what he was thanking me for. I lit a
cheroot.

"Isaacs," I said, "you are a pretty cool hand, upon
my word."

"Why?"

"Why, indeed! Here you and Miss Westonhaugh
have been calmly planning an extensive tiger-hunt,
when you have promised to be in the neighbourhood
of Keitung in three weeks, wherever that may be.
I suppose it is in the opposite direction from here,
for you will not find any tigers nearer than the Terai
at this time of year."

"I do not see the difficulty," he answered. "We
can be in Oude in two days from here; shoot tigers
for ten days, and be here again in two days more.
That is just a fortnight. It will not take me a week
to reach Keitung. I am much mistaken if I do not
get there in three days. I shall lay a *dâk* by messengers before I go to Oude, and between a double
set of coolies and lots of ponies wherever the roads
are good enough, I shall be at the place of meeting
soon enough, never fear."

"Oh, very well; but I hardly think Ghyrkins will want to return under three weeks; and — I did not think you would want to leave the party." He had evidently planned the whole three weeks' business carefully. I did not continue the conversation. He was naturally absorbed in the arrangement of his numerous schemes — no easy matter, when affairs of magnitude have to be ordered to suit the exigencies of a *grande passion*. I shrank from intruding on his reflections, and I had quite enough to do in keeping my horse on his feet in the thick darkness. Suddenly he reared violently, and then stood still, quivering in every limb. Isaacs' horse plunged and snorted by my side, and cannoned heavily against me. Then all was quiet. I could see nothing. Presently a voice, low and musical, broke on the darkness, and I thought I could distinguish a tall figure on foot at Isaacs' knee. Whoever the man was he must be on the other side of my companion, but I made out a head from which the voice proceeded.

"Peace, Abdul Hafiz!" it said.

"Aleikum Salaam, Ram Lal!" answered Isaacs. He must have recognised the man by his voice.

"Abdul," continued the stranger, speaking Persian. "I have business with thee this night; thou art going home. If it is thy pleasure I will be with thee in two hours in thy dwelling."

"Thy pleasure is my pleasure. Be it so." I thought the head disappeared.

"Be it so," the voice echoed, growing faint, as if

moving rapidly away from us. The horses, momentarily startled by the unexpected pedestrian, regained their equanimity. I confess the incident gave me a curiously unpleasant sensation. It was so very odd that a man on foot — a Persian, I judged, by his accent — should know of my companion's whereabouts, and that they should recognise each other by their voices. I recollected that our coming to Mr. Ghyrkins' bungalow was wholly unpremeditated, and I was sure Isaacs had spoken to none but our party — not even to his saice — since our meeting with the Westonhaughs on the Annandale road an hour and a half before.

"I wonder what he wants," said my friend, apparently soliloquising.

"He seems to know where to find you, at all events," I answered. "He must have second sight to know you had been to Carisbrooke."

"He has. He is a very singular personage altogether. However, he has done me more than one service before now, and though I do not comprehend his method of arriving at conclusions, still less his mode of locomotion, I am always glad of his advice."

"But what is he? Is he a Persian? — you called him by an Indian name, but that may be a disguise — is he a wise man from Irân?"

"He is a very wise man, but not from Irân. No. He is a Brahmin by birth, a Buddhist by adopted religion, and he calls himself an 'adept' by profession, I suppose, if he can be said to have any. He comes and goes unexpectedly, with amazing rapidity. His visits are brief, but he always seems to be perfectly conversant with the matter in hand, whatever it be. He will come to-night and give me about twenty words of advice, which I may follow or may not, as my judgment dictates; and before I have answered or recovered from my surprise, he will have vanished, apparently into space; for if I ask my servants where he is gone they will stare at me as if I were crazy, until I show them that the room is empty, and accuse them of going to sleep instead of seeing who goes in and out of my apartment. He speaks more languages than I do, and better. He once told me he was educated in Edinburgh, and his perfect knowledge of European affairs and of European topics leads me to think he must have been there a long time. Have you ever looked into the higher phases of Buddhism? It is a very interesting study."

"Yes, I have read something about it. Indeed I have read a good deal, and have thought more. The subject is full of interest, as you say. If I had been an Asiatic by birth, I am sure I should have sought to attain *moksha*, even if it required a lifetime to pass through all the degrees of initiation. There is something so rational about their theories, disclaiming, as they do, all supernatural power; and, at the same time, there is something so pure and high in their conception of life, in their ideas about the ideal, if you will allow me the expression, that I do

not wonder Edwin Arnold has set our American
transcendentalists and Unitarians and freethinkers
speculating about it all, and wondering whether the
East may not have had men as great as Emerson
and Channing among its teachers." I paused. My
greatest fault is that if any one starts me upon a subject I know anything about, I immediately become
didactic. So I paused and reflected that Isaacs,
being, as he himself declared, frequently in the
society of an "adept" of a high class, was sure to
know a great deal more than I.

"I too," he said, "have been greatly struck, and
sometimes almost converted, by the beauty of the
higher Buddhist thoughts. As for their apparently
supernatural powers and what they do with them, I
care nothing about phenomena of that description.
We live in a land where marvels are common enough.
Who has ever explained the mango trick, or the
basket trick, or the man who throws a rope up into
the air and then climbs up it and takes the rope after
him, disappearing into blue space? And yet you
have seen those things — I have seen them, every one
has seen them, — and the performers claim no supernatural agency or assistance. It is merely a difference of degree, whether you make a mango grow from
the seed to the tree in half an hour, or whether you
transport yourself ten thousand miles in as many
seconds, passing through walls of brick and stone on
your way, and astonishing some ordinary mortal by
showing that you know all about his affairs. I see

no essential difference between the two 'phenomena,' as the newspapers call them, since Madame Blavatsky has set them all by the ears in this country. It is just the difference in the amount of power brought to bear on the action. That is all. I have seen, in a workshop in Calcutta, a hammer that would crack an eggshell without crushing it, or bruise a lump of iron as big as your head into a flat cake. 'Phenomena' may amuse women and children, but the real beauty of the system lies in the promised attainment of happiness. Whether that state of supreme freedom from earthly care gives the fortunate initiate the power of projecting himself to the antipodes by a mere act of volition, or of condensing the astral fluid into articles of daily use, or of stimulating the vital forces of nature to an abnormal activity, is to me a matter of supreme indifference. I am tolerably happy in my own way as things are. I should not be a whit happier if I were able to go off after dinner and take a part in American politics for a few hours, returning to business here to-morrow morning."

"That is an extreme case," I said. "No man in his senses ever connects the idea of happiness with American politics."

"Of one thing I am sure, though." He paused as if choosing his words. "I am sure of this. If any unforeseen event, whether an act of folly of my own, or the hand of Allah, who is wise, should destroy the peace of mind I have enjoyed for ten years, with very trifling interruption,— if anything should occur to make me permanently unhappy, beyond the possibility of ordinary consolation,— I should seek comfort in the study of the pure doctrines of the higher Buddhists. The pursuit of a happiness, so immeasurably beyond all earthly considerations of bodily comfort or of physical enjoyment, can surely not be inconsistent with my religion — or with yours."

"No indeed," said I. "But, considering that you are the strictest of Mohammedans, it seems to me you are wonderfully liberal. So you have seriously contemplated the possibility of your becoming one of the 'brethren' — as they style themselves?"

"It never struck me until to-day that anything might occur by which my life could be permanently disturbed. Something to-day has whispered to me that such an existence could not be permanent. I am sure that it cannot be. The issue must be either to an infinite happiness or to a still more infinite misery. I cannot tell which." His clear, evenly modulated voice trembled a little. We were in sight of the lights from the hotel.

"I shall not dine with you to-night, Griggs. I will have something in my own rooms. Come in as soon as you have done — that is if you are free. There is no reason why you should not see Ram Lal the adept, since we think alike about his religion, or school, or philosophy — find a name for it while you are dining." And we separated for a time.

It had been a long and exciting day to me. I felt no more inclined than he did for the din and racket

and lights of the public dining-room. So I followed
his example and had something in my own apartment. Then I settled myself to a hookah, resolved
not to take advantage of Isaacs' invitation until near
the time when he expected Ram Lal. I felt the need
of an hour's solitude to collect my thoughts and to
think over the events of the last twenty-four hours.
I recognised that I was fast becoming very intimate
with Isaacs, and I wanted to think about him and
excogitate the problem of his life; but when I tried
to revolve the situation logically, and deliver to myself a verdict, I found myself carried off at a tangent
by the wonderful pictures that passed before my eyes.
I could not detach the events from the individual.
His face was ever before me, whether I thought of
Miss Westonhaugh, or of the wretched old maharajah,
or of Ram Lal the Buddhist. Isaacs was the central
figure in every picture, always in the front, always
calm and beautiful, always controlling the events
around him. Then I entered on a series of trite
reflections to soothe my baffled reason, as a man will
who is used to understanding what goes on before
him and suddenly finds himself at a loss. Of course,
I said to myself, it is no wonder he controls things,
or appears to. The circumstances in which I find
this three days' acquaintance are emphatically those
of his own making. He has always been a successful man, and he would not raise spirits that he could
not keep well in hand. He knows perfectly well
what he is about in making love to that beautiful

creature, and is no doubt at this moment laughing
in his sleeve at my simplicity in believing that he
was really asking my advice. Pshaw! as if any
advice could influence a man like that! Absurd.

I sipped my coffee in disgust with myself. All
the time, while trying to persuade myself that Isaacs
was only a very successful schemer, neither better
nor worse than other men, I was conscious of the
face that would not be banished from my sight. I
saw the beautiful boyish look in his deep dark eyes,
the gentle curve of the mouth, the grand smooth
architrave of the brows. No — I was a fool! I had
never met a man like him, nor should again. How
could Miss Westonhaugh save herself from loving
such a perfect creature? I thought, too, of his generosity. He would surely keep his promise and
deliver poor Shere Ali, hunted to death by English
and Afghan foes, from all his troubles. Had he not
the Maharajah of Baithopoor in his power? He
might have exacted the full payment of the debt,
principal and interest, and saved the Afghan chief
into the bargain. But he feared lest the poor
Mohammedans should suffer from the prince's extor-
tion, and he forgave freely the interest, amounting
now to a large sum, and put off the payment of the
bond itself to the maharajah's convenience. Did
ever an Oriental forgive a debt before even to his own
brother? Not in my experience.

I rose and went down to Isaacs. I found him as
on the previous evening, among his cushions with a

manuscript book. He looked up smiling and motioned me to be seated, keeping his place on the page with one finger. He finished the verse before he spoke, and then laid the book down and leaned back.

"So you have made up your mind that you would like to see Ram Lal. He will be here in a minute, unless he changes his mind and does not come after all."

There was a sound of voices outside. Some one asked if Isaacs were in, and the servant answered. A tall figure in a gray *caftán* and a plain white turban stood in the door.

"I never change my mind," said the stranger, in excellent English, though with an accent peculiar to the Hindoo tongue when struggling with European languages. His voice was musical and high in pitch, though soft and sweet in tone. The quality of voice that can be heard at a great distance, with no apparent effort to the speaker. "I never change my mind. I am here. Is it well with you?"

"It is well, Ram Lal. I thank you. Be seated, if you will stay with us a while. This is my friend Mr. Griggs, of whom you probably know. He thinks as I do on many points, and I was anxious that you should meet."

While Isaacs was speaking, Ram Lal advanced into the room and stood a moment under the soft light, a gray figure, very tall, but not otherwise remarkable. He was all gray. The long *caftán* wrapped round him, the turban which I had first

thought white, the skin of his face, the pointed beard
and long moustache, the heavy eyebrows — a study
of grays against the barbaric splendour of the richly
hung wall — a soft outline on which the yellow
light dwelt lovingly, as if weary of being cast back
and reflected from the glory of gold and the thousand
facets of the priceless gems.   Ram Lal looked toward
me, and as I gazed into his eyes I saw that they too
were gray — a very singular thing in the East — and
that they were very far apart, giving his face a look
of great dignity and fearless frankness.   To judge
by his features he seemed to be very thin, and his
high shoulders were angular, though the long loose
garment concealed the rest of his frame from view.
I had plenty of time to note these details, for he
stood a full minute in the middle of the room, as if
deciding whether to remain or to go.   Then he moved
quietly to a divan and sat down cross-legged.

"Abdul, you have done a good deed to-day, and
I trust you will not change your mind before you
have carried out your present intentions."

"I never change my mind, Ram Lal," said Isaacs,
smiling as he quoted his visitor's own words.   I was
startled at first.   What good deed was the Buddhist
referring to if not to the intended liberation of Shere
Ali? How could he know of it?   Then I reflected
that this man was, according to Isaacs' declaration,
an adept of the higher grades, a seer and a knower of
men's hearts.   I resolved not to be astonished at anything that occurred, only marvelling that it should

have pleased this extraordinary man to make his entrance like an ordinary mortal, instead of through the floor or the ceiling.

"Pardon me," answered Ram Lal, "if I venture to contradict you. You do change your mind sometimes. Who was it who lately scoffed at women, their immortality, their virtue, and their intellect? Will you tell me now, friend Abdul, that you have not changed your mind? Do you think of anything, sleeping or waking, but the one woman for whom you *have* changed your mind? Is not her picture ever before you, and the breath of her beauty upon your soul? Have you not met her in the spirit as well as in the flesh? Surely we shall hear no more of your doubts about women for some time to come. I congratulate you, as far as that goes, on your conversion. You have made a step towards a higher understanding of the world you live in."

Isaacs did not seem in the least surprised at his visitor's intimate acquaintance with his affairs. He bowed his head in silence, acquiescing to what Ram Lal had said, and waited for him to proceed.

"I have come," continued the Buddhist, "to give you some good advice — the best I have for you. You will probably not take it, for you are the most self-reliant man I know, though you have changed a little since you have been in love, witness your sudden intimacy with Mr. Griggs." He looked at me, and there was a faint approach to a smile in his gray eyes. "My advice to you is, do not let this pro-

jected tiger-hunt take place if you can prevent it.
No good can come of it, and harm may. Now I have
spoken because my mind would not be at rest if I
did not warn you. Of course you will do as you
please, only never forget that I pointed out to you
the right course in time."

"Thank you, Ram Lal, for your friendly concern
in my behalf. I do not think I shall act as you sug-
gest, but I am nevertheless grateful to you. There
is one thing I want to ask you, and consult you
about, however."

"My friend, what is the use of my giving you
advice that you will not follow? If I lived with
you, and were your constant companion, you would
ask me to advise you twenty times a day, and then
you would go and do the diametric opposite of what
I suggested. If I did not see in you something that
I see in few other men, I would not be here. There
are plenty of fools who have wit enough to take
counsel of a wise man. There are few men of wit
wise enough to be guided by their betters, as if they
were only fools for the time. Yet because you are
so wayward I will help you once or twice more, and
then I will leave you to your own course — which
you, in your blindness, will call your kismet, not
seeing that your fate is continually in your own
hands — more so at this moment than ever before.
Ask, and I will answer."

"Thanks, Ram Lal. It is this I would know.
You are aware that I have undertaken a novel kind of

bargain. The man you wot of is to be delivered to me near Keitung. I am anxious for the man's safety afterwards, and I would be glad of some hint about disposing of him. I must go alone, for I do not want any witness of what I am going to do, and as a mere matter of personal safety for myself and the man I am going to set free, I must decide on some plan of action when I meet the band of sowars who will escort him. They are capable of murdering us both if the maharajah instructs them to. As long as I am alive to bring the old man into disgrace with the British, the captive is safe; but it would be an easy matter for those fellows to dispose of us together, and there would be an end of the business."

"Of course they could," replied Ram Lal, adding in an ironical tone "and if you insist upon putting your head down the tiger's throat, how do you expect me to prevent the brute from snapping it off? That would be a 'phenomenon,' would it not? And only this evening you were saying that you despised 'phenomena.'"

"I said that such things were indifferent to me. I did not say I despised them. But I think that this thing may be done without performing any miracles."

"If it were not such a good action on your part I would have nothing to do with it. But since you mean to risk your neck for your own peculiar views of what is right, I will endeavour that you shall not break it. I will meet you a day's journey before you reach Keitung, somewhere on the road, and we will

go together and do the business. But if I am to
help you I will not promise not to perform some
miracles, as you call them, though you know very
well they are no such thing. Meanwhile, do as you
please about the tiger-hunt; I shall say no more
about it." He paused, and then, withdrawing one
delicate hand from the folds of his *caftán*, he pointed
to the wall behind Isaacs and me, and said, "What
a very singular piece of workmanship is that yataghan!"

We both naturally turned half round to look at
the weapon he spoke of, which was the central piece
in a trophy of jewelled sabres and Afghan knives.

"Yes," said Isaacs, turning back to answer his
guest, "it is a —— " He stopped, and I, who had
not seen the weapon before, lost among so many, and
was admiring its singular beauty, turned too; to
my astonishment I saw that Isaacs was gazing into
empty space. The divan where Ram Lal had been
sitting an instant before, was vacant. He was gone.

"That is rather sudden," I said.

"More so than usual," was the reply. "Did you
see him go? Did he go out by the door?"

"Not I," I answered, "when I looked round at the
wall he was placidly sitting on that divan pointing
with one hand at the yataghan. Does he generally
go so quickly?"

"Yes, more or less. Now I will show you some
pretty sport." He rose to his feet and went to the
door. "Narain!" he cried. Narain, the bearer,

who was squatting against the door-post outside, sprang up and stood before his master. "Narain, why did you not show that pundit the way down-stairs? What do you mean? have you no manners?"

Narain stood open mouthed. "What pundit, sahib?" he asked.

"Why, the pundit who came a quarter of an hour ago, you donkey! He has just gone out, and you did not even get up and make a salaam, you impertinent vagabond!" Narain protested that no pundit, or sahib, or any one else, had passed the threshold since Ram Lal had entered. "Ha! you *budmash*. You lazy dog of a Hindoo! you have been asleep again, you swine, you son of a pig, you father of piglings! Is that the way you do your work in my service?" Isaacs was enjoying the joke in a quiet way im-mensely.

"Sahib," said the trembling Narain, apparently forgetting the genealogy his master had thrust upon him, "Sahib, you are protector of the poor, you are my father and my mother, and my brother, and all my relations," the common form of Hindoo supplica-tion, "but, Sri Krishnaji! by the blessed Krishna, I have not slept a wink."

"Then I suppose you mean me to believe that the pundit went through the ceiling, or is hidden under the cushions. Swear not by your false idols, slave; I shall not believe you for that, you dog of an unbeliever, you soor-be-iman, you swine without faith!"

"Han, sahib, han!" cried Narain, seizing at the idea that the pundit had disappeared mysteriously through the walls. "Yes, sahib, the pundit is a great yogi, and has made the winds carry him off." The fellow thought this was a bright idea, not by any means beneath consideration. Isaacs appeared somewhat pacified.

"What makes you think he is a yogi, dog?" he inquired in a milder tone. Narain had no answer ready, but stood looking rather stupidly through the door at the room whence the unearthly visitor had so suddenly disappeared. "Well," continued Isaacs, "you are more nearly right than you imagine. The pundit is a bigger yogi than any your idiotic religion can produce. Never mind, there is an eight anna bit for you, because I said you were asleep when you were not." Narain bent to the ground in thanks, as his master turned on his heel. "Not that he minds being told that he is a pig, in the least," said Isaacs. "I would not call a Mussulman so, but you can insult these Hindoos so much worse in other ways that I think the porcine simile is quite merciful by comparison." He sat down again among the cushions, and putting off his slippers, curled himself comfortably together for a chat.

"What do you think of Ram Lal?" he asked, when Narain had brought hookahs and sherbet.

"My dear fellow, I have hardly made up my mind what to think. I have not altogether recovered from my astonishment. I confess that there was nothing

startling about his manner or his person. He behaved and talked like a well educated native, in utter
contrast to the amazing things he said, and to his
unprecedented mode of leave-taking. It would have
seemed more natural — I would say, more fitting —
if he had appeared in the classic dress of an astrolo-
ger, surrounded with zodiacs, and blue lights, and
black cats. Why do you suppose he wants you to
abandon the tiger-hunt?"

"I cannot tell. Perhaps he thinks something may
happen to me to prevent my keeping the other
engagement. Perhaps he does not approve ——" he
stopped, as if not wanting to approach the subject of
Ram Lal's disapprobation. "I intend, nevertheless,
that the expedition come off, and I mean, moreover,
to have a very good time, and to kill a tiger if I see
one."

"I thought he seemed immensely pleased at your
conversion, as he calls it. He said that your newly
acquired belief in woman was a step towards a better
understanding of life."

"Of the world, he said," answered Isaacs, correct-
ing me. "There is a great difference between the
'world' and 'life.' The one is a finite, the other an
infinite expression. I believe, from what I have
learned of Ram Lal, that the ultimate object of the
adepts is happiness, only to be attained by wisdom,
and I apprehend that by wisdom they mean a knowledge of the world in the broadest sense of the word.
The world to them is a great repository of facts,

physical and social, of which they propose to acquire a specific knowledge by transcendental methods. If that seems to you a contradiction of terms, I will try and express myself better. If you understand me, I am satisfied. Of course I use transcendental in the sense in which it is applied by Western mathematicians to a mode of reasoning which I very imperfectly comprehend, save that it consists in reaching finite results by an adroit use of the infinite."

"Not a bad definition of transcendental analysis for a man who professes to know nothing about it," said I. "I would not accuse you of a contradiction of terms, either. I have often thought that what some people call the 'philosophy of the nineteenth century,' is nothing after all but the unconscious application of transcendental analysis to the everyday affairs of life. Consider the theories of Darwin, for instance. What are they but an elaborate application of the higher calculus? He differentiates men into protoplasms, and integrates protoplasms into monkeys, and shows the caudal appendage to be the independent variable, a small factor in man, a large factor in monkey. And has not the idea of successive development supplanted the early conception of spontaneous perfection? Take an illustration from India — the new system of competition, which the natives can never understand. Formerly the members of the Civil Service received their warrants by divine authority, so to speak. They were born perfect, as Aphrodite from the foam of the sea; they sprang armed and ready from the head of old John Company as Pallas Athene from the head of Zeus. Now all that is changed; they are selected from a great herd of candidates by methods of extreme exactness, and when they are chosen they represent the final result of infinite probabilities for and against their election. They are all exactly alike; they are a formula for taxation and the administration of justice, and so long as you do not attempt to use the formula for any other purpose, such, for instance, as political negotiation or the censorship of the public press, the equation will probably be amenable to solution."

"As I told you," said Isaacs, "I know nothing, or next to nothing, of Western mathematics, but I have a general idea of the comparison you make. In Asia and in Asiatic minds, there prevails an idea that knowledge can be assimilated once and for all. That if you can obtain it, you immediately possess the knowledge of everything — the pass-key that shall unlock every door. That is the reason of the prolonged fasting and solitary meditation of the ascetics. They believe that by attenuating the bond between soul and body, the soul can be liberated and can temporarily identify itself with other objects, animate and inanimate, besides the especial body to which it belongs, acquiring thus a direct knowledge of those objects, and they believe that this direct knowledge remains. Western philosophers argue that the only acquaintance a man can have with

K

bodies external to his mind is that which he acquires by the medium of his bodily senses — though these are themselves external to his mind, in the truest sense. The senses not being absolutely reliable, knowledge acquired by means of them is not absolutely reliable either. So the ultimate difference between the Asiatic saint and the European man of science is, that while the former believes all knowledge to be directly within the grasp of the soul, under certain conditions, the latter, on the other hand, denies that any knowledge can be absolute, being all obtained indirectly through a medium not absolutely reliable. The reasoning, by which the Western mind allows itself to act fearlessly on information which is not (according to its own verdict) necessarily accurate, depends on a clever use of the infinite in unconsciously calculating the probabilities of that accuracy — and this entirely falls in with what you said about the application of transcendental analysis to the affairs of everyday life."

"I see you have entirely comprehended me," I said. "But as for the Asiatic mind — you seem to deny to it the use of the calculus of thought, and yet you defined adepts as attempting to acquire specific knowledge by general and transcendental methods. Here is a real contradiction."

"No; I see no confusion, for I do not include the higher adepts in either class, since they have the wisdom to make use of the learning and of the methods of both. They seem to me to be endeavouring, roughly speaking, to combine the two. They believe absolute knowledge attainable, and they devote much time to the study of nature, in which pursuit they make use of highly analytical methods. They subdivide phenomena to an extent that would surprise and probably amuse a Western thinker. They count fourteen distinct colours in the rainbow, and invariably connect sound, even to the finest degrees, with shades of colour. I could name many other peculiarities of their mode of studying natural phenomena, which displays a much more minute subdivision and classification of results than you are accustomed to. But beside all this they consider that the senses of the normal man are susceptible of infinite refinement, and that upon a greater or less degree of acquired acuteness of perception the value of his results must depend. To attain this high degree of sensitiveness, necessary to the perception of very subtle phenomena, the adepts find it necessary to train their faculties, bodily and mental, by a life of rigid abstention from all pleasures or indulgences not indispensable in maintaining the relation between the physical and intellectual powers."

"The common *fakir* aims at the same thing," I remarked.

"But he does not attain it. The common *fakir* is an idiot. He may, by fasting and self-torture, of a kind no adept would approve, sharpen his senses till he can hear and see some sounds and sights inaudible and invisible to you and me. But his whole system

lacks any intellectual basis: he regards knowledge
as something instantaneously attainable when it
comes at last; he believes he will have a vision, and
that everything will be revealed to him. His devotion to his object is admirable, when he is a genuine
ascetic and not, as is generally the case, a good-for-
nothing who makes his piety pay for his subsistence;
but it is devotion of a very low intellectual order.
The true adept thinks the training of the mind in
intellectual pursuits no less necessary than the mod-
erate and reasonable mortification of the flesh, and
higher Buddhism pays as much attention to the one
as to the other."

"Excuse me," said I, "if I make a digression. I
think there are two classes of minds commonly to be
found among thinkers all over the world. The one
seek to attain to knowledge, the others strive to
acquire it. There is a class of commonplace intellects
who regard knowledge of all kinds in the light of a
ladder, one ladder for each science, and the rungs of
the ladders are the successive facts mastered by an
effort and remembered in the order they have been
passed. These persons think it is possible to attain to
high eminence on one particular ladder, that is, in
one particular science, without having been up any
of the other ladders, that is, without a knowledge of
other branches of science. This is the mind of the
plodder, the patient man who climbs, step by step,
in his own unvarying round of thought; not seeing
that it is but the wheel of a treadmill over which he

is labouring, and that though every step may pass, and repass, beneath his toiling feet, he can never obtain a birdseye view of what he is doing, because his eyes are continually fixed on the step in front."

"But," I continued, as Isaacs assented to my simile by a nod, "there is another class of minds also. There are persons who regard the whole imaginable and unimaginable knowledge of mankind, past, present, and future, as a boundless plain over which they hang suspended and can look down. Immediately beneath them there is a map spread out which represents, in the midst of the immense desert, the things they themselves know. It is a puzzle map, like those they make for children, where each piece fits into its appointed place, and will fit nowhere else; every piece of knowledge acquired fits into the space allotted to it, and when there is a piece, that is, a fact, wanting, it is still possible to define its extent and shape by the surrounding portions, though all the details of colour and design are lacking. These are the people who regard knowledge as a whole, harmonious, when every science and fragment of a science has its appointed station and is necessary to completeness of perfect knowledge. I hope I have made clear to you what I mean, though I am conscious of only sketching the outlines of a distinction which I believe to be fundamental."

"Of course it is fundamental. Broadly, it is the difference between analytic and synthetic thought; between the subjective and the objective views;

between the finite conception of a limited world and the infinite ideal of perfect wisdom. I understand you perfectly."

"You puzzle me continually, Isaacs. Where did you learn to talk about 'analytic' and 'synthetic,' and 'subjective' and 'objective,' and transcendental analysis, and so forth?" It seemed so consistent with his mind that he should understand the use of philosophical terms, that I had not realised how odd it was that a man of his purely Oriental education should know anything about the subject. His very broad application of the words 'analytic' and 'synthetic' to my pair of illustrations attracted my attention and prompted the question I had asked.

"I read a good deal," he said simply. Then he added in a reflective tone, "I rather think I have a philosophical mind. The old man who taught me theology in Istamboul when I was a boy used to talk philosophy to me by the hour, though I do not believe he knew much about it. He was a plodder, and went up ladders in search of information, like the man you describe. But he was very patient and good to me; the peace of Allah be with him."

It was late, and soon afterwards we parted for the night. The next day was Sunday, and I had a heap of unanswered letters to attend to, so we agreed to meet after tiffin and ride together before dining with Mr. Ghyrkins and the Westonhaughs.

I went to my room and sat a while over a volume of Kant, which I always travel with — a sort of phi-

losopher's stone on which to whet the mind's tools
when they are dulled with boring into the geological
strata of other people's ideas. I was too much occupied with the personality of the man I had been talking with to read long, and so I abandoned myself
to a reverie, passing in review the events of the long
day.

CHAPTER VII.

The Sabbatarian tendency of the English mind at home and abroad is proverbial, and if they are well-behaved on Sunday in London they are models of virtue in Simla on the same day. Whether they labour and are well-fed and gouty in their island home, or suffer themselves to be boiled for gain in the tropical kettles of Ceylon and Singapore; whether they risk their lives in hunting for the north pole or the northwest passage, or endanger their safety in the pursuit of tigers in the Terai, they will have their Sunday, come rain, come shine. On the deck of the steamer in the Red Sea, in the cabin of the inbound Arctic explorer, in the crowded Swiss hotel, or the straggling Indian hill station, there is always a parson of some description, in a surplice of no description at all, who produces a Bible and a couple of well-thumbed sermons from the recesses of his trunk or his lunch basket, or his gun-case, and goes at the work of weekly redemption with a will. And, what is more, he is listened to, and for the time being — though on week days he is styled a bore by the old and a prig by the young — he becomes temporarily invested with a dignity not his own, with an authority he could not claim on any other day. It is the dignity of a people who with all their faults have the courage of their opinions, and it is the authority that they have been taught from their childhood to reverence, whenever their traditions give it the right to assert itself. Not otherwise. It is a fine trait of national character, though it is one which has brought upon the English much unmerited ridicule. One may differ from them in faith and in one's estimate of the real value of these services, which are often only saved from being irreverent in their performance by the perfect sincerity of parson and congregation. But no one who dispassionately judges them can deny that the custom inspires respect for English consistency and admiration for their supreme contempt of surroundings.

I presume that the periodical manifestations of religious belief to which I refer are intimately and indissolubly connected with the staid and funereal solemnity which marks an Englishman's dress, conversation, and conduct on Sunday. He is a different being for the nonce, and must sustain the entire character of his dual existence, or it will fall to the ground and forsake him altogether. He cannot take his religion in the morning and enjoy himself the rest of the day. He must abstain from everything that could remind him that he has a mind at all, besides a soul. No amusement will he tolerate, no reading of even the most harmless fiction can he suffer, while he is in the weekly devotional trance.

I cannot explain these things; they are race questions, problems for the ethnologist. Certain it is,
however, that the partial decay of strict Sabbatari-
anism which seems to have set in during the last
quarter of a century has not been attended by any
notable development of power in English thought of
that class. The first Republic tried the experiment
of the decimal week, and it was a failure. The
English who attempt to put off even a little of the
quaint armour of righteousness, which they have
been accustomed to buckle on every seventh day for
so many generations, are not so successful in the
attempt as to attract many to follow them. They
are not graceful in their holiday gambols.

Meditating somewhat on this wise I lay in my long
chair by the open door that Sunday morning in September. It was a little warmer again and the sun
shone pleasantly across the lawn on the great branches
and bright leaves of the rhododendron. The house
was very quiet. All the inmates were gone to the
church on the mall, and the servants were basking in
the last few days of warmth they would enjoy before
their masters returned to the plains. The Hindoo
servant hates the cold. He fears it as he fears cobras, fever, and freemasons. His ideal life is nothing to do, nothing to wear, and plenty to eat, with the
thermometer at 135 degrees in the verandah and 110
inside. Then he is happy. His body swells with
much good rice and *dal*, and his heart with pride;
he will wear as little as you will let him, and

whether you will let him or not, he will do less work
in a given time than any living description of servant. So they basked in rows in the sunshine, and
did not even quarrel or tell yarns among themselves;
it was quiet and warm and sleepy. I dozed lazily,
dropped my book in my lap, struggled once, and then
fairly fell asleep.

I was roused by Kiramat Ali pulling at my foot,
as natives will when they are afraid of the consequences of waking their master. When I opened my
eyes he presented a card on a salver, and explained
that the gentleman wanted to see me. I looked, and
was rather surprised to see it was Kildare's card.
"Lord Steepleton Kildare, 33d Lancers "— there was
no word in pencil, or any message. I told Kiramat
to show the sahib in, wondering why he should call
on me. By Indian etiquette, if there was to be any
calling, it was my duty to make the first visit.
Before I had time to think more I heard the clank-
ing of spurs and sabre on the verandah, and the
young man walked in, clad in the full uniform of
his regiment. I rose to greet him, and was struck by
his soldierly bearing and straight figure, as I had
been at our first meeting. He took off his bearskin
— for he was in the fullest of full dress — and sat
down.

"I am so glad to find you at home," he said: "I
feared you might have gone to church, like everybody else in this place."

"No. I went early this morning. I belong to a

different persuasion. I suppose you are on your way to Peterhof?"

"Yes. There is some sort of official reception to somebody, — I forget who, — and we had notice to turn out. It is a detestable nuisance."

"I should think so."

"Mr. Griggs, I came to ask you about something. You heard of my proposal to get up a tiger-hunt? Mr. Ghyrkins was speaking of it."

"Yes. He wanted us to go, — Mr. Isaacs and me, — and suggested leaving his niece, Miss Weston-haugh, with Lady Smith-Tompkins."

"It would be so dull without a lady in the party. Nothing but tigers and shikarries and other native abominations to talk to. Do you not think so?"

"Why, yes. I told Mr. Ghyrkins that all the little Smith-Tompkins children had the measles, and the house was not safe. If they have not had them, they will, I have no doubt. Heaven is just, and will not leave you to the conversational mercies of the entertaining tiger and the engaging shikarry."

"By Jove, Mr. Griggs, that was a brilliant idea; and, as you say, they may all get the measles yet. The fact is, I have set my heart on this thing. Miss Westonhaugh said she had never seen a tiger, except in cages and that kind of thing, and so I made up my mind she should. Besides, it will be no end of a lark; just when nobody is thinking about tigers, you go off and kill a tremendous fellow, fifteen or sixteen feet long, and come back covered with glory and mosquito bites, and tell everybody that Miss Westonhaugh shot him herself with a pocket pistol. That will be glorious!"

"I should like it very much too; and I really see no reason why it should not be done. Mr. Ghyrkins seemed in a very cheerful humour about tigers last night, and I have no doubt a little persuasion from you will bring him to a proper view of his obligations to Miss Westonhaugh." He looked pleased and bright and hopeful, thoroughly enthusiastic, as became his Irish blood. He evidently intended to have quite as "good" a "time" as Isaacs proposed to enjoy. I thought the spectacle of those rivals for the beautiful girl's favour would be extremely interesting. Lord Steepleton was doubtless a good shot and a brave man, and would risk anything to secure Miss Westonhaugh's approval; Isaacs, on the other hand, was the sort of man who is very much the same in danger as anywhere else.

"That is what I came to ask you about. We shall all meet there at dinner this evening, and I wanted to secure as many allies as possible."

"You may count on me, Lord Steepleton, at all events. There is nothing I should enjoy better than such a fortnight's holiday, in such good company."

"All right," said Lord Steepleton, rising, "I must be off now to Peterhof. It is an organised movement on Mr. Ghyrkins this evening, then. Is it understood?" He took his bearskin from the table, and prepared to go, pulling his straps and belts into place, and dusting a particle of ash from his sleeve.

"Perfectly," I answered. "We will drag him forth into the arena before three days are past." We shook hands, and he went out.

I was glad he had come, though I had been waked from a pleasant nap to receive him. He was so perfectly gay, and natural, and healthy, that one could not help liking him. You felt at once that he was honest and would do the right thing in spite of any one, according to his light; that he would stand by a friend in danger, and face any odds in fight, with as much honest determination to play fair and win, as he would bring to a cricket match or a steeple-chase. His Irish blood gave him a somewhat less formal manner than belongs to the Englishman; more enthusiasm and less regard for "form," while his good heart and natural courtesy would lead him right in the long-run. He seemed all sunshine, with his bright blue eyes and great fair moustache and brown face; the closely fitting uniform showed off his erect figure and elastic gait, and the whole impression was fresh and exhilarating in the extreme. I was sorry he had gone. I would have liked to talk with him about boating and fishing and shooting; about athletics and horses and tandem-driving, and many things I used to like years ago at college, before I began my wandering life. I watched him as he swung himself into the military saddle, and he threw up his hand in a parting salute as he rode away. Poor fellow! was he, too, going to be food for powder and Afghan knives in the avenging army on its way to Kabul? I went back to my books and remained reading until the afternoon sun slanted in through the open door, and falling across my book warned me it was time to keep my appointment with Isaacs.

As we passed the church the people were coming out from the evening service, and I saw Kildare, once more in the garb of a civilian, standing near the door, apparently watching for some one to appear. I knew that, with his strict observance of Catholic rules — often depending more on pride of family than on religious conviction, in the house of Kildare — he would not have entered the English Church at such a time, and I was sure he was lying in wait for Miss Westonhaugh, probably intending to surprise her and join her on her homeward ride. The road winds down below the Church, so that for some minutes after passing the building you may get a glimpse of the mall above and of the people upon it — or at least of their heads — if they are moving near the edge of the path. I was unaccountably curious this evening, and I dropped a little behind Isaacs, craning my neck and turning back in the saddle as I watched the stream of heads and shoulders, strongly foreshortened against the blue sky above, moving ceaselessly along the parapet over my head. Before long I was rewarded; Miss Westonhaugh's fair hair and broad hat entered the field of my vision, and a moment later Lord Steepleton, who must have pushed through the crowd from the other side,

appeared struggling after her. She turned quickly,
and I saw no more, but I did not think she had
changed colour.

I began to be deeply interested in ascertaining
whether she had any preference for one or the other
of the two young men. Kildare's visit in the morning — though he had said very little — had given me
a new impression of the man, and I felt that he was
no contemptible rival. I saw from the little incident I had just witnessed that he neglected no opportunity of being with Miss Westonhaugh, and that he
had the patience to wait and the boldness to find her
in a crowd. I had seen very little of her myself;
but I had been amply satisfied that Isaacs was capable of interesting her in a *tête-à-tête* conversation.
"The talker has the best chance, if he is bold enough,"
I said to myself; but I was not satisfied, and I
resolved that if I could manage it Isaacs should have
another chance that very evening after the dinner.
Meanwhile I would involve Isaacs in a conversation
on some one of those subjects that seemed to interest
him most. He had not seen the couple on the mall,
and was carelessly ambling along with his head in
the air and one hand in the pocket of his short coat,
the picture of unconcern.

I was trying to make up my mind whether I would
open fire upon the immortality of the soul, matrimony, or the differential calculus, when, as we
passed from the narrow street into the road leading
round Jako, Isaacs spoke.

"Look here, Griggs," said he, "there is something I want to impress upon your mind."

"Well, what is it?"

"It is all very well for Ram Lal to give advice about things he understands. I have a very sincere regard for him, but I do not believe he was ever in my position. I have set my heart on this tiger-hunt. Miss Westonhaugh said the other day that she had never seen a tiger, and I then and there made up my mind that she should."

I laughed. There seemed to be no essential difference of opinion between the Irishman and the Persian in regard to the pleasures of the chase. Miss Westonhaugh was evidently anxious to see tigers, and meant to do it, since she had expressed her wish to the two men most likely to procure her that innocent recreation. Lord Steepleton Kildare by his position, and Isaacs by his wealth, could, if they chose, get up such a tiger-hunt for her benefit as had never been seen. I thought she might have waited till the spring — but I had learned that she intended to return to England in April, and was to spend the early months of the year with her brother in Bombay.

"You want to see Miss Westonhaugh, and Miss Westonhaugh wants to see tigers! My dear fellow, go in and win; I will back you."

"Why do you laugh, Griggs?" asked Isaacs, who saw nothing particularly amusing in what he had said.

"Oh, I laughed because another young gentleman

expressed the same opinions to me, in identically the same words, this morning."

"Mr. Westonhaugh?"

"No. You know very well that Mr. Westonhaugh cares nothing about it, one way or the other. The little plan for 'amusing brother John' is a hoax. The thing cannot be done. You might as well try to amuse an undertaker as to make a man from Bombay laugh. The hollowness of life is ever upon them. No. It was Kildare; he called and said that Miss Westonhaugh had never seen a tiger, and he seemed anxious to impress upon me his determination that she should. Pshaw! what does Kildare care about brother John?"

"Brother John, as you call him, is a better fellow than he looks. I owe a great deal to brother John." Isaacs' olive skin flushed a little, and he emphasised the epithet by which I had designated Mr. John Westonhaugh as if he were offended by it.

"I mean nothing against Mr. Westonhaugh," said I half apologetically. "I remember when you met yesterday afternoon you said you had seen him in Bombay a long time ago."

"Do you remember the story I told you of myself the other night?"

"Perfectly."

"Westonhaugh was the young civil servant who paid my fine and gave me a rupee, when I was a ragged sailor from a Mocha craft, and could not speak a word of English. To that rupee I ultimately owe my entire fortune. I never forget a face, and I am sure it is he — do you understand me now? I owe to his kindness everything I possess in the world."

"The unpardonable sin is ingratitude," I answered, "of which you will certainly not be accused. That is a very curious coincidence."

"I think it is something more. A man has always at least one opportunity of repaying a debt, and, besm Illah! I will repay what I can of it. By the beard of the apostle, whose name is blessed, I am not ungrateful!" Isaacs was excited as he said this. He was no longer the calm Mr. Isaacs; he was Abdul Hafiz the Persian, fiery and enthusiastic.

"You say well, my friend," he continued earnestly, "that the unpardonable sin is ingratitude. Doubtless, had the blessed prophet of Allah lived in our day, he would have spoken of the doom that hangs over the ungrateful. It is the curse of this age; for he who forgets or refuses to remember the kindness done to him by others sets himself apart, and worships his miserable self; and he makes an idol of himself, saying, 'I am of more importance than my fellows in the world, and it is meet and right that they should give and that I should receive.' Ingratitude is selfishness, and selfishness is the worship of oneself, the setting of oneself higher than man and goodness and God. And when man perishes and the angel Al Sijil, the recorder, rolls up his scroll, what is written therein is written; and Israfil shall call men to judgment, and the scrolls shall be unfolded, and he that has taken of others and not given in return, but has ungratefully forgotten and put away the remembrance of the kindness received, shall be counted among the unbelievers and the extortioners and the unjust, and shall broil in raging flames. By the hairs of the prophet's beard, whose name is blessed."

I had not seen Isaacs so thoroughly roused before upon any subject. The flush had left his face and given place to a perfect paleness, and his eyes shone like coals of fire as he looked upward in pronouncing the last words. I said to myself that there was a strong element of religious exaltation in all Asiatics, and put his excitement down to this cause. His religion was a very beautiful and real thing to him, ever present in his life, and I mused on the future of the man, with his great endowments, his exquisite sensitiveness, and his high view of his obligations to his fellows. I am not a worshipper of heroes, but I felt that, for the first time in my life, I was intimate with a man who was ready to stand in the breach and to die for what he thought and believed to be right. After a pause of some minutes, during which we had ridden beyond the last straggling bungalows of the town, he spoke again, quietly, his temporary excitement having subsided.

"I feel very strongly about these things," he said, and then stopped short.

"I can see you do, and I honour you for it. I

think you are the first grateful person I have ever met; a rare and unique bird in the earth."

"Do not say that."

"I do say it. There is very little of the philosophy of the nineteenth century about you, Isaacs. Your belief in the obligations of gratitude and in the general capacity of the human race for redemption, savours little of 'transcendental analysis.'"

"You have too much of it," he answered seriously. "I do not think you see how much your cynicism involves. You would very likely, if you are the man I take you for, be very much offended if I accused you of not believing any particular dogma of your religion. And yet, with all your faith, you do not believe in God."

"I cannot see how you get at that conclusion," I replied. "I must deny your hypothesis, at the risk of engaging you in an argument." I could not see what he was driving at.

"How can you believe in God, and yet condemn the noblest of His works as altogether bad? You are not consistent."

"What makes you think I am so cynical?" I inquired, harking back to gain time.

"A little cloud, a little sultriness in the air, is all that betrays the coming *khemsin*, that by and by shall overwhelm and destroy man and beast in its sandy darkness. You have made one or two remarks lately that show little faith in human nature, and if you do not believe in human nature what is there left for

you to believe in? You said a moment ago that I
was the first grateful person you had ever met. Then
the rest of humanity are all selfish, and worshippers
of themselves, and altogether vile, since you yourself say, as I do, that ingratitude is the unpardonable sin; and God has made a world full of unpardonable sinners, and unless you include yourself in
the exception you graciously make in my favour, no
one but I shall be saved. And yet you say also with
me that God is good. Do you deny that you are
utterly inconsistent?"

"I may make you some concession in a few minutes,
but I am not going to yield to such logic. You have
committed the fallacy of the undistributed middle
term, if you care to know the proper name for it. I
did not say that all men, saving you, were ungrateful.
I said that, saving you, the persons I have met in
my life have been ungrateful. You ought to distinguish."

"All I can say is, then, that you have had a very
unfortunate experience of life," retorted Isaacs
warmly.

"I have," said I, "but since you yield the technical point of logic, I will confess that I made the
assertion hastily and overshot the mark. I do not
remember, however, to have met any one who felt
so strongly on the point as you do."

"Now you speak like a rational being," said Isaacs,
quite pacified. "Extraordinary feelings are the result of unusual circumstances. I was in such dis-

tress as rarely falls to the lot of an innocent man of fine temperament and good abilities. I am now in a position of such wealth and prosperity as still more seldom are given to a man of my age and antecedents. I remember that I obtained the first step on my road to fortune through the kindness of John Weston-haugh, though I could never learn his name, and I met him at last, as you saw, by an accident. I call that accident a favour, and an opportunity bestowed on me by Allah, and the meeting has roused in me those feelings of thankfulness which, for want of an object upon which to show them, have been put away out of sight as a thing sacred for many years. I am willing you should say that, were my present fortune less, my gratitude would be proportionately less felt — it is very likely — though the original gift remain the same, one rupee and no more. You are entitled to think of any man as grateful in proportion to the gift, so long as you allow the gratitude at all." He made this speech in a perfectly natural and uncon-cerned way, as if he were contemplating the case of another person.

"Seriously, Isaacs, I would not do so for the world. I believe you were as grateful twelve years ago, when you were poor, as you are now that you are rich." Isaacs was silent, but a look of great gentleness crossed his face. There was at times something almost angelic in the perfect kindness of his eyes.

"To return," I said at last, "to the subject from which we started, the tigers. If we are really going,

we must leave here the day after to-morrow morning
— indeed, why not to-morrow?"

"No; to-morrow we are to play that game of polo,
which I am looking forward to with pleasure. Besides, it will take the men three days to get the
elephants together, and I only telegraphed this morning to the collector of the district to make the
arrangements."

"So you have already taken steps? Does Kildare
know you have sent orders?"

"Certainly. He came to me this morning at daybreak, and we determined to arrange everything and
take uncle Ghyrkins for granted. You need not
look astonished; Kildare and I are allies, and very
good friends." What a true Oriental! How wise
and far-sighted was the Persian, how bold and reckless the Irishman! It was odd, I thought, that Kildare had not mentioned the interview with Isaacs.
Yet there was a certain rough delicacy — contra-
dictory and impulsive — in his silence about this
coalition with his rival. We rode along and dis-
cussed the plans for the expedition. All the men
in the party, except Lord Steepleton, who had not
been long in India, had killed tigers before. There
would be enough of us, without asking any one
else to join. The collector to whom Isaacs had telegraphed was an old acquaintance of his, and would
probably go out for a few days with us. It all
seemed easy enough and plain sailing. In the
course of time we returned to our hotel, dressed,

and made our way through the winding roads to
Mr. Currie Ghyrkins' bungalow.

We were met on the verandah by the old commissioner, who welcomed us warmly and praised our
punctuality, for the clock was striking seven in the
drawing-room, as we divested ourselves of our light
top-coats. In the vestibule, Miss Westonhaugh and
her brother came forward to greet us.

"John," said the young lady, "you know I told
you there was some one here whom you got out of
trouble ever so many years ago in Bombay. Here he
is. This is a new introduction. Mr. John Westonhaugh, Mr. Abdul Hafiz-ben-Isâk, commonly known
to his friends as Mr. Isaacs." Her face beamed with
pleasure, and I thought with pride, as she led her
brother to Isaacs, and her eyes rested long on the
Persian with a look that, to me, argued something
more than a mere interest. The two men clasped
hands and stood for some seconds looking at each
other in silence, but with very different expressions.
Westonhaugh wore a look of utter amazement, though
he certainly seemed pleased. The good heart that
had prompted the good action twelve years before was
still in the right place, above any petty considerations about nationality. His astonishment gradually
changed to a smile of real greeting and pleasure,
as he began to shake the hand he still held. I
thought that even the faintest tinge of blood coloured
his pale cheek.

"God bless my soul," said he, " I remember you

perfectly well now. But it is so unexpected; my sister reminded me of the story, which I had not forgotten, and now I look at you I remember you perfectly. I am so glad."

As Isaacs answered, his voice trembled, and his face was very pale. There was a moisture in the brilliant eyes that told of genuine emotion.

"Mr. Westonhaugh, I consider that I owe to you everything I have in the world. This is a greater pleasure than I thought was in store for me. Indeed I thank you again."

His voice would not serve him. He stopped short and turned away to look for something in his coat.

"Indeed," said Westonhaugh, "it was a very little thing I did for you." And presently the two men went together into the drawing-room, Westonhaugh asking all manner of questions, which Isaacs, who was himself again, began to answer. The rest of us remained in the vestibule to meet Lord Steepleton, who at that moment came up the steps. There were more greetings, and then the head *khitmatgar* appeared and informed the "*Sahib log*, protectors of the poor, that their meat was ready." So we filed into the dining-room.

Isaacs was placed at Miss Westonhaugh's right, and her brother sat on his other side. Ghyrkins was opposite his niece at the other end, and Kildare and I were together, facing Westonhaugh and Isaacs, a party of six. Of course Kildare sat beside the lady.

The dinner opened very pleasantly. I could see

that Isaacs' undisguised gratitude and delight in having at last met the man who had helped him had strongly predisposed John Westonhaugh in his favour. Who is it that is not pleased at finding that some deed of kindness, done long ago with hardly a thought, has borne fruit and been remembered and treasured up by the receiver as the turning-point in his life? Is there any pleasure greater than that we enjoy through the happiness of others — in those rare cases where kindness is not misplaced? I had had time to reflect that Isaacs had most likely told a part of his story to Miss Westonhaugh on the previous afternoon as soon as he had recognised her brother. He might have told her before; I did not know how long he had known her, but it must have been some time. Presently she turned to him.

"Mr. Isaacs," said she, "some of us know something of your history. Why will you not tell us the rest now? My uncle has heard nothing of it, and I know Lord Steepleton is fond of novels."

Isaacs hesitated long, but as every one pressed him in turn, he yielded at last. And he told it well. It was exactly the narrative he had given me, in every detail of fact, but the whole effect was different. I saw how true a mastery he had of the English language, for he knew his audience thoroughly, and by a little colour here and an altered expression there he made it graphic and striking, not without humour, and altogether free of a certain mystical tinge he had imparted to it when we were alone. He talked

easily, with no more constraint than on other occasions, and his narrative was a small social success.
I had not seen him in evening dress before, and I
could not help thinking how much more thoroughly
he looked the polished man of the world than the
other men.   Kildare never appeared to greater advantage than in the uniform and trappings of his profession.   In a black coat and a white tie he looked like
any other handsome young Englishman, utterly without individuality.   But Isaacs, with his pale complexion and delicate high-bred features, bore himself
like a noble of the old school.   Westonhaugh beside
him looked washed-out and deathly, Kildare was too
coarsely healthy, and Ghyrkins and I, representing
different types of extreme plainness, served as foils
to all three.

I watched Miss Westonhaugh while Isaacs was
speaking.   She had evidently heard the whole story,
for her expression showed beforehand the emotion
she expected to feel at each point.   Her colour came
and went softly, and her eyes brightened with a warm
light beneath the dark brows that contrasted so
strangely yet delightfully with the mass of flaxen-
white hair.   She wore something dark and soft, cut
square at the neck, and a plain circlet of gold was
her only ornament.   She was a beautiful creature,
certainly; one of those striking-looking women of
whom something is always expected, until they drop
quietly out of youth into middle age, and the world
finds out that they are, after all, not heroines of

romance, but merely plain, honest, good women; good wives and good mothers who love their homes and husbands well, though it has pleased nature in some strange freak to give them the form and feature of a Semiramis, a Cleopatra, or a Jeanne d'Arc.

"Dear me, how very interesting!" exclaimed Mr. Ghyrkins, looking up from his hill mutton as Isaacs finished, and a little murmur of sympathetic applause went round the table.

"I would give a great deal to have been through all that," said Lord Steepleton, slowly proceeding to sip a glass of claret.

"Just think!" ejaculated John Westonhaugh. "And I was entertaining such a Sinbad unawares!" and he took another green pepper from the dish his servant handed him.

"Upon my word, Isaacs," I said, "some one ought to make a novel of that story; it would sell like wildfire."

"Why don't you do it yourself, Griggs?" he asked. "You are a pressman, and I am sure you are welcome to the whole thing."

"I will," I answered.

"Oh do, Mr. Griggs," said the young lady, "and make it wind up with a tiger-hunt. You could lay the scene in Australia or the Barbadoes, or some of those places, and put us all in—and kill us all off, if you like, you know. It would be such fun." Poor Miss Westonhaugh!

"It is easy to see what you are thinking about

most, Miss Westonhaugh," said Lord Steepleton:
"the tigers are uppermost in your mind; and therefore in mine also," he added gallantly.

"Indeed, no — I was thinking about Mr. Isaacs."
She blushed scarlet — the first time I had ever seen
her really embarrassed.   It was very natural that she
should be thinking of Isaacs and the strange adven-
tures he had just recounted; and if she had not cared
about him she would not have changed colour.   So
I thought, at all events.

"My dear, drink some water immediately, this
curry is very hot — deuced hot, in fact," said Mr.
Ghyrkins, in perfectly good faith.

John Westonhaugh, who was busy breaking up
biscuits and green peppers and "Bombay ducks"
into his curry, looked up slowly at his sister and
smiled.

"Why, you are quite a griffin, Katharine," said
he, "how they will laugh at you in Bombay!"   I
was amused; of course the remarks of her uncle and
brother did not make the blush subside — on the
contrary.   Kildare was drinking more claret, to conceal his annoyance.   Isaacs had a curious expression.
There was a short silence, and for one instant he
turned his eyes to Miss Westonhaugh.   It was only
a look, but it betrayed to me — who knew what he
felt — infinite surprise, joy, and sympathy.   His
quick understanding had comprehended that he had
scored his first victory over his rival.

As her eyes met those of Isaacs, the colour left her

cheeks as suddenly as it had come, leaving her face
dead white. She drank a little water, and presently
seemed at ease again. I was beginning to think she
cared for him seriously.

"And pray, John," she asked, "what may a griffin
be? It is not a very pretty name to call a young
lady, is it?"

"Why, a griffin," put in Mr. Ghyrkins, "is the
'Mr. Verdant Green' of the Civil Service. A young
civilian—or anybody else—who is just out from
home is called a griffin. John calls you a griffin
because you don't understand eating pepper. You
don't find it as *chilly* as he does! Ha! ha! ha!" and
the old fellow laughed heartily, till he was red in
the face, at his bleared old pun. Of course every one
was amused or professed to be, for it was a diversion
welcomed by the three men of us who had seen the
young girl's embarrassment.

"A griffin," said I, "is a thing of joy. Mr.
Westonhaugh was a griffin when he gave Mr. Isaacs
that historical rupee." I cast my little bombshell
into the conversation, and placidly went on manipu-
lating my rice.

Isaacs was in too gay a humour to be offended, and
he only said, turning to Miss Westonhaugh—

"Mr. Griggs is a cynic, you know. You must not
believe anything he says."

"If doing kind things makes one a griffin, I hope I
may be one always," said Miss Westonhaugh quickly,
"and I trust my brother is as much a griffin as ever."

"I am, I assure you," said he. "But Mr. Griggs is quite right, and shows a profound knowledge of Indian life. No one but a griffin of the greenest ever gave anybody a rupee in Bombay — or ever will now, I should think."

"Oh, John, are you going to be cynical too?"

"No, Katharine, I am not cynical at all. I do not think you are quite sure what a 'cynic' is."

"Oh yes, I know quite well. Diogenes was a cynic, and Saint Jerome, and other people of that class."

"A man who lives in a tub, and abuses Alexander the Great, and that sort of thing," remarked Kildare, who had not spoken for some time.

"Mr. Griggs," said John Westonhaugh, "since you are the accused, pray define what you mean by a cynic, and then Mr. Isaacs, as the accuser, can have a chance too."

"Very well, I will. A man is a cynic if he will do no good to any one because he believes every one past improvement. Most men who do good actions are also cynics, because they well know that they are doing more harm than good by their charity. Mr. Westonhaugh has the discrimination to appreciate this, and therefore he is not a cynic."

"It is well you introduced the saving clause, Griggs," said Isaacs to me from across the table. "I am going to define you now; for I strongly suspect that you are the very ideal of a philosopher of that class. You are a man who believes in all that is good and beautiful in theory, but by too much indifference to good in small measures — for you want a thing perfect, or you want it not at all — you have abstracted yourself from perceiving it anywhere, except in the most brilliant examples of heroism that history affords. You set up in your imagination an ideal which you call the good man, and you are utterly dissatisfied with anything less perfect than perfection. The result is that, though you might do a good action from your philosophical longing to approach the ideal in your own person, you will not suffer yourself to believe that others are consciously or unconsciously striving to make themselves better also. And you do not believe that any one can be made a better man by any one else, by any exterior agency, by any good that you or others may do to him. What makes you what you are is the fact that you really cherish this beautiful ideal image of your worship and reverence, and love it; but for this, you would be the most insufferable man of my acquaintance, instead of being the most agreeable."

Isaacs was gifted with a marvellous frankness of speech. He always said what he meant, with a supreme indifference to consequences; but he said it with such perfect honesty and evident appreciation of what was good, even when he most vehemently condemned what he did not like, that it was impossible to be annoyed. Every one laughed at his attack on me, and having satisfied my desire to observe Miss Westonhaugh, which had prompted my first

M

remark about griffins, I thought it was time to turn the conversation to the projected hunt.

"My dear fellow," I said, "I think that in spite of your Parthian shaft, your definition of a cynic is as complimentary to the school at large as to me in particular. Meanwhile, however," I added, turning to Mr. Ghyrkins, "I am inclined to believe with Lord Steepleton that the subject uppermost in the thoughts of most of us is the crusade against the tigers. What do you say? Shall we not all go as we are, a neat party of six?"

"Well, well, Mr. Griggs, we shall see, you know. Now, if we are going at all, when do you mean to start?"

"The sooner the better of course," broke in Kildare, and he launched into a host of reasons for going immediately, including the wildest statistics about the habits of tigers in winter. This was quite natural, however, as he was a thorough Irishman and had never seen a tiger in his life. Mr. Currie Ghyrkins vainly attempted to stem the torrent of his eloquence, but at last pinned him on some erratic statement about tigers moulting later in the year and their skins not being worth taking. Kildare would have asserted with equal equanimity that all tigers shed their teeth and their tails in December; he was evidently trying to rouse Mr. Ghyrkins into a discussion on the subject of tiger shooting in general, a purpose very easily accomplished. The old gentleman was soon goaded to madness by Kildare's wonderful opinions, and before long he vowed that the youngster had never seen a tiger, — not one in his whole life, sir, — and that it was high time he did, high time indeed, and he swore he should see one before he was a week older. Yes, sir, before he was a week older, "if I have to carry you among 'em like a baby in arms, sir, by gad, sir — I should think so!"

This was all we wanted, and in another ten minutes we were drinking a bumper to the health of the whole tiger-hunt and of Miss Westonhaugh in particular. Isaacs joined with the rest, and though he only drank some sherbet, as I watched his bright eyes and pale cheek, I thought that never knight drank truer toast to his lady. Miss Westonhaugh rose and went out, leaving us to smoke for a while. The conversation was general, and turned on the chase, of course. In a few minutes Isaacs dropped his cigarette and went quietly out. I determined to detain the rest as long as possible, and I seconded Mr. Ghyrkins in passing the claret briskly round, telling all manner of stories of all nations and peoples — ancient tales that would not amuse a schoolboy in America, but which were a revelation of profound wit and brilliant humour to the unsophisticated British mind. By immense efforts — and I hate to exert myself in conversation — I succeeded in prolonging the session through a cigar and a half, but at last I was forced to submit to a move; and with a somewhat ancient remark from Mr. Ghyrkins, to the effect that all good things

must come to an end, we returned to the drawing-
room.

Isaacs and Miss Westonhaugh were looking over
some English photographs, and she was enthusiasti-
cally praising the beauties of Gothic architecture,
while Isaacs was making the most of his opportunity,
and taking a good look at her as she bent over the
album.   After we came in, she made a little music
at the tuneless piano — there never was a piano in
India yet that had any tune in it — playing and singing a little, very prettily.   She sang something about
a body in the rye, and then something else about
drinking only with the eyes, to which her brother
sang a sort of second very nicely.   I do not understand much about music, but I thought the allusion
to Isaacs' temperance in only drinking with his eyes
was rather pointed.   He said, however, that he liked
it even better with a second than when she sang it
alone, so I argued that it was not the first time he
had heard it.

"Mr. Isaacs," said she, "you have often promised
to sing something Persian for us.   Will you not
keep your word now?"

"When we are among the tigers, Miss Westonhaugh, next week.   Then I will try and borrow a
lute and sing you something."

It was late for an Indian dinner-party, so we took
our departure soon afterwards, having agreed to meet
the following afternoon at Annandale for the game
of polo, in which Westonhaugh said he would also

play. He and Isaacs made some appointment for the morning; they seemed to be very sympathetic to each other. Kildare mounted and rode homeward with us, though he had much farther to go than we. If he felt any annoyance at the small successes Isaacs had achieved during the evening, he was far too courteous a gentleman to show it; and so, as we groped our way through the trees by the starlight, chiefly occupied in keeping our horses on their legs, the snatches of conversation that were possible were pleasant, if not animated, and there was a cordial "Good-night" on both sides, as we left Kildare to pursue his way alone.

CHAPTER VIII.

IT was nearly four o'clock in the afternoon when Isaacs and I emerged from the narrow road upon the polo ground. We were clad in the tight-fitting garments which are necessary for the game, and wrapped in light top-coats; as we came out on the green we saw a number of other men in similar costume standing about, and a great many native grooms leading ponies up and down. Miss Westonhaugh was there in her gray habit and broad hat, and by her side, on foot, Lord Steepleton Kildare was making the most of his time, as he waited for the rest of the players. Mr. Currie Ghyrkins was ambling about on his broad little horse, and John Westonhaugh stood with his hands in his pockets and a large Trichinopoli cheroot between his lips, apparently gazing into space. Several other men, more or less known to us and to each other, moved about or chatted disconnectedly, and one or two arrived after us. Some of them wore coloured jerseys that showed brightly over the open collars of their coats, others were in ordinary dress and had come to see the game. Farther off, at one side of the ground, one or two groups of ladies and their escorting cavaliers haunted at a short distance by their saices in many-coloured turbans and belts, or *cummer-bunds,* as the sash is called in India, moved slowly about, glancing from time to time towards the place where the players and their ponies were preparing for the contest.

Few games require so little preparation and so few preliminaries as polo, descended as it is from an age when more was thought of good horsemanship and quick eye than of any little refinements depending on an accurate knowledge of fixed rules. Any one who is a firstrate rider and is quick with his hands can learn to play polo. The stiffest of arms can be limbered and the most recalcitrant wrist taught to turn nimbly in its socket; but the essential condition is, that the player should know how to ride. This being established, there is no reason why anybody who likes should not play the game, if he will only use a cetrain amount of caution, and avoid braining the other players and injuring the ponies by too wild a use of his mallet. Presently it was found that all who were to play had arrived — eight of us all told. Kildare had arranged the sides and had brought the other men necessary to make the number complete, so we mounted and took up our positions on the ground. Kildare and Isaacs were together, and Westonhaugh and I on the other side, with two men I knew slightly. We won the charge, and Westonhaugh, who was a celebrated player, struck the ball off cleverly, and I followed him up with a rush as he raced after it. Isaacs, on the other side, swept

along easily, and as the ball swerved on striking the
ground bent far over till he looked as though he
were out of the saddle and stopped it cleverly, while
Kildare, who was close behind, got a good stroke in
just in time, as Westonhaugh and I galloped down on
him, and landed the ball far to the rear near our goal.
As we wheeled quickly, I saw that one of the other
two men on our side had stopped it and was beginning to "dribble" it along.   This was very bad play,
both Westonhaugh and I being so far forward, and it
met its reward.   Isaacs and Kildare raced down on
him, but the latter soon pulled up on finding himself
passed, and waited.   Isaacs rushed upon the tem-
porising player and got the ball away from him in no
time; eluded the other man, and with a neat stroke
sent the ball right between the poles.   The game
had hardly lasted three minutes, and a little sound
of clapping was heard from where the spectators were
standing, far off on one side.   I could see Miss
Westonhaugh plainly, as she cantered with her uncle
to where the victors were standing together on the
other side, patting their ponies and adjusting stirrup
and saddle.   Isaacs had his back turned, but wheeled
round as he heard the sound of hoofs behind him and
bowed low in his saddle to the fair girl, whose face,
I could see even at that distance, was flushed with
pleasure.   They remained a few minutes in conversation, and then the two spectators rode away, and
we took up our positions once more.

The next game was a much longer one.   It was

the turn of the other party to hit off, for Kildare
won the charge. There were encounters of all kinds;
twice the ball was sent over the line, but outside the
goal, by long sweeping blows from Isaacs, who ever
hovered on the edge of the scrimmage, and, by his
good riding, and the help of a splendid pony, often
had a chance where another would have had none.
At last it happened that I was chasing the ball back
towards our goal, from one of his hits, and he was
pursuing me. I had the advantage of a long start,
and before he could reach me I got in a heavy "back-
hander" that sent the ball far away to one side,
where, as good luck would have it, Westonhaugh
was waiting. Quick as thought he carried it along,
and in another minute we had scored a goal, amidst
enthusiastic shouts from the spectators, who had
been kept long in suspense by the protracted game.
This time it was to our side that the young girl
came, riding up to her brother to congratulate him
on his success. I thought she had less colour as she
came nearer, and though she smiled sweetly as she
said, "It was splendidly played, John," there was
not so much enthusiasm in her voice as the said
John, who had really won the game with masterly
neatness, might have expected. Then she sat quietly
looking over the ground, while we dismounted from
our ponies, breathless, and foaming, and lathery,
from the hard-fought battle. The grooms ran up
with blankets and handfuls of grass to give the poor
beasts a rub, and covering them carefully after
removing the saddles, led them away. Vol. I

The sun leaves Annandale early, and I put on a
coat and lit a cigarette, while the saice saddled our
second mounts.   There are few prettier sights than
an English game, of any kind, on a beautiful stretch
of turf.   The English live, and move and have their
being out of doors.   A cricket-match, tennis, a race-
course, or a game of polo, show them at their greatest
advantage, whether as players or spectators.   Their
fresh complexions suit the green of the grass and of
the trees as naturally as a bed of roses, or cyclamens,
or any fresh and healthy flower will combine with
the grass and the ferns in garden or glen.   The glorious vitality that belongs to their race seems to blos-
som freshly in the contact with their mother earth,
and the physical capacity for motion with which
nature endows them makes them graceful and fascinating to watch, when in some free and untrammelled dress of white they are at their games, batting
and bowling and galloping and running; they have
the same natural grace then as a herd of deer or
antelopes; they are beautiful animals in the full enjoyment of life and vigour, of health and strength;
they are intensely alive.   Something of this kind
passed through my mind, in all probability, and,
combined with the delightful sensation any strong
man feels in the pause after great exertion, disposed me well towards my fellows and towards mankind at large.   Besides we had won the last game.

"You look pleased, Mr. Griggs," said Miss Westonhaugh, who had probably been watching me for a

moment or two. "I did not know cynics were ever pleased."

"I remember who it was that promised to crown the victors of this match, Miss Westonhaugh, and I cherish some hopes of being one of them. Would you mind very much?"

"Mind? Oh dear no; you had better try. But if you stand there with your coat on, you will not have much chance. They are all mounted, and waiting for you."

"Well, here goes," I said to myself, as I got into the saddle again. "I hope he may win, but he would find me out in a minute if I tried to play into his hands." We were only to play the best out of three goals, and the score was "one all." All eight of us had fresh mounts, and the experience of each other's play we had got in the preceding games made it likely that the game would be a long one. And so it turned out.

From the first things went badly. John Weston-haugh's fresh pony was very wild, and he had to take him a breather half over the ground before he could take his place for the charge. When at last the first stroke was made, the ball went low along the ground, spinning and twisting to right and left. Both Kildare and Isaacs missed it and wheeled across to return, when a prolonged scrimmage ensued less than thirty yards from their goal. Every one played his best, and we wheeled and spun round in a way that reminded one of a cavalry skirmish. Strokes and back-strokes followed quickly, till at last I got the ball as it came rolling out between my horse's legs, and, hotly pursued, beyond the possibility of making a fair stroke, I moved away with it in front of me.

Then began one of those interminable circular games that all polo players know so well, round and round the battlefield, riding close together, sometimes one succeeding in driving the ball a little, only to be foiled by the next man's ill-delivered backstroke; racing, and pulling up short, and racing again, till horses and riders were in a perspiration and a state of madness not to be attained by any peaceful means. At last, as we were riding near our own goal, some one, I could not see who, struck the ball out into the open. Isaacs, who had just missed, and was ahead, rode for it like a madman, his club raised high for a back-stroke. He was hotly pressed by the man who had roused my wrath in the first game by his "dribbling" policy. He was a light weight and had kept his best horse for the last game, so that as Isaacs spun along at lightning speed the little man was very close to him, his club well back for a sweeping hit. He rode well, but was evidently not so old a hand in the game as the rest of us. They neared the ball rapidly and Isaacs swerved a little to the left in order to get it well under his right hand, thus throwing himself somewhat across the track of his pursuer. As the Persian struck with all his force downwards and backwards, his adversary, excited by the chase, beyond all judgment or reckoning of his chances, hit out wildly, as beginners will. The long elastic handle of his weapon struck Isaacs' horse on the flank and glanced upward, the head of the club striking Isaacs just above the back of the neck. We saw him throw up his arms, the club in his right hand hanging to his wrist by the strap. The infuriated little arab pony tore on, and in a moment more the iron grip of the rider's knees relaxed, Isaacs swayed heavily in the saddle and fell over on the near side, his left foot hanging in the stirrup and dragging him along some paces before the horse finally shook himself clear and scampered away across the turf. The whole catastrophe occurred in a moment; the man who had done the mischief threw away his club to reach the injured player the sooner, and as we thundered after him, my pony stumbled over the long handle, and falling, threw me heavily over his head. I escaped with a very slight kick from one of the other horses, and leaving my beast to take care of himself, ran as fast as I could to where Isaacs lay, now surrounded by the six players as they dismounted to help him. But there was some one there before them.

The accident had occurred near the middle of the ground, and opposite the place where Miss Weston-haugh and her uncle had taken up their stand to watch the contest. With a shake of the reins and a blow of the hand that made the thoroughbred bound his length as he plunged into a gallop, the girl rode

wildly to where Isaacs lay, and reining the animal
back on his haunches, sprang to the ground and knelt
quickly down, so that before the others had reached
them she had propped up his head and was rubbing
his hands in hers. There was no mistaking the
impulse that prompted her. She had seen many an
accident in the hunting-field, and knew well that
when a man fell like that it was ten to one he was
badly hurt.

Isaacs was ghastly pale, and there was a little
blood on Miss Westonhaugh's white gauntlet. Her
face was whiter even than his, though not a quiver
of mouth or eyelash betrayed emotion. The man
who had done it knelt on the other side, rubbing one
of the hands. Kildare and Westonhaugh galloped
off at full speed, and presently returned bearing a
brandy-flask and a smelling-bottle, and followed by
a groom with some water in a native *lota*. I wanted
to make him swallow some of the liquor, but Miss
Westonhaugh took the flask from my hands.

"He would not like it. He never drinks it, you
know," she said in a quiet low voice, and pouring
some of the contents on her handkerchief, moistened
all his brows and face and hair with the powerful
alcohol.

"Loosen his belt! pull off his boots, some of you!"
cried Mr. Currie Ghyrkins, as he came up breathless.
"Take off his belt — damn it, you know! Dear,
dear!" and he got off his *tat* with all the alacrity he
could muster.

Miss Westonhaugh never took her eyes from the face of the prostrate man — pressing the wet handkerchief to his brow, and moistening the palm of the hand she held with brandy. In a few minutes Isaacs breathed a long heavy breath, and opened his eyes.

"What is the matter?" he said; then, recollecting himself and trying to move his head — "Oh! I have had a tumble. Give me some water to drink." There was a sigh of relief from every one present as he spoke, quite naturally, and I held the *lota* to his lips. "What became of the ball?" he asked quickly, as he sat up. Then turning round, he saw the beautiful girl kneeling at his side. The blood rushed violently to his face, and his eyes, a moment ago dim with unconsciousness, flashed brightly. "What! Miss Westonhaugh — you?" he bounded to his feet, but would have fallen back if I had not caught him in my arms, for he was still dizzy from the heavy blow that had stunned him. The blood came and went in his cheeks, and he hung on my arm confused and embarrassed, looking on the ground.

"I really owe you all manner of apologies ——" he began.

"Not a bit of it, my dear boy," broke in Ghyrkins, "my niece was nearest to you when you fell, and so she came up and did the right thing, like the brave girl she is." The old fellow helped her to rise as he said this, and he looked so pleased and proud of her that I was delighted with him. "And now," he went on, "we must see how much you are hurt—

the deuce of a knock, you know, enough to kill you
— and if you are not able to ride, why, we will carry
you home, you know; the devil of a way off it is,
too, confound it all." As he jerked out his sentences he was feeling the back of Isaacs' head, to
ascertain, if he could, how much harm had been
done. All this time the man who had done the mischief was standing by, looking very penitent, and
muttering sentences of apology as he tried to perform any little office for his victim that came in his
way. Isaacs stretched out his arm, while Ghyrkins
was feeling and twisting his head, and taking the
man's hand, held it a moment.

"My dear sir," he said, "I am not in the least
hurt, I assure you, and it was my fault for crossing
you at such a moment. Please do not think anything more about it." He smiled kindly at the young
fellow, who seemed very grateful, and who from that
day on would have risked everything in the world
for him. I heard behind me the voice of Kildare,
soliloquising softly.

"Faith," said he, "that fellow is a gentleman if I
ever saw one. I am afraid I should not have let that
infernal duffer off so easily. By-the-bye, Isaacs,"
he said aloud, coming up to us, "you know you won
the game. Nobody stopped the ball after you hit it,
and the saices say it ran right through the goal. So
cheer up; you have got something for your pains and
your tumble." It was quite true; the phlegmatic
saices had watched the ball instead of the falling

man. Miss Westonhaugh, who was really a sensible and self-possessed young woman, and had begun to be sure that the accident would have no serious results, expressed the most unbounded delight.

"Thank you, Miss Westonhaugh," said Isaacs; "you have kept your promise; you have crowned the victor."

"With brandy," I remarked, folding up a scarf which somebody had given me wherewith to tie a wet compress to the back of his head.

"There is nothing the matter," said Ghyrkins; "no end of a bad bruise, that's all. He will be all right in the morning, and the skin is only a little broken."

"Griggs," said Isaacs, who could now stand quite firm again, "hold the wet handkerchief in place, and give me that scarf." I did as he directed, and he took the white woollen shawl, and in half a dozen turns wound it round his head in a turban, deftly and gracefully. It was wonderfully becoming to his Oriental features and dark eyes, and I could see that Miss Westonhaugh thought so. There was a murmur of approbation from the native grooms who were looking on, and who understood the thing.

"You see I have done it before," he said, smiling. "And now give me my coat, and we will be getting home. Oh yes! I can ride quite well."

"That man has no end of pluck in him," said John Westonhaugh to Kildare.

"By Jove! yes," was the answer. "I have seen

men at home make twice the fuss over a tumble in a
ploughed field, when they were not even stunned. I
would not have thought it."

"He is not the man to make much fuss about anything of that kind."

Isaacs stoutly refused any further assistance, and
after walking up and down a few minutes, he said
he had got his legs back, and demanded a cigarette.
He lit it carefully, and mounted as if nothing had
happened, and we moved homeward, followed by the
spectators, many of whom, of course, were acquaint-
ances, and who had ridden up more or less quickly to
make polite inquiries about the accident. No one
disputed with Isaacs the right to ride beside Miss
Westonhaugh on the homeward road. He was the
victor of the day, and of course was entitled to the
best place. We were all straggling along, but without any great intervals between us, so that the two
were not able to get away as they had done on Saturday evening, but they talked, and I heard Miss
Westonhaugh laugh. Isaacs was determined to show
that he appreciated his advantage, and though, for
all I know, he might be suffering a good deal of
pain, he talked gaily and sat his horse easily, rather
a strange figure in his light-coloured English over-
coat, surmounted by the large white turban he had
made out of the shawl. As we came out on the mall
at the top of the hill, Mr. Ghyrkins called a council
of war.

"Of course we shall have to put off the tiger-
hunt."

"I suppose so," muttered Kildare, disconsolately.

"Why?" said Isaacs. "Not a bit of it. Head or no head, we will start to-morrow morning. I am well enough, never fear."

"Nonsense, you know it's nonsense," said Ghyrkins, "you will be in bed all day with a raging headache. Horrid things, knocks on the back of the head."

"Not I. My traps are all packed, and my servants have gone down to Kalka, and I am going to-morrow morning."

"Well, of course, if you really think you can," etc. etc. So he was prevailed upon to promise that if he should be suffering in the morning he would send word in time to put off the party. "Besides," he added, "even if I could not go, that is no reason why you should not."

"Stuff," said Ghyrkins.

"Oh!" said Miss Westonhaugh, looking rather blank.

"That would never do," said John.

"Preposterous! we could not think of going without you," said Lord Steepleton Kildare loudly; he was beginning to like Isaacs in spite of himself. And so we parted.

"I shall not dine to-night, Griggs," said Isaacs, as we paused before his door. "Come in for a moment: you can help me." We entered the richly carpeted room, and he went to a curious old Japanese cabinet, and after opening various doors and divi-

sions, showed a small iron safe. This he opened by
some means known to himself, for he used no key,
and he took out a small vessel of jade and brought it
to the light. "Now," he said, "be good enough to
warm this little jar in your hands while I go into the
next room and get my boots and spurs and things off.
But do not open it on any account — not on any
account, until I come back," he added very emphatically.

"All right, go ahead," said I, and began to warm
the cold thing that felt like a piece of ice between
my hands. He returned in a few minutes robed in
loose garments from Kashmir, with the low Eastern
slippers he generally wore indoors. He sat down
among his cushions and leaned back, looking pale
and tired; after ordering the lamps to be lit and the
doors closed, he motioned me to sit down beside him.

"I have had a bad shaking," he said, "and my
head is a good deal bruised. But I mean to go to-
morrow in spite of everything. In that little vial
there is a powerful remedy unknown in your Western medicine. Now I want you to apply it, and to
follow with the utmost exactness my instructions.
If you fear you should forget what I tell you, write
it down, for a mistake might be fatal to you, and
would certainly be fatal to me."

I took out an old letter and a pencil, not daring to
trust my memory.

"Put the vial in your bosom while you write: it
must be near the temperature of the body. Now

listen to me. In that silver box is wax. Tie first
this piece of silk over your mouth, and then stop
your nostrils carefully with the wax. Then open
the vial quickly and pour a little of the contents into
your hand. You must be quick, for it is very volatile. Rub that on the back of my head, keeping the
vial closed. When your hand is dry, hold the vial
open to my nostrils for two minutes by your watch.
By that time, I shall be asleep. Put the vial in
this pocket of my *caftán;* open all the doors and
windows, and tell my servant to leave them so, but
not to admit any one. Then you can leave me; I
shall sleep very comfortably. Come back and wake
me a little before midnight. You will wake me
easily by lifting my head and pressing one of my
hands. Remember, if you should forget to wake
me, and I should still be asleep at one o'clock, I
should never open my eyes again, and should be
dead before morning. Do as I tell you, for friendship's sake, and when I wake I shall bathe and
sleep naturally the rest of the night."

I carefully fulfilled his instructions. Before I
had finished rubbing his head he was drowsy, and
when I took the vial from his nostrils he was sound
asleep. I placed the precious thing where he had
told me, and arranged his limbs on the cushions.
Then I opened everything, and leaving the servant
in charge went my way to my rooms. On removing
the silk and the wax which had protected me from
the powerful drug, an indescribable odour which

permeated my clothes ascended to my nostrils; aromatic, yet pungent and penetrating. I never smelt anything that it reminded me of, but I presume the compound contained something of the nature of an opiate. I took some books down to Isaacs' rooms and passed the evening there, unwilling to leave him to the care of an inquisitive servant, and five minutes before midnight I awoke him in the manner he had directed. He seemed to be sleeping lightly, for he was awake in a moment, and his first action was to replace the vial in the curious safe. He professed himself perfectly restored; and, indeed, on examining his bruise I found there was no swelling or inflammation. The odour of the medicament, which, as he had said, seemed to be very volatile, had almost entirely disappeared. He begged me to go to bed, saying that he would bathe and then do likewise, and I left him for the night; speculating on the nature of this secret and precious remedy.

CHAPTER IX.

THE Himalayan *tonga* is a thing of delight. It is easily described, for in principle it is the ancient Persian war-chariot, though the accommodation is so modified as to allow four persons to sit in it back to back; that is, three besides the driver. It is built for great strength, the wheels being enormously heavy, and the pole of the size of a mast. Harness the horses have none, save a single belt with a sort of lock at the top, which fits into the iron yoke through the pole, and can slide from it to the extremity; there is neither breeching nor trace nor collar, and the reins run from the heavy curb bit directly through loops on the yoke to the driver's hands. The latter, a wiry, long-bearded Mohammedan, is armed with a long whip attached to a short thick stock, and though he sits low, on the same level as the passenger beside him on the front seat, he guides his half broken horses with amazing dexterity round sharp curves and by giddy precipices, where neither parapet nor fencing give the startled mind even a momentary impression of security. The road from Simla to Kalka at the foot of the hills is so narrow that if two vehicles meet, the one has to draw up to the edge of the road, while the other passes on its way. In view of the frequent encounters, every tonga-driver is provided with a post horn of tremendous power and most discordant harmony; for the road is covered with bullock carts bearing provisions and stores to the hill station. Smaller loads, such as trunks and other luggage, are generally carried by coolies, who follow a shorter path, the carriage road being ninety-two miles from Umballa, the railroad station, to Simla, but a certain amount may be stowed away in the tonga, of which the capacity is considerable.

In three of these vehicles our party of six began the descent on Tuesday morning, wrapped in linen "dusters" of various shades and shapes, and armed with countless varieties of smoking gear. The roughness of the road precludes all possibility of reading, and, after all, the rapid motion and the constant appearance of danger — which in reality does not exist — prevent any overpowering *ennui* from assailing the dusty traveller. So we spun along all day, stopping once or twice for a little refreshment, and changing horses every five or six miles. Everybody was in capital spirits, and we changed seats often, thus obtaining some little variety. Isaacs, who to every one's astonishment, seemed not to feel any inconvenience from his accident, clung to his seat in Miss Westonhaugh's tonga, sitting in front with the driver, while she and her uncle or brother occupied the seat behind, which is far more comfortable. At last, however, he was obliged to give his place to Kildare, who had been very patient, but at last said it "really wasn't fair, you know," and so Isaacs courteously yielded. At last we reached Kalka, where the tongas are exchanged for *dâk gharry* or mail carriage, a thing in which you can sit up in the daytime and lie down at night, there being an extension under the driver's box calculated for the accommodation of the longest legs. When lying down in one of these vehicles the sensation is that of being in a hearse and playing a game of funeral. On this occasion, however, it was still early when we made the change, and we paired off, two and two, for the last part of the drive. By the well planned arrangements of Isaacs and Kildare, two carriages were in readiness for us on the express train, and though the difference in temperature was enormous between Simla and the plains, still steaming from the late rainy season, the travelling was made easy for us, and we settled ourselves for the journey, after dining at the little hotel; Miss Westonhaugh bidding us all a cheery "good-night" as she retired with her *ayah* into the carriage prepared for her. I will not go into tedious details of the journey — we slept and woke and slept again, and smoked, and occasionally concocted iced drinks from our supplies, for in India the carriages are so large that the traveller generally provides himself with a generous basket of provisions and a travelling ice-chest full of bottles, and takes a trunk or two with

him in his compartment. Suffice it to say that we
arrived on the following day at Fyzabad in Oude,
and that we were there met by guides and shikarries
— the native huntsmen — who assured us that there
were tigers about near the outlying station of Pegnugger, where the elephants, previously ordered,
would all be in readiness for us on the following day.
The journey from Fyzabad to Pegnugger was not a
long one, and we set out in the cool of the evening,
sending our servants along in that "happy-go-lucky"
fashion which characterises Indian life. It has
always been a mystery to me how native servants
manage always to turn up at the right moment. You
say to your man, "Go there and wait for me," and
you arrive and find him waiting; though how he
transferred himself thither, with his queer-looking
bundle, and his lota, and cooking utensils, and your
best teapot wrapped up in a newspaper and ready for
use, and with all the other hundred and one things
that a native servant contrives to carry about without breaking or losing one of them, is an unsolved
puzzle. Yet there he is, clean and grinning as ever,
and if he were not clean and grinning and provided
with tea and cheroots, you would not keep him in
your service a day, though you would be incapable
of looking half so spotless and pleased under the
same circumstances yourself.

On the following day, therefore, we found ourselves at Pegnugger, surrounded by shikarries and
provided with every instrument of the chase that the

ingenuity of man and the foresight of Isaacs and
Ghyrkins could provide. There were numbers of
tents, sleeping tents, cooking tents, and servants'
tents; guns and ammunition of every calibre likely
to be useful; *kookries*, broad strong weapons not
unlike the famous American bowie knives (which
are all made in Sheffield, to the honour, glory, and
gain, of British trade); there were huge packs of
provisions edible and potable; baskets of utensils
for the kitchen and the table, and piles of blankets
and tenting gear for the camp. There was also the
little collector of Pegnugger, whose small body
housed a stout heart, for he had shot tigers on foot
before now in company with a certain German doctor
of undying sporting fame, whose big round spectacles
seemed to direct his bullets with unerring precision.
But the doctor was not here now, and so the sturdy
Englishman condescended to accept a seat in the
howdah, and to kill his game with somewhat less
risk than usual.

This first day was occupied in transferring our
party, now swelled by countless beaters and numerous huntsmen, not to mention all the retinue of
servants necessary for an Indian camp, to the neighbourhood of the battlefield. There is not much conversation on these occasions, for the party is apt to
become scattered, and there is a general tone of
expectancy in the air, the old hands conversing more
with the natives who know the district than with
each other, and the young ones either wondering how

many tigers they will kill, or listening open mouthed
to the tales of adventure reeled off by the yard by the
old bearded shikarry, who has slain the king of the
jungle with a *kookrie* in hand to hand struggle when
he was young, and bears the scars of the deadly
encounter on his brown chest to this day. Old
Ghyrkins, who was evidently in his element, rode
about on a little *tat*, questioning beaters and shikarries, and coming back every now and then to bawl up
some piece of information to the little collector, who
had established himself on one of the elephants and
looked down over the edge of the howdah, the great
pith hat on his head making him look like an
immense mushroom with a very thin stem sprouting
suddenly from the back of the huge beast. He
smiled pleasantly at the old sportsman from his elevation, and seemed to know all about it. It so
chanced that when he received Isaacs' telegrams he
had been planning a little excursion on his own
account, and had been sending out scouts and beaters
for some days to ascertain where the game lay. This,
of course, was so much clear gain to us, and the
little man was delighted at the opportune coincidence which enabled him, by the unlimited money
supplied, to join in such a hunt as he had not seen
since the time when the Prince of Wales disported
himself among the royal game, three years before.
As for Miss Westonhaugh, she was in the gayest of
spirits, as she sat with her brother on an elephant's
back, while Isaacs, who loved the saddle, circled

round her and kept up a fire of little compliments
and pretty speeches, to which she was fast becoming
inured. Kildare and I followed them closely on
another elephant, discoursing seriously about the
hunt, and occasionally shouting some question to
John Westonhaugh, ahead, about sport in the south.

Before evening we had arrived at our first camping
ground, near a small village on the outskirts of the
jungle, and the tents were pitched on a little elevation covered with grass, now green and waving.
The men had mowed a patch clear, and were busy
with the pegs and all the paraphernalia of a canvas
house, and we strolled about, some of us directing
the operations, others offering a sacrifice of cooling
liquids and tobacco to the setting sun. Miss Westonhaugh had heard about living in tents ever since
she came to India, and had often longed to sleep in
one of those temporary chambers that are set up anywhere in the "compound" of an English bungalow
for the accommodation of the bachelor guests whom
the house itself is too small to hold; now she was
enchanted at the prospect of a whole fortnight under
canvas, and watched with rapt interest the driving
of the pegs, the raising of the poles, and the careful
furnishing of her dwelling. There was a carpet,
and armchairs, and tables, and even a small book-
case with a few favourite volumes. To us in civilised life it seems a great deal of trouble to transport
a lunch basket and a novel to some shady glen to
enjoy a day's rest in the open air, and we would

almost rather starve than take the trouble to carry
provisions. In India you speak the word, and as by
magic there arises in the wilderness a little village
of tents, furnished with every necessary luxury —
and the luxuries necessary to our degenerate age are
many — a kitchen tent is raised, and a skilled dark-
skinned artist provides you in an hour with a dinner
such as you could eat in no hotel. The treasures of
the huge portable ice-chest reveal cooling wines and
soda water to the thirsty soul, and if you are going
very far beyond the reach of the large towns, a small
ice-machine is kept at work day and night to increase
the supply while you sleep, and to maintain it while
you wake. In the *connât* or verandah of the tent,
long chairs await you after your meal, and as you
smoke the fragrant cigarette and watch the stars
coming out, you feel as comfortable as though you
had been dining in your own spacious bungalow in
Mudnugger.

It was not long before all was ready, and having
made many ablutions and a little toilet, we assembled round the dinner table in the eating tent,
the same party that had dined at Mr. Currie Ghyrkins' house on Sunday night, with the addition of
the little collector of Pegnugger, whose stories of his
outlying district were full of humour and anecdote.
The talk bending in the direction of adventure, Kildare, who had been lately in South Africa with his
regiment, told some tales of Zulus and assegais and
Boers in the Hibernian style of hyperbole. The

Irish blood never comes out so strongly as when a story is to be told, and no amount of English education and Oxford accent will suppress the tendency. The brogue is gone, but the love of the marvellous is there still. Isaacs related the experience of "a man he knew," who had been pulled off his elephant, howdah and all, and had killed the tiger with a revolver at half arm's length.

"Ah yes," said the little collector, who had not caught the names of all the party when introduced, "I read about it at the time; I remember it very well. It happened in Purneah two years ago. The gentleman was a Mr. Isaacs of Delhi. Queer name too — remember perfectly." There was a roar of laughter at this, in which the collector joined vociferously on being informed that the man with the "queer name" was his neighbour at table.

"You see what you get for your modesty," cried old Ghyrkins, laughing to convulsions.

"And is it really true, Mr. Isaacs?" asked Miss Westonhaugh, looking admiringly across at the young man, who seemed rather annoyed.

And so the conversation went round and all were merry, and some were sleepy after dinner, and we sat in long chairs under the awning or *connât*. There was no moon yet, but the stars shone out as they shine nowhere save in India, and the evening breeze played pleasantly through the ropes after the long hot day. Miss Westonhaugh assured everybody for the hundredth time that day that she rather liked the smell of cigars, and so we smoked and chatted a little, and presently there was a jerk and a sputtering sneeze from Mr. Ghyrkins, who, being weary with the march and the heat and the good dinner, and on the borders of sleep, had put the wrong end of his cigar in his mouth with destructive results. Then he threw it away with a small volley of harmless expletives, and swore he would go to bed, as he could not stand our dulness any longer; but he merely shifted his position a little, and was soon snoring merrily.

"What a pity it is we have no piano, Katharine," said John Westonhaugh, who was fond of music. "Could you not sing something without any accompaniment?"

"Oh no. Mr. Isaacs," she said, turning her voice to where she could see the light of his cigarette and the faint outline of his chair in the starlight, "here we are in the camp. Now where is the 'lute' you promised to produce for us? I think the time has come at last for you to keep your promise."

"Well," said he, "I believe there really is an old guitar or something of the kind among my traps somewhere. But it might wake Mr. Ghyrkins, who, I understand from his tones, is asleep."

Various opinions were expressed to the effect that Mr. Ghyrkins was not so easily disturbed, and a voice like Kildare's was heard to mumble that "it would not hurt him if he was," a sentence no one attempted to construe. So the faithful Narain was

summoned, and instructed to bring the instrument if
he could find it. I was rather surprised at Isaacs'
readiness to sing; but in the first place I had never
heard him, and besides I did not make allowance for
the Oriental courtesy of his character, which would
not refuse anything, or make any show of refusal in
order to be pressed. Narain returned with a very
modern-looking guitar-case, and, opening the box,
presented his master with the instrument, which, as
Isaacs took it to the light in the door of the tent to
see if it had travelled safely, appeared to be a perfectly new German guitar. I suspected him of having purchased it at the little music shop at Simla,
for the especial amusement of our party.

"I thought it was a lute you played on," said Miss
Westonhaugh, "a real, lovely, ancient Assyrian lute,
or something of that kind."

"Oh, a plain guitar is infinitely better and less
troublesome," said Isaacs as he returned to his seat
in the dark and began to tune the strings softly.
"It takes so long to tune one of those old things,
and then nothing will make them stand. Now this
one, you see, — or rather you cannot see, — has an
ingenious contrivance of screws by which you may
tune it in a moment." While he was speaking he
was altering the pitch of the strings, and presently
he added, "There, it is done now," and two or three
sounding chords fell on the still air. "Now what
shall I sing? I await your commands."

"Something soft, and sweet, and gentle."

"A love-song?" asked he quietly.

"Well yes — a love-song if you like. Why not?" said she.

"No reason in the world that I can think of," I remarked. Whereat Lord Steepleton Kildare threw his cigar away, and began lighting another a moment after, as if he had discarded his weed by mistake.

Isaacs struck a few chords softly, and then began a sort of running accompaniment. His voice, which seemed to me to be very high, was wonderfully smooth and round, and produced the impression of being much more powerful than he cared to show. He sang without the least effort, and yet there was none of that effeminate character that I have noticed in European male singers when producing high notes very softly. I do not understand music, but I am sure I never heard an opera tenor with a voice of such quality. The words of his song were Persian, and the pure accents of his native tongue seemed well suited to the half passionate, half plaintive air he had chosen. I afterwards found a translation of the sonnet by an English officer, which I here give, though it conveys little idea of the music of the original verse.

Last night, my eyes being closed in sleep, but my good fortune awake,
The whole night, the livelong night, the image of my beloved one was
    the companion of my soul.
The sweetness of her melodious voice still remains vibrating on my
    soul;
Heavens! how did the sugared words fall from her sweeter lips;
Alas! all that she said to me in that dream has escaped from my
    memory,

Although it was my care till break of day to repeat over and over
    her sweet words.
The day, unless illuminated by her beauty, is, to my eyes, of noc-
    turnal darkness.
Happy day that first I gazed upon that lovely face !
May the eyes of Jami long be blessed with pleasing visions, since
    they presented to his view last night
The object, on whose account he passed his waking life in expec-
    tation.[1]

His beautiful voice ceased, and with infinite skill
he wove a few strains of the melody into the final
chords he played when he had finished singing. It
was all so entirely novel, so unlike any music most
of us had ever heard, and it was so undeniably good,
that every one applauded and said something to the
singer in turn, expressing the greatest admiration
and appreciation. Miss Westonhaugh was the last
to speak.

"It is perfectly lovely," she said. "I wish I could
understand the words — are they as sweet as the
music?"

"Sweeter," he answered, and he gave an offhand
translation of two or three verses.

"Beautiful indeed," she said; "and now sing me
another, please." There was no resisting such an
appeal, with the personal pronoun in the singular
number. He moved a little nearer, and emphatically
sang to her, and to no one else. A song of the same
character as the first, but, I thought, more passionate
and less dreamy, as his great sweet voice swelled
and softened and rose again in burning vibrations

---

[1] Sir Gore Ousely, *Notices of the Persian Poets.*

and waves of sound. She did not ask a translation this time, but some one else did, after the applause had subsided.

"I cannot translate these things," said Isaacs, "so as to do them justice, or give you any idea of the strength and vitality of the Persian verses. Perhaps Griggs, who understands Persian very well and is a literary man, may do it for you. I would rather not try." I professed my entire inability to comply with the request, and to turn the conversation asked him where he had learned to play the guitar so well.

"Oh," he answered, "in Istamboul, years ago. Everybody plays in Istamboul — and most people sing love-songs. Besides it is so easy," and he ran scales up and down the strings with marvellous rapidity to illustrate what he said.

"And do you never sing English songs, Mr. Isaacs?" asked the collector of Pegnugger, who was enchanted, not having heard a note of music for months.

"Oh, sometimes," he answered. "I think I could sing 'Drink to me only with thine eyes' — do you know it?" He began to play the melody on the guitar while he spoke.

"Rather — I should think so!" Kildare was heard to say. He was beginning to think the concert had lasted long enough.

"Oh, do sing it, Mr. Isaacs," said the young girl, "and my brother and I will join in. It will be so pretty!"

It certainly sounded very sweetly as he gave the melody in his clear, high tones, and Miss Weston-haugh and John sang with him. Having heard it several thousand times myself, I was beginning to recognise the tune well enough to enjoy it a good deal.

"That is very nice," said Kildare, who was sorry he had made an impatient remark before, and wanted to atone.

"Eh? what? how's that?" said Mr. Ghyrkins just waking up. "Oh! of course. My niece sings charm-ingly. Quite an artist, you know." And he strug-gled out of his chair and said it was high time we all went to bed if we meant to shoot straight in the morning. The magistrate of Pegnugger concurred in the opinion, and we reluctantly separated for the night to our respective quarters, Isaacs and I occupy-ing a tent together, which he had caused to be sent on from Delhi, as being especially adapted to his comfort.

On the following day at dawn we were roused by the sound of preparations, and before we were dressed the voices of Mr. Currie Ghyrkins and the collector were heard in the camp, stirring up the sleepy ser-vants and ordering us to be waked. The two old sportsmen felt it their duty to be first on such an occasion as this, and in the calm security that they would do everything that was right, Isaacs and I dis-cussed our tea and fruit — the *chota haziri* or "little breakfast" usually taken in India on waking — sit-

ting in the door of our tent, while Kiramat Ali and
Narain and Mahmoud and the rest of the servants
were giving a final rub to the weapons of the chase,
and making all the little preparations for a long day.
And we sat looking out and sipping our tea.

In the cool of the dawn Miss Westonhaugh came
tripping across the wet grass to where her uncle was
giving his final directions about the furnishing of
his howdah for the day; a lovely apparition of freshness in the gray morning, all dressed in dark blue, a
light pith helmet-shaped hat pressing the rebellious
white-gold hair almost out of sight. She walked so
easily it seemed as if her dainty little feet had wings,
as Hermes' of old, to ease the ground of their feather
weight. A broad belt hung across her shoulder with
little rows of cartridges set all along, and at the end
hung a very business-like revolver case of brown
leather and of goodly length. No toy miniature
pistol would she carry, but a full-sized, heavy "six-
shooter," that might really be of use at close quarters. She stood some minutes talking with Mr.
Ghyrkins, not noticing us in the shadow of the tent
some thirty yards away; Isaacs and I watched her
intently — with very different feelings, possibly, but
yet intensely admiring the fair creature, so strong
and pliant, and yet so erect and straight. She turned
half round towards us, and I saw there were flowers
in the front of her dress. I wondered where they
had come from; they were roses — of all flowers in
the world to be blooming in the desert. Perhaps she

had brought them carefully from Fyzabad, but that was improbable; or from Pegnugger — yes, there would be roses in the collector's garden there. Isaacs rose to his feet.

"Oh, come along, Griggs. You have had quite enough tea!"

"Go ahead; I will be with you in a moment." But a sudden thought struck me, and I went with him, bareheaded, to greet Miss Westonhaugh. She smiled brightly as she held out her hand.

"Good morning, Mr. Isaacs. Thank you so much for the roses. How *did* you do it? They are *too* lovely!" So it was just as I thought. Isaacs had probably despatched a man back to Pegnugger in the night.

"Very easy I assure you. I am so glad you like them. They are not very fresh after all though, I see," he added depreciatingly, as men do when they give flowers to people they care about. I never heard a man find fault with flowers he gave out of a sense of duty. It is perhaps that the woman best loved of all things in the world has for him a sweetness and a beauty that kills the coarser hues of the rose, and outvies the fragrance of the double violets.

"Oh no!" she said, emphasising the negative vigorously. "I think they are perfectly beautiful, but I want you to tell me where you got them." I began talking to Ghyrkins, who was intent on the arrangement of his guns which was going on under his eyes, but I heard the answer, though Isaacs spoke in a low voice.

"You must not say that, Miss Westonhaugh. You yourself are the most perfect and beautiful thing God ever made." By a superhuman effort I succeeded in keeping my eyes fixed on Ghyrkins, probably with a stony, unconscious stare, for he presently asked what I was looking at. I do not think Isaacs cared whether I heard him or not, knowing that I sympathised, but Mr. Ghyrkins was another matter. The Persian had made progress, for there was no trace of annoyance in Miss Westonhaugh's answer, though she entirely overlooked her companion's pretty speech.

"Seriously, Mr. Isaacs, if you mean to have one of them for your badge to-day, you must tell me how you got them." I turned slowly round. She was holding a single rose in her fingers, and looking from it to him, as if to see if it would match his olive skin and his Karkee shooting-coat. He could not resist the bribe.

"If you really want to know I will tell you, but it is a profound secret," he said, smiling. "Griggs, swear!"

I raised my hand and murmured something about the graves of my ancestors.

"Well," he continued, "yesterday morning at the collector's house I saw a garden; in the garden there were roses, carefully tended, for it is late. I took the gardener apart and said, 'My friend, behold, here is silver for thee, both rupees and pais. And if thou wilt pick the best of thy roses and deliver them to the swift runner whom I will send to thee at supper

time when the stars are coming out, I will give thee
as much as thou shalt earn in a month with thy
English master. But if thou wilt not do it, or if
thou failest to do it, having promised, I will cause
the grave of thy father to be defiled with the slaugh-
ter of swine, and, moreover, I will return and beat
thee with a thick stick!' The fellow was a Mussulman, and there was a merry twinkle in his eye as he
took the money and swore a great oath. I left a
running man at Pegnugger with a basket, and that is
how you got the roses. Don't tell the collector, that
is all."

We all laughed, and Miss Westonhaugh gave the
rose to Isaacs, who touched it to his lips, under pretence of smelling it, and put it in his buttonhole.
Kildare came up at this moment and created a diversion; then the collector joined us and scattered us
right and left, saying it was high time we were in the
howdahs and on the way. So we buckled on our
belts, and those who wore hats put them on, and
those who preferred turbans bent while their bearers
wound them on, and then we moved off to where the
elephants were waiting and got into our places, and
the *mahouts* urged the huge beasts from their knees to
their feet, and we went swinging off to the forest.
The pad elephants, who serve as beaters and move
between the howdah animals, joined us, and presently
we went splashing through the reedy patches of fern,
and crashing through the branches, towards the heart
of the jungle.

Mr. Currie Ghyrkins, whose long experience had made him as cool when after tigers as when reading the *Pioneer* in his shady bungalow at Simla, had taken Miss Westonhaugh with him in his howdah, and as an additional precaution for her safety, the little collector of Pegnugger, who was a dead shot, only allowed two pad elephants to move between himself and Ghyrkins. As there were thirty-seven animals in all, the rest of the party were much scattered. I thought there were too many elephants for our six howdahs, but it turned out that I was mistaken, for we had capital sport. The magistrate of Pegnugger, who knew the country thoroughly, was made the despot of the day. His orders were obeyed unquestioningly and unconditionally, and we halted in long line or marched onwards, forcing a passage through every obstacle, at his word. We might have been out a couple of hours, watching every patch of jungle and blade of long rank grass for a sight of the striped skin, writhing through the reeds, that we so longed to see, when the quick, short crack of a rifle away to the right brought us to a halt, and every one drew a long breath and turned, gun in hand, in the direction whence the sound had come. It was Kildare; he had met his first tiger, and the first also of the hunt. He had put up the animal not five paces in front of him, stealing along in the cool grass and hoping to escape between the elephants, in the cunning way they often do. He had fired a snap shot too quickly, inflicting a wound in the flank which only served to rouse the tiger to madness. With a leap that seemed to raise its body perpendicularly from the ground, the gorgeous creature flew into the air and settled right on the head of Kildare's elephant, while the terrified *mahout* wound himself round the howdah. It would have been a trying position for the oldest sportsman, but to be brought into such terrific encounter at arm's length, almost, at one's very first experience of the chase, was a terrible test of nerve. Those who were near said that in that awful moment Kildare never changed colour. The elephant plunged wildly in his efforts to shake off the beast from his head, but Kildare had seized his second gun the moment he had discharged the first, and aiming for one second only, as the tossing head and neck of the tusker brought the gigantic cat opposite him, fired again. The fearful claws, driven deep and sure into the thick hide of the poor elephant, relaxed their hold, the beautiful lithe limbs straightened by their own perpendicular weight, and the first prize of the day dropped to the ground like lead, dead, shot through the head.

A great yell of triumph arose all along the line, and the little *mahout* crept cautiously back from his lurking-place behind the howdah to see if the coast were clear. Kildare had behaved splendidly, and shouts of congratulation reached his ears from all sides. Miss Westonhaugh waved her handkerchief in token of approbation, every one applauded, and far away to the left Isaacs, who was in the last how-

dah, clapped his hands vigorously, and sent his high
clear voice ringing like a trumpet down the line.

"Well done, Kildare! well done, indeed!" and
his rival's praise was not the least grateful to Lord
Steepleton on that day. Meanwhile the shikarries
gathered around the fallen beast. It proved to be a
young tigress some eight feet long, and the clean
bright coat showed that she was no man-eater. So
the pad elephant came alongside, to use a nautical
phrase not inappropriate, and kneeling down received
its burden willingly, well knowing that the slain
beauty was one of his deadly foes. The *mahout* pronounced the elephant on which Kildare was mounted
able to proceed, and only a few huge drops of blood
marked where the tigress had kept her hold. We
moved on again, beating the jungle, wheeling and
doubling the long line, wherever it seemed likely
that some striped monster might have eluded us.
Marching and counter-marching through the heat of
the day, we picked up another prize in the afternoon.
It was a large old tiger, nine feet six as he lay; he
fell an easy prey to the gun of the little collector of
Pegnugger, who sent a bullet through his heart at the
first shot, and smiled rather contemptuously as he
removed the empty shell of the cartridge from his
gun. He would rather have had Kildare's chance in
the morning.

After all, two tigers in a day was not bad sport for
the time of year. I knew Isaacs would be disappointed at not having had a shot, where his rival in

a certain quarter had had so good an opportunity for displaying skill and courage; and I confessed to myself that I preferred a small party, say, a dozen elephants and three howdahs, to this tremendous and expensive *battue*. I had a shot-gun with me, and consoled myself by shooting a peacock or two as we rolled and swayed homewards. We had determined to keep to the same camp for a day or two, as we could enter the forest from another point on the morrow, and might even beat some of the same ground again with success.

It was past five when we got down to the tents and descended from our howdahs, glad to stretch our stiffened limbs in a brisk walk. The dead tigers were hauled into the middle of the camp, and the servants ran together to see the result of the *sahib log's* day out. We retired to dress and refresh ourselves for dinner.

CHAPTER X.

In Isaacs' tent I was pulling off my turban, all
shapeless and crumpled by the long day, while Isaacs
stood disconsolately looking at the clean guns and
unbroken rows of cartridges which Narain deposited
on the table. The sun was very low, and shone
horizontally through the raised door of the tent on
my friend's rather gloomy face. At that moment
something intercepted the sunshine, and a dark
shadow fell across the floor. I looked, and saw a
native standing on the threshold, salaaming and
waiting to be spoken to. He was not one of our
men, but a common ryot, clad simply in a *dhoti* or
waist-cloth, and a rather dirty turban.

"Kya chahte ho?" — "What do you want?" asked
Isaacs impatiently. He was not in a good humour
by any means. "Wilt thou deprive thy betters of the
sunlight thou enjoyest thyself?"

"The sahib's face is like the sun and the moon,"
replied the man deprecatingly. "But if the great
lord will listen I will tell him what shall rejoice his
heart."

"Speak, unbeliever," said Isaacs.

"Protector of the poor! you are my father and my

mother! but I know where there lieth a great tiger, an eater of men, hard-hearted, that delighteth in blood."

"Dog," answered Isaacs, calmly removing his coat, "the tiger you speak of was seen by you many moons since; what do you come to me with idle tales for?" Isaacs was familiar with the native trick of palming off old tigers on the unwary stranger, in the hope of a reward.

"Sahib, I am no liar. I saw the tiger, who is the king of the forest, this morning." Isaacs' manner relaxed a little, and he sat down and lighted the eternal cigarette. "Slave," he said meditatively, "if it is as you say, I will kill the tiger, but if it is not as you say, I will kill you, and cause your body to be buried with the carcass of an ox, and your soul shall not live." The man did not seem much moved by the threat. He moved nearer, and salaamed again.

"It is near to the dwelling of the sahib, who is my father," said the man, speaking low. "The day before yesterday he destroyed a man from the village. He has eaten five men in the last moon. I have seen him enter his lair, and he will surely return before the dawn; and the sahib shall strike him by his lightning; and the sahib will not refuse me the ears of the man-eater, that I may make a *jādu*, a charm against sudden death?"

"Hound! if thou speakest the truth, and I kill the tiger, the monarch of game, I will make thee a rich man; but thou shalt not have his ears. I desire the *jādu* for myself. I have spoken; wait thou here my

pleasure." The ryot bent low to the earth, and then
squatted by the tent-door to wait, in the patient way
that a Hindoo can, for Isaacs to go and eat his
dinner. As the latter came out ten minutes later,
he paused and addressed the man once more. "Speak
not to any man of thy tiger while I am gone, or I
will cut off thine ears with a pork knife." And we
passed on.

The sun was now set and hovering in the after-
glow, the new moon was following lazily down. I
stopped a moment to look at her, and was surprised
by Miss Westonhaugh's voice close behind me.

"Are you wishing by the new moon, Mr. Griggs?"
she asked.

"Yes," said I, "I was. And what were you wishing, Miss Westonhaugh, if I may ask?" Isaacs came
up, and paused beside us. The beautiful girl stood
quite still, looking to westward, a red glow on the
white-gold masses of her hair.

"Did you say you were wishing for something,
Miss Westonhaugh?" he asked. "Perhaps I can get
it for you. More flowers, perhaps? They are very
easily got."

"No — that is, not especially. I was wishing —
well, that a tiger-hunt might last for ever; and I
want a pair of tiger's ears. My old *ayah* says they
keep off evil spirits and sickness; and all sorts of
things."

"I know; it is a curious idea. I suppose both
those beasts there have lost theirs already. These
fellows cut them off in no time."

"Yes. I have looked. So I suppose I must wait till to-morrow. But promise me, Mr. Isaacs, if you shoot one to-morrow, let me have the ears!"

"I will promise that readily enough. I would promise anything you ——" The last part of the sentence was lost to me, as I moved away and left them.

At dinner, of course, every one talked of the day's sport, and compliments of all kinds were showered on Lord Steepleton, who looked very much pleased, and drank a good deal of wine. Ghyrkins and the little magistrate expressed their opinion that he would make a famous tiger-killer one of these days, when he had learned to wait. Every one was hungry and rather tired, and after a somewhat silent cigar, we parted for the night, Miss Westonhaugh rising first. Isaacs went to his quarters, and I remained alone in a long chair, by the deserted dining-tent. Kiramat Ali brought me a fresh hookah, and I lay quietly smoking and thinking of all kinds of things —— things of all kinds, tigers, golden hair, more tigers, Isaacs, Shere Ali, Baithop——, what was his name — Baithop—p——. I fell asleep.

Some one touched my hand, waking me suddenly. I sprang to my feet and seized the man by the throat, before I recognised in the starlight that it was Isaacs.

"You are not a nice person to rouse," remarked he in a low voice, as I relaxed my grasp. "You will have fever if you sleep out-of-doors at this time of year. Now look here; it is past midnight, and I am going out a little way." I noticed that he had a *kookrie* knife at his waist, and that his cartridge-belt was on his chest.

"I will go with you," said I, guessing his intention. "I will be ready in a moment," and I began to move towards the tent.

"No. I must go alone, and do this thing single-handed. I have a particular reason. I only wanted to warn you I was gone, in case you missed me. I shall take that ryot fellow with me to show me the way."

"Give him a gun," I suggested.

"He could not use one if I did. He has your *kookrie* in case of accidents."

"Oh, very well! do not let me interfere with any innocent and childlike pastime you may propose for your evening hours. I will attend to your funeral in the morning. Good-night."

"Good-night; I shall be back before you are up." And he walked quickly off to where the ryot was waiting and holding his guns. He had the sense to take two. I was angry at the perverse temerity of the man. Why could he not have an elephant out and go like a sensible thinking being, instead of sneaking out with one miserable peasant to lie all night among the reeds, in as great danger from cobras as from the beast he meant to kill? And all for a girl — an English girl — a creature all fair hair and eyes, with no more intelligence than a sheep! Was it not she who sent him out to his death in the jungle, that

her miserable caprice for a pair of tiger's ears might
be immediately satisfied? If a woman ever loved
me, Paul Griggs, — thank heaven no woman ever
did, — would I go out into bogs and desert places
and risk my precious skin to find her a pair of cat's
ears? Not I; — wait a moment, though. If I were
in his place, if Miss Westonhaugh loved *me* — I
laughed at the conceit. But supposing she did.
Just for the sake of argument, I would allow it. I
think that I would risk something after all. What
a glorious thing it would be to be loved by a woman,
once, wholly and for ever. To meet the creature I
described to him the other night, waiting for me to
come into her life, and to be to her all I could be to
the woman I should love. But she has never come;
never will, now; still, there is a sort of rest to me in
thinking of rest. Hearth, home, wife, children; the
worn old staff resting in the corner, never to wander
again. What a strange thing it is that men should
have all these, and more, and yet never see that they
have the simple elements of earthly happiness, if they
would but use them. And we, outcasts and wan-
derers, children of sin and darkness, in whose hands
one commandment seems hardly less fragile than
another, would give anything — had we anything to
give — for the happiness of a home, to call our own.
How strange it is that what I said to Isaacs should
be true. "Do not marry unless you must depend on
each other for daily bread, or unless you are rich
enough to live apart." Yes, it is true, in ninety-

nine cases out of a hundred. But then, I should add a saving clause, "and unless you are quite sure that you love each other." Ay, there is the *pons asinorum*, the bridge whereon young asses and old fools come to such terrible grief. They are perfectly sure they love eternally; they will indignantly scorn the suggestions of prudence; love any other woman? never, while I live, answers the happy and unsophisticated youth. Be sorry I did it? Do you think I am a schoolboy in my first passion? demands the aged bridegroom. And so they marry, and in a year or two the enthusiastic young man runs away with some other enthusiastic man's wife, and the octogenarian spouse finds himself constituted into a pot of honey for his wife's swarming relations to settle on, like flies. But a man in strong middle prime of age, like me, knows his own mind; and — yes, on the whole I was unjust to Isaacs and to Miss Weston-haugh. If a woman loved me, she should have all the tiger's ears she wanted. "Still, I hope he will get back safely," I added, in afterthought to my reverie, as I turned into bed and ordered Kiramat Ali to wake me half an hour before dawn.

I was restless, sleeping a little and dreaming much. At last I struck a light and looked at my watch. Four o'clock. It would not be dawn for more than an hour. I knew Isaacs had made for the place where the tiger passed his days, certain that he would return near daybreak, according to all common probability. He need not have gone so early, I thought. However, it might be a long way off. I lay still for a while, but it seemed very hot and close under the canvas. I got up and threw a *caftán* round me, drew a chair into the *connát* and sat, or rather lay, down in the cool morning breeze. Then I dozed again until Kiramat Ali woke me by pulling at my foot. He said it would be dawn in half an hour. I had passed a bad night, and went out, as I was, to walk on the grass. There was Miss Weston-haugh's tent away off at the other end. She was sleeping calmly enough, never doubting that at that very moment the man who loved her was risking his life for her pleasure — her slightest whim. She would be wide awake if she knew it, staring out into the darkness and listening for the crack of his rifle. A faint light appeared behind the dining-tent, over the distant trees, like the light of London seen from twenty or thirty miles' distance in the country, a faint, suggestive, murky grayness in the sky, making the stars look dimmer.

The sound of a shot rang true and clear through the chill air; not far off I thought. I held my breath, listening for a second report, but none came. So it was over. Either he had killed the tiger with his first bullet, or the tiger had killed him before he could fire a second. I was intensely excited. If he were safe I wished him to have the glory of coming home quite alone. There was nothing for it but to wait, so I went into my tent and took a bath — a very simple operation where the bathing consists in

pouring a huge jar of water over one's head. Tents
in India have always a small side tent with a ditch
dug to drain off the water from the copious ablutions
of the inmate. I emerged into the room feeling
better. It was now quite light, and I proceeded to
dress leisurely to spin out the time. As I was drawing on my boots, Isaacs sauntered in quietly and laid
his gun on the table. He was pale, and his Karkee
clothes were covered with mud and leaves and bits of
creeper, but his movements showed he was not hurt
in any way; he hardly seemed tired.

"Well?" I said anxiously.

"Very well, thank you. Here they are," and he
produced from the pocket of his coat the *spolia opima*
in the shape of a pair of ears, that looked very large
to me. There was a little blood on them and on his
hands as he handed the precious trophies to me for
inspection. We stood by the open door, and while I
was turning over the ears curiously in my hands, he
looked down at his clothes.

"I think I will take a bath," he said; "I must
have been in a dirty place."

"My dear fellow," I said, taking his hand, "this is
absurd. I mean all this affected calmness. I was
angry at your going in that way, to risk your head
in a tiger's mouth; but I am sincerely glad to see
you back alive. I congratulate you most heartily."

"Thank you, old man," he said, his pale face
brightening a little. "I am very glad myself. Do
you know I have a superstition that I must fulfil

every wish of — like that — even half expressed, to the very letter?"

"The 'superstition,' as you call it, is worthy of the bravest knight that ever laid lance in rest. Don't part with superstitions like that. They are noble and generous things."

"Perhaps," he answered, "but I really am very superstitious," he added, as he turned into the bathing *connât.* Soon I heard him splashing among the water jars.

"By-the-bye, Griggs," he called out through the canvas, "I forgot to tell you. They are bringing that beast home on an elephant. It was much nearer than we supposed. They will be here in twenty minutes." A tremendous splashing interrupted him. "You can go and attend to that funeral you were talking about last night," he added, and his voice was again drowned in the swish and souse of the water. "He was rather large — over ten feet — I should say. Measure him as soon as he ——" another cascade completed the sentence. I went out, taking the measuring tape from the table.

In a few minutes the procession appeared. Two or three matutinal shikarries had gone out and come back, followed by the elephant, for which Isaacs had sent the ryot at full speed the moment he was sure the beast was dead. And so they came up the little hill behind the dining-tent. The great tusker moved evenly along, bearing on the pad an enormous yellow carcass, at which the little *mahout* glanced occasionally over his shoulder. Astride of the dead king sat the ryot, who had directed Isaacs, crooning a strange psalm of victory in his outlandish northern dialect, and occasionally clapping his hands over his head with an expression of the most intense satisfaction I have ever seen on a human face. The little band came to the middle of the camp where the other tigers, now cut up and skinned elsewhere, had been deposited the night before, and as the elephant knelt down, the shikarries pulled the whole load over, pad, tiger, ryot and all, the latter skipping nimbly aside. There he lay, the great beast that had taken so many lives. We stretched him out and measured him — eleven feet from the tip of his nose to the end of his tail, all but an inch — as a little more straightening fills the measure, eleven feet exactly.

Meanwhile, the servant and shikarries collected, and the noise of the exploit went abroad. The sun was just rising when Mr. Ghyrkins put his head out of his tent and wanted to know "what the deuce all this *tamāsha* was about."

"Oh, nothing especial," I called out. "Isaacs has killed an eleven foot man-eater in the night. That is all."

"Well I'm damned," said Mr. Ghyrkins briefly, and to the point, as he stared from his tent at the great carcass, which lay stretched out for all to see, the elephant having departed.

"Clear off those fellows and let me have a look at him, can't you?" he called out, gathering the tent curtains round his neck; and there he stood, his jolly red face and dishevelled gray hair looking as if they had no body attached at all.

I went back to our quarters. Isaacs was putting the ears, which he had carefully cleansed from blood, into a silver box of beautiful workmanship, which Narain had extracted from his master's numerous traps.

"Take that box to Miss Westonhaugh's tent," he said, giving it to the servant, "with a greeting from me — with 'much peace.'" The man went out.

"She will send the box back," said I. "Such is the Englishwoman. She will take a pair of tiger's ears that nearly cost you your life, and she would rather die than accept the bit of silver in which you enclose them, without the 'permission of her uncle.'"

"I do not care," he said, "so long as she keeps the ears. But unless I am much mistaken, she will keep the box too. She is not like other Englishwomen in the least."

I was not sure of that. We had some tea in the door of our tent, and Isaacs seemed hungry and thirsty, as well he might be. Now that he was refreshed by bathing and the offices of the camp barber, he looked much as usual, save that the extreme paleness I had noticed when he came in had given place to a faint flush beneath the olive, probably due to his excitement, the danger being past. As we sat there, the rest of the party, who had slept rather later than usual after their fatigues of the previous

day, came out one by one and stood around the dead
tiger, wondering at the tale told by the delighted
ryot, who squatted at the beast's head to relate the
adventure to all comers. We could see the group
from where we sat, in the shadow of the *connât*, and
the different expressions of the men as they came
out. The little collector of Pegnugger measured
and measured again; Mr. Ghyrkins stood with his
hands in his coat pockets and his legs apart, then
going to the other side he took up the same position
again. Lord Steepleton Kildare sauntered round and
twirled his big moustache, saying nothing the while,
but looking rather serious. John Westonhaugh,
who seemed to be the artistic genius of the party,
sent for a chair and made his servant hold an umbrella
over him while he sketched the animal in his note-
book, and presently his sister came out, a big bunch
of roses in her belt, and a broad hat half hiding her
face, and looked at the tiger and then round the party
quickly, searching for Isaacs. In her hand she held
a little package wrapped in white tissue paper. I
strolled up to the group, leaving Isaacs in his tent.
I thought I might as well play innocence.

"Of course," I remarked, "those fellows have
bagged his ears as usual."

"They never omit that," said Ghyrkins.

"Oh no, uncle," broke in Miss Westonhaugh, "he
gave them to me!"

"Who?" asked Ghyrkins, opening his little eyes
wide.

"Mr. Isaacs. Did not he kill the tiger? He sent me the ears in a little silver box. Here it is — the box, I mean. I am going to give it back to him, of course."

"How did Mr. Isaacs know you wanted them?" asked her uncle, getting red in the face.

"Why, we were talking about them last night before dinner, and he promised that if he shot a tiger to-day he would give me the ears." Mr. Ghyrkins was redder and redder in the morning sun. There was a storm of some kind brewing. We were collected together on the other side of the dead tiger and exchanged all kinds of spontaneous civilities and remarks, not wishing to witness Mr. Ghyrkins' wrath, nor to go away too suddenly. I heard the conversation, however, for the old gentleman made no pretence of lowering his voice.

"And do you mean to say you let him go off like that? He must have been out all night. That beast of a nigger says so. On foot, too. I say on foot! Do you know what you are talking about? Eh? Shooting tigers on foot? What? Eh? Might have been killed as easily as not! And then what would you have said? Eh? What? Upon my soul! You girls from home have no more hearts than a parcel of old Juggernauts!" Ghyrkins was now furious. We edged away towards the dining-tent, making a great talk about the terrible heat of the sun in the morning. I caught the beginning of Miss Westonhaugh's answer. She had hardly appreciated the situation yet, and probably thought her uncle was joking, but she spoke very coldly, being properly annoyed at his talking in such a way.

"You cannot suppose for a moment that I meant him to go," I heard her say, and something else followed in a lower tone. We then went into the dining-tent.

"Now look here, Katharine," Mr. Ghyrkins' irate voice rang across the open space, "if any young woman asked me ——" John Westonhaugh had risen from his chair and apparently interrupted his uncle. Miss Westonhaugh walked slowly to her tent, while her male relations remained talking. I thought Isaacs had shown some foresight in not taking part in the morning discussion. The two men went into their tents together and the dead tiger lay alone in the grass, the sun rising higher and higher, pouring down his burning rays on man and beast and green thing. And soon the shikarries came with a small elephant and dragged the carcass away to be skinned and cut up. Kildare and the collector said they would go and shoot some small game for dinner. Isaacs, I supposed, was sleeping, and I was alone in the dining-tent. I shouted for Kiramat Ali and sent for books, paper, and pens, and a hookah, resolved to have a quiet morning to myself, since it was clear we were not going out to-day. I saw Ghyrkins' servant enter his tent with bottles and ice, and I suspected the old fellow was going to cool his wrath with a "peg," and would be asleep most of the morn-

ing. John would take a peg too, but he would not
sleep in consequence, being of Bombay, iron-headed
and spirit-proof. So I read on and wrote, and was
happy, for I like the heat of the noon-day and the
buzzing of the flies, and the smell of the parched
grass, being southern born.

About twelve o'clock, when I was beginning to
think I had done enough work for one day, I saw
Miss Westonhaugh's native maid come out of her
mistress's tent and survey the landscape, shading her
eyes with her hand. She was dressed, of course, in
spotless white drapery, and there were heavy anklets
on her feet and bangles of silver on her wrist. She
seemed satisfied by her inspection and went in again,
returning presently with Miss Westonhaugh and a
large package of work and novels and letter-writing
materials. They came straight to where I was sitting under the airy tent where we dined, and Miss
Westonhaugh established herself at one side of the
table at the end of which I was writing.

"It is so hot in my tent," she said almost apologetically, and began to unroll some worsted work.

"Yes, it is quite unbearable," I answered politely,
though I had not thought much about the temperature. There was a long silence, and I collected my
papers in a bundle and leaned back in my chair. I
did not know what to say, nor was anything expected
of me. I looked occasionally at the young girl, who
had laid her hat on the table, allowing the rich coils
of dazzling hair to assert their independence. Her

dark eyes were bent over her work as her fingers deftly pushed the needle in and out of the brown linen she worked on.

"Mr. Griggs," she began at last without looking up, "did you know Mr. Isaacs was going out last night to kill that horrid thing?" I had expected the question for some time.

"Yes; he told me about midnight, when he started."

"Then why did you let him go?" she asked, looking suddenly at me, and knitting her dark eyebrows rather fiercely.

"I do not think I could have prevented him. I do not think anybody could prevent him from doing anything he had made up his mind to. I nearly quarrelled with him, as it was."

"I am sure I could have stopped him, if I had been you," she said innocently.

"I have not the least doubt that you could. Unfortunately, however, you were not available at the time, or I would have suggested it to you."

"I wish I had known," she went on, plunging deeper and deeper. "I would not have had him go for — for anything."

"Oh! Well, I suppose not. But, seriously, Miss Westonhaugh, are you not flattered that a man should be willing and ready to risk life and limb in satisfying your lightest fancy?"

"Flattered?" she looked at me with much astonishment and some anger. I was sure the look was genuine and not assumed.

"At all events the tiger's ears will always be a charming reminiscence, a token of esteem that any one might be proud of."

"I am not proud of them in the least, though I shall always keep them as a warning not to wish for such things. I hope that the next time Mr. Isaacs is going to do a foolish thing you will have the common sense to prevent him." She returned to her starting-point; but I saw no use in prolonging the skirmish, and turned the talk upon other things. And soon John Westonhaugh joined us, and found in me a sympathetic talker and listener, as we both cared a great deal more for books than for tigers, though not averse to a stray shot now and then.

In this kind of life the week passed, shooting to-day and staying in camp to-morrow. We shifted our ground several times, working along the borders of the forest and crashing through the jungle after tiger with varying success. In the evenings, when not tired with the day's work, we sat together, and Isaacs sang, and at last even prevailed upon Miss Weston-haugh to let him accompany her with his guitar, in which he proved very successful. They were constantly together, and Ghyrkins was heard to say that Isaacs was "a very fine fellow, and it was a pity he wasn't English," to which Kildare assented somewhat mournfully, allowing that it was quite true. His chance was gone, and he knew it, and bore it like a gentleman, though he still made use of every opportunity he had to make himself acceptable to

Miss Westonhaugh. The girl liked his **manly ways,** **and** was always grateful for any little attention from him that attracted her **notice,** but it was **evident that** all her interest ceased **there.** She liked him in **the** same way she liked her brother, but rather less, **if** anything. She hardly knew, for she had seen so little of John since she was a small child. I suppose **Isaacs must** have talked **to** her about me, for she **treated me with a certain consideration,** and often referred questions to me, **on** which I thought she might as well have consulted some one else. For my part, I served the lovers in every way I could think of. I would have done anything for **Isaacs** then as now, and I liked her for the honest good feeling she had shown about him, especially in the matter of the tiger's ears, for which she could not forgive **herself** — though in truth she had been innocent enough. **And they were really** lovers, those two. Any one might **have seen it, and but** for the wondrous fascination Isaacs exercised over every one who came near him, and the circumstances of his spotless **name and** reputation for integrity in the large transactions in which he was frequently known **to** be engaged, it is certain that Mr. Ghyrkins would have looked askance at the whole affair, and very likely would have broken up the party.

In the course of time we became a little *blasé* about tigers, till on the eighth day from the beginning **of** the **hunt,** which was a Thursday, I remember, **an** **incident occurred which left a lasting impression on**

the mind of every one who witnessed it. It was a
very hot morning, the hottest day we had had, and
we had just crossed a *nullah* in the forest, full from
the recent rains, wherein the elephants lingered lovingly to splash the water over their heated sides,
drowning the swarms of mosquitoes from which they
suffer such torments, in spite of their thick skins.
The collector called a halt on the opposite side; our
line of march had become somewhat disordered by
the passage, and numerous tracks in the pasty black
mud showed that the *nullah* was a favourite resort of
tigers — though at this time of day they might be a
long distance off. I had come next to the collector
after we emerged from the stream, the pad elephants
having lingered longer in the water, and Mr. Ghyrkins with Miss Westonhaugh was three or four places
beyond me. It was shady and cool under the thick
trees, and the light was not good. The collector bent
over his howdah, looking at some tracks.

"Those tracks look suspiciously fresh, Mr. Griggs,"
said the collector, scrutinising the holes, not yet filled
by the oozing back water of the *nullah*. "Don't you
think so?"

"Indeed, yes. I do not understand it at all," I
replied. At the collector's call a couple of beaters
came forward and stooped down to examine the trail.
One of them, a good-looking young *gowala*, or cow-
herd, followed along the footprints, examining each
to be sure he was not going on a false spoor; he moved
slowly, scrutinising each hole, as the traces grew

Q

shallower on the rising ground, approaching a bit of
small jungle.   My sight followed the probable course
of the track ahead of him and something caught my
eyes, which are remarkably good, even at a great
distance.   The object was brown and hairy; a dark
brown, not the kind of colour one expects to see in
the jungle in September.   I looked closely, and was
satisfied that it must be part of an animal; still more
clearly I saw it, and no doubt remained in my mind;
it was the head of a bullock or a heifer.   I shouted
to the man to be careful, to stop and let the elephants
plough through the undergrowth, as only elephants
can.   But he did not understand my Hindustani,
which was of the civilised *Urdu* kind learnt in the
North-West Provinces.   The man went quickly
along, and I tried to make the collector comprehend
what I saw.   But the pad elephants were coming
out of the water and forcing themselves between our
beasts, and he hardly caught what I said in the confusion.   The track led away to my left, nearly opposite to the elephant bearing Mr. Ghyrkins and his
niece.   The little Pegnugger man was on my right.
The native held on, moving more and more rapidly
as he found himself following a single track.   I
shouted to him — to Ghyrkins — to everybody, but
they could not make the doomed man understand
what I saw — the freshly slain head of the tiger's
last victim.   There was little doubt that the king
himself was near by — probably in that suspicious-
looking bit of green jungle, slimy green too, as green

is, that grows in sticky chocolate-coloured mud. The young fellow was courageous, and ignorant of the immediate danger, and, above all, he was on the look out for bucksheesh. He reached the reeds and unclean vegetables that grew thick and foul together in the little patch. He put one foot into the bush.

A great fiery yellow and black head rose cautiously above the level of the green and paused a moment, glaring. The wretched man, transfixed with terror, stood stock still, expecting death. Then he moved, as if to throw himself on one side, and at the same instant the tiger made a dash at his naked body, such a dash as a great relentless cat makes at a gold-fish trying to slide away from its grip. The tiger struck the man a heavy blow on the right shoulder, felling him like a log, and coming down to a standing position over his prey, with one paw on the native's right arm. Probably the parade of elephants and bright coloured howdahs, and the shouts of the beaters and shikarries, distracted his attention for a moment. He stood whirling his tail to right and left, with half dropped jaw and flaming eyes, half pressing, half grabbing the fleshy arm of the senseless man beneath him — impatient, alarmed, and horrible.

"Pack! ! ! Pi-i-i-i-ing . . . " went the crack and the sing of the merry rifle, and the scene changed.

With a yell like a soul in everlasting torment the great beast whirled himself into the air ten feet at least, and fell dead beside his victim, shot through

breast and breastbone and heart. A dead silence fell
on the spectators. Then I looked, and saw Miss
Westonhaugh holding out a second gun to Mr.
Ghyrkins, while he, seeing that the first had done
its work, leaned forward, his broad face pale with the
extremity of his horror for the man's danger, and his
hands gripping at the empty rifle.

"You've done it this time," cried the collector from
the right. "Take six to four the man's dead!"

"Done," called Kildare from the other end. I was
the nearest to the scene, after Ghyrkins. I dropped
over the edge of the howdah and made for the spot,
running. I think I reflected as I ran that it was
rather low for men to bet on the poor fellow's life
in that way. Tigers are often very deceptive and
always die hard, and I am a cautious person, so when
I was near I pulled out my long army six-shooter,
and, going within arm's length, quietly put a bullet
through the beast's eye as a matter of safety. When
he was cut up, however, the ball from the rifle of Mr.
Ghyrkins was found in his heart; the old fellow was
a dead shot still. I went up and examined the prostrate man. He was lying on his face, and so I picked
him up and propped his head against the dead tiger.
He was still breathing, but a very little examination
proved that his right collar-bone and the bone of his
upper arm were broken. A little brandy revived
him, and he immediately began to scream with pain.
I was soon joined by the collector, who with characteristic promptitude had torn and hewed some broad

slats of bamboo from his howdah, and with a little pulling and wrenching, and the help of my long, tough turban-cloth, a real native pugree, we set and bound the arm as best we could, giving the poor fellow brandy all the while. The collar-bone we left to its own devices; an injury there takes care of itself.

An elephant came up and received the dead tiger, and the man was carried off and placed in my howdah. The other animals with their riders had gathered near the scene, and every one had something to say to Ghyrkins, who by his brilliant shot and the life he had saved, had maintained his reputation, and come off the hero of the whole campaign. Miss Weston-haugh was speechless with horror at the whole thing, and seemed to cling to her uncle, as if fearing something of the same kind might happen to her at any moment. Isaacs, as usual the last on the line of beating, came up and called out his congratulations.

"After saving a life so well, Mr. Ghyrkins, you will not grudge me the poor honour of risking one, will you?"

"Not I, my boy!" answered the delighted old sportsman, "only if that mangy old man-eater had got you down the other day, I should not have been there to pot him!"

"Great shot, sir! I envy you," said Kildare.

"Splendid shot. A hundred yards at least," said John Westonhaugh meditatively, but in a loud voice.

So we swung away toward the camp, though it was early. Ghyrkins chuckled, and the man with the broken bones groaned. But between the different members of the party he would be a rich man before he was well. I amused myself with my favourite sport of potting peacocks with bullets; it is very good practice. Isaacs had told me that morning when we started that he would leave us the next day to meet Shere Ali near Keitung. We reached camp about three o'clock, in the heat of the afternoon. The injured beater was put in a servant's tent to be sent off to Pegnugger in a litter in the cool of the night. There was a doctor there who would take care of him under the collector's written orders.

The camp was in a shady place, quite unlike the spot where we had first pitched our tents. There was a little grove of mango-trees, rather stunted, as they are in the north, and away at one corner of the plantation was a well with a small temple where a Brahmin, related to all the best families in the neighbouring village, dwelt and collected the gifts bestowed on him and his simple shrine by the superstitious, devout, or worldly pilgrims who yearly and monthly visited him in search of counsel, spiritual or social. The men had mowed the grass smooth under the trees, and the shade was not so close as to make it damp. Some ryots had been called in to dig a ditch and raised a rough *chapudra* or terrace, some fifteen feet in diameter, opposite the dining-tent, on which elevation we could sit, even late at night, in reasonable security from cobras and other evil beasts. It was a pleasant place in the afternoon, and pleasanter still at night. As I turned into our tent after we got back, I thought I would go and sit there when I had bathed, and send for a hookah and a novel, and go to sleep.

CHAPTER XI.

I OBSERVED that Isaacs was very quick about his
toilet, and when I came out and ascended the terrace,
followed by Kiramat Ali with books and tobacco, I
glanced lazily over the quiet scene, settling myself
in my chair, and fully expecting to see my friend
somewhere among the trees, not unaccompanied by
some one else. I was not mistaken. Turning my
eyes towards the corner of the grove where the old
Brahmin had his shrine, I saw the two well-known
figures of Isaacs and Miss Westonhaugh sauntering
towards the well. Having satisfied the expectations
of my curiosity, I turned over the volume of philosophy, well thumbed and hard used as a priest's brevi-
ary, and I inhaled long draughts of tobacco, debating
whether I should read, or meditate, or dream. Deciding in favour of the more mechanical form of intel-
lectuality, I fixed on a page that looked inviting, and
followed the lines, from left to right, lazily at first,
then with increased interest, and finally in that
absorbed effort of continued comprehension which con-
stitutes real study. Page after page, syllogism after
syllogism, conclusion after conclusion, I followed for
the hundredth time in the book I love well — the

book of him that would destroy the religion I believe, but whose brilliant failure is one of the grandest efforts of the purely human mind. I finished a chapter and, in thought still, but conscious again of life, I looked up. They were still down there by the well, those two, but while I looked the old priest, bent and white, came out of the little temple where he had been sprinkling his image of Vishnu, and dropped his aged limbs from one step to the other painfully, steadying his uncertain descent with a stick. He went to the beautiful couple seated on the edge of the well, built of mud and sun-dried bricks, and he seemed to speak to Isaacs. I watched, and became interested in the question whether Isaacs would give him a two-anna bit or a copper, and whether I could distinguish with the naked eye at that distance between the silver and the baser metal. Curious, thought I, how odd little trifles will absorb the attention. The interview which was to lead to the expected act of charity seemed to be lasting a long time.

Suddenly Isaacs turned and called to me; his high, distinct tones seeming to gather volume from the hollow of the well. He was calling me to join them. I rose, rather reluctantly, from my books and moved through the trees to where they were.

"Griggs," Isaacs called out before I had reached him, "here is an old fellow who knows something. I really believe he is something of a yogi."

"What ridiculous nonsense," I said impatiently,

"who ever heard of a yogi living in a temple and feeding on the fat of the land in the way all these men do? Is that all you wanted?" Miss Weston-haugh, peering down into the depths of the well, laughed gaily.

"I told you so! Never try to make Mr. Griggs swallow that kind of thing. Besides, he is a 'cynic' you know."

"As far as personal appearance goes, Miss Weston-haugh, I think your friend the Brahmin there stands more chance of being taken for a philosopher of that school. He really does not look particularly well fed, in spite of the riches I thought he possessed." He was a strange-looking old man, with a white beard and a small badly-rolled pugree. His black eyes were filmy and disagreeable to look at. I addressed him in Hindustani, and told him what Isaacs said, that he thought he was a yogi. The old fellow did not look at me, nor did the bleared eyes give any sign of intelligence. Nevertheless he answered my question.

"Of what avail that I do wonders for you who believe not?" he asked, and his voice sounded cracked and far off.

"It will avail thee several coins, friend," I answered, "both rupees and pais. Reflect that there may be bucksheesh in store for thee, and do a miracle."

"I will not do wonders for bucksheesh," said the priest, and began to hobble away. Isaacs stepped lightly to his side and whispered something in his ear. The ancient Brahmin turned.

"Then I will do a wonder for you, but I want no bucksheesh. I will do it for the lady with white hair, whose face resembles Chunder." He looked long and fixedly at Miss Westonhaugh. "Let the *sáhib log* come with me a stone's throw from the well, and let one sáhib call his servant and bid him draw water that he may wash his hands. And I will do this wonder; the man shall not draw any water, though he had the strength of Siva, until I say the word." So we moved away under the trees, and I shouted for Kiramat Ali, who came running down, and I told him to send a *bhisti*, a water-carrier, with his leathern bucket. Then we waited. Presently the man came, with bucket and rope.

"Draw water, that I may wash my hands," said I.

"Achhá, sáhib," and he strode to the well and lowered his pail by the rope. The priest looked intently at him as he shook the rope to turn the bucket over and let it fill; then he began to pull. The bucket seemed to be caught. He jerked, and then bent his whole weight back, drawing the rope across the edge of the brickwork. The thing was immovable. He seemed astonished and looked down into the well, thinking the pail was caught in a stone. I could not resist the temptation to go down and inspect the thing. No. The bucket was full and lying in the middle of the round sheet of water at the bottom of the well. The man tugged, while the

Brahmin never took his eyes, now bright and fiery, off him. I went back to where they all stood. The thing had lasted five minutes. Then the priest's lips moved silently.

Instantly the strain was released and the stout water-carrier fell headlong backwards on the grass, his heels in the air, jerking the bucket right over the edge of the well. He bounded to his feet and ran up the grove, shouting " Bhūt, Bhūt," "devils, devils," at the top of his voice. His obstinacy had lasted so long as the bucket would not move, but then his terror got the better of him and he fled.

" Did you ever see anything of that kind before, Miss Westonhaugh?" I inquired.

" No indeed; have you? How is it done?"

" I have seen similar things done, but not often. There are not many of them that know how. But I cannot tell you the process any more than I can explain the mango trick, which belongs, distantly, to the same class of phenomena."

The Brahmin, whose eyes were again dim and filmy, turned to Isaacs.

" I have done a wonder for you. I will also tell you a saying. You have done wrong in not taking the advice of your friend. You should not have come forth to kill the king of game, nor have brought the white-haired lady into the tiger's jaws. I have spoken. Peace be with you." And he moved away.

" And with you peace, friend," answered Isaacs mechanically, but as I looked at him he turned white to the very lips.

Miss Westonhaugh did not understand the language, and Isaacs would have been the last person to translate such a speech as the Brahmin had made. We turned and strolled up the hill, and presently I bethought me of some errand, and left them together under the trees. They were so happy and so beautiful together, the fair lily from the English dale and the deep red rose of Persian Gulistán. The sun slanted low through the trees and sank in rose-coloured haze, and the moon, now just at the half, began to shine out softly through the mangoes, and still the lovers walked, pacing slowly to and fro near the well. No wonder they dallied long; it was their last evening together, and I doubted not that Isaacs was telling her of his sudden departure, necessary for reasons which I knew he would not explain to her or to any one else.

At last we all assembled in the dining-tent. Mr. Currie Ghyrkins was among the first, and his niece was the last to enter the room. He was glorious that evening, his kindly red face beamed on every one, and he carried himself like a victorious general at a ladies' tea-party. He had reason to be happy, and his jerky good spirits were needed to counterbalance the deep melancholy that seemed to have settled upon his niece. The colour was gone from her cheeks, and her dark eyes, heavily fringed by the black brows and lashes, shone out strangely; the contrast between the white flaxen hair, drawn back in simple massive waves like a Greek statue, and the broad level eyes as dark as night, was almost startling this evening in the singularity of its beauty. She sat like a queenly marble at the end of the table, not silent, by any means, but so evidently out of spirits that John Westonhaugh, who did not know that Isaacs was going in the morning, and would not have supposed that his sister could care so much, if he had known, remarked upon her depression.

"What is the matter, Katharine?" he asked kindly. "Have you a headache this evening?" She was just then staring rather blankly into space.

"Oh no," she said, trying to smile. "I was thinking."

"Ah," said Mr. Ghyrkins merrily, "that is why you look so unlike yourself, my dear!" And he laughed at his rough little joke.

"Do I?" asked the girl absently.

But Ghyrkins was not to be repressed, and as Kildare and the Pegnugger man were gay and wide awake, the dinner was not as dull as might have been expected. When it was over, Isaacs announced his intention of leaving early the next morning. Very urgent business recalled him suddenly, he explained. A messenger had arrived just before dinner. He must leave without fail in the morning. Miss Westonhaugh of course was forewarned; but the others were not. Lord Steepleton Kildare, in the act of lighting a cheroot, dropped the vesuvian incontinently, and stood staring at Isaacs with an indescribable expression of empty wonder in his face, while the match sputtered and smouldered and died away in the grass by the door. John Westonhaugh, who liked Isaacs sincerely, and had probably contemplated the possibility of the latter marrying Katharine, looked sorry at first, and then a half angry expression crossed his face, which softened instantly again. Currie Ghyrkins swore loudly that it was out of the question — that it would break up the party — that he would not hear of it, and so on.

"I must go," said Isaacs quietly. "It is a very serious matter. I am sorry — more sorry than I can tell you; but I must."

"But you cannot, you know. Damn it, sir, you are the life of the party, you know! Come, come, this will never do!"

"My dear sir," said Isaacs, addressing Ghyrkins, "if, when you were about to fire this morning to save that poor devil's life, I had begged you not to shoot, would you have complied?"

"Why, of course not," ejaculated Ghyrkins angrily.

"Well, neither can I comply, though I would give anything to stay with you all."

"But nobody's life depends on your going away to-morrow morning. What do you mean? The deuce and all, you know, I don't understand you a bit."

"I cannot tell you, Mr. Ghyrkins; but something depends on my going, which is of as great importance to the person concerned as life itself. Believe me," he said, going near to the old gentleman and laying a hand on his arm, "I do not go willingly."

"Well, I hope not, I am sure," said Ghyrkins gruffly, though yielding. "If you will, you will, and there's no holding you; but we are all very sorry. That's all. Mahmoud! bring fire, you lazy pigling, that I may smoke." And he threw himself into a chair, the very creaking of the cane wicker expressing annoyance and dissatisfaction.

So there was an end of it, and Isaacs strode off through the moonlight to his quarters, to make some arrangement, I supposed. But he did not come back. Miss Westonhaugh retired also to her tent, and no one was surprised to see her go. Kildare rose presently and asked if I would not stroll to the well, or anywhere, it was such a jolly night. I went with him, and arm in arm we walked slowly down. The young moon was bright among the mango-trees, striking the shining leaves, that reflected a strange greenish light. We moved leisurely, and spoke little. I understood Kildare's silence well enough, and I had nothing to say. The ground was smooth and even, for the men had cut the grass close, and the little humped cow that belonged to the old Brahmin cropped all she could get at.

We skirted round the edge of the grove, intending to go back to the tents another way. Suddenly I saw something in front that arrested my attention. Two figures, some thirty yards away. They stood quite still, turned from us. A man and a woman between the trees, an opening in the leaves just letting a ray of moonlight slip through on them. His arm around her, the tall lissome figure of her bent, and her head resting on his shoulder. I have good eyes and was not mistaken, but I trusted Kildare had not seen. A quick twitch of his arm, hanging carelessly through mine, told me the mischief was done before I could turn his attention. By a common instinct we wheeled to the left, and passing into the open strolled back in the direction whence we had come. I did not look at Kildare, but after a minute he began to talk about the moonlight and tigers, and whether tigers were ever shot by moonlight, and altogether was rather incoherent; but I took up the question, and we talked bravely till we got back to the dining-tent, where we sat down again, secretly wishing we had not gone for a stroll after all. In a few minutes Isaacs came from his tent, which he must have entered from the other side. He was perfectly at his ease, and at once began talking about the disagreeable journey he had before him. Then, after a time, we broke up, and he said good-bye to every one in turn, and Ghyrkins told John to call his sister, if she were still visible, for " Mr. Isaacs wanted to say good-bye." So she came and took his hand, and made a simple speech about " meeting again before long," as she stood with her uncle; and my friend and I went away to our tent.

We sat long in the *connât*. Isaacs did not seem to

want rest, and I certainly did not. For the first half
hour he was engaged in giving directions to the faithful Narain, who moved about noiselessly among the
portmanteaus and gun-cases and boots which strewed
the floor. At last all was settled for the start before
dawn, and he turned to me.

" We shall meet again in Simla, Griggs, of course?"

" I hope so. Of course we shall, unless you are
killed by those fellows at Keitung. I would not
trust them."

" I do not trust them in the least, but I have an all-
powerful ally in Ram Lal. Did you not think it
very singular that the Brahmin should know all
about Ram Lal's warning? and that he should have
the same opinion?"

" We live in a country where nothing should
astonish us, as I remember saying to you a fortnight
ago, when we first met," I answered. " That the
Brahmin possesses some knowledge of *yog-vidya* is
more clearly shown by his speech about Ram Lal than
by that ridiculous trick with my water-carrier."

" You are not easily astonished, Griggs. But I
agree with you as to that. I am still at a loss to
understand why I should not have come or let the
others come. I was startled at the Brahmin."

" I saw you were; you were as white as a sheet,
and yet you turned up your nose at Ram Lal when
he told you not to come."

" The Brahmin said something more than Ram
Lal. He said I should not have brought the white-

haired lady into the tiger's jaws. I saw that the first warning had been on her account, and I suppose the impression of possible danger for her frightened me."

"It would not have frightened you three weeks ago about any woman," I said. "It appears to me that your ideas in certain quarters have undergone some little change. You are as different from the Isaacs I knew at first as Philip drunk was different from Philip sober. Such is human nature — scoffing at women the one day, and risking life and soul for their whims the next."

"I hate your reflections about the human kind, Griggs, and I do not like your way of looking at women. You hate women so!"

"No. You like my descriptions of the 'ideal creatures I rave about' much better, it seems. Upon my soul, friend, if you want a criterion of yourself, take this conversation. A fortnight ago to-day — or to-morrow, will it be? — I was lecturing you about the way to regard women; begging you to consider that they had souls and were capable of loving, as well as of being loved. And here you are accusing me of hating the whole sex, and without the slightest provocation on my part, either. Here is Birnam wood coming to Dunsinane with a vengeance!"

"Oh, I don't deny it. I don't pretend to argue about it. I have changed a good deal in the last month." He pensively crossed one leg over the other as he lay back on the long chair and pulled at his slipper. "I suppose I have — changed a good deal."

"No wonder. I presume your views of immortality, the future state of the fair sex, and the application of transcendental analysis to matrimony, all changed about the same time?"

"Don't be unreasonable," he answered. "It all dates from that evening when I had that singular fit and the vision I related to you. I have never been the same man since; and I am glad of it. I now believe women to be much more adorable than you painted them, and not half enough adored." Suddenly he dropped the extremely English manner which he generally affected in the idiom and construction of his speech, and dropped back into something more like his own language. "The star that was over my life is over it no longer. I have no life-star any longer. The jewel of the southern sky withdraws his light, paling before the white gold from the northern land. The gold that shall be mine through all the cycles of the sun, the gold that neither man nor monarch shall take from me. What have I to do with stars in heaven? Is not my star come down to earth to abide with me through life? And when life is over and the scroll is full, shall not my star bear me hence, beyond the fiery foot-bridge, beyond the paradise of my people and its senseless sensuality of houris and strong wine? Beyond the very memory of limited and bounded life, to that life eternal where there is neither limit, nor bound, nor sorrow? Shall our two souls not unite and be one soul to roam through the countless circles of revolv-

ing outer space? Not through years, or for times,
or for ages — but for ever? The light of life is
woman, the love of life is the love of woman; the
light that pales not, the life that cannot die, the love
that can know not any ending; *my* light, *my* life,
and *my* love!" His whole soul was in his voice,
and his whole heart; the twining white fingers, the
half-closed eyes, and the passionate quivering tone,
told all he had left unsaid. It was surely a high and
a noble thing that he felt, worthy of the man in his
beauty of mind and body. He loved an ideal, revealed
to him, as he thought, in the shape of the fair English
girl; he worshipped his ideal through her, without a
thought that he could be mistaken. Happy man!
Perhaps he had a better chance of going through life
without any cruel revelation of his mistake than falls
to the lot of most lovers, for she was surpassingly
beautiful, and most good and true hearted. But are
not people always mistaken who think to find the
perfect comprehended in the imperfect, the infinite
enchained and made tangible in the finite? Bah!
The same old story, the same old vicious circle, the
everlastingly recurring mathematical view of things
that cannot be treated mathematically; the fruitless
attempt to measure the harmonious circle of the soul
by the angular square of the book. What poor
things our minds are, after all. We have but one
way of thinking derived from what we know, and
we incontinently apply it to things of which we can
know nothing, and then we quarrel with the result,

which is a mere *reductio ad absurdum*, showing how utterly false and meagre are our hypotheses, premisses, and so-called axioms. Confucius, who began his system with the startling axiom that "man is good," arrived at much more really serviceable conclusions than Schopenhauer and all the pessimists put together. Meanwhile, Isaacs was in love, and, I supposed, expected me to say something appreciative.

"My dear friend," I began, "it is a rare pleasure to hear any one talk like that; it refreshes a man's belief in human nature, and enthusiasm, and all kinds of things. I talked like that some time ago because you would not. I think you are a most satisfactory convert."

"I am indeed a convert. I would not have believed it possible, and now I cannot believe that I ever thought differently. I suppose it is the way with all converts — in religion as well — and with all people who are taken up by a fair-winged genius from an arid desert and set down in a garden of roses." He could not long confine himself to ordinary language. "And yet the hot sand of the desert, and the cool of the night, and the occasional patch of miserable, languishing green, with the little kindly spring in the camel-trodden oasis, seemed all so delightful in the past life that one was quite content, never suspecting the existence of better things. But now — I could almost laugh to think of it. I stand in the midst of the garden that is filled with all things fair, and the tree of life is beside me, blossoming straight and broad with the flowers that wither not, and the fruit that is good to the parched lips and the thirsty spirit. And the garden is for us to dwell in now, and the eternity of the heavenly spheres is ours hereafter." He was all on fire again. I kept silence for some time; and his hands unfolded, and he raised them and clasped them under his head, and drew a deep long breath, as if to taste the new life that was in him.

"Forgive my bringing you down to earth again," I said after a while, "but have you made all necessary arrangements? Is there anything I can do, after you are gone? Anything to be said to these good people, if they question me about your sudden departure?"

"Yes. I was forgetting. If you will be so kind, I wish you would see the expedition out, and take charge of the expenses. There are some bags of rupees somewhere among my traps. Narain knows. I shall not take him with me — or, no; on second thoughts I will hand you over the money, and take him to Simla. Then, about the other thing. Do not tell any one where I have gone, unless it be Miss Westonhaugh, and use your own discretion about her. We shall all be in Simla in ten days, and I do not want this thing known, as you may imagine. I do not think there is anything else, thanks." He paused, as if thinking. "Yes, there is one more consideration. If anything out of the way should occur in this transaction with Baithopoor, I should

want your assistance, if you will give it. **Would
you mind?**"

"Of course not. Anything ——"

"In that case, if Ram Lal thinks **you are wanted,**
he will send a swift messenger to you with a letter
signed by me, in the Persian *shikast* — which you
read. — Will you come by the way he will direct you,
if I send? He will answer for your safety."

"**I will come,**" I said, though I thought it was
rather rash of me, who am a cautious man, to trust
my life in the hands of a shadowy person like Ram
Lal, who seemed to come and go in strange ways,
and was in communication with suspicious old Brahmin jugglers. But I trusted **Isaacs** better than his
adept friend.

"I suppose," I said, vaguely hoping there might
yet be a possibility of detaining him, "that there
is no way of doing this business so that you could
remain here."

"No, friend Griggs. If there were any other way,
I would not go now. I would not go to-day, of all
days in the year — of all days in my life. There
is no other way, by the grave of my father, on whom
be the peace of Allah." So we went to bed.

At four o'clock Narain waked us, and in twenty
minutes Isaacs was on horseback. I had ordered a
tat to be in readiness for me, thinking I would ride
with him an hour or two in the cool of the morning.
So we passed along by the quiet tents, Narain disappearing in the manner peculiar to Hindoo servants,

to be found at the end of the day's march, smiling as ever. The young moon had set some time before, but the stars were bright, though it was dark under the trees.

Twenty yards beyond the last tent, a dark figure swept suddenly out from the blackness and laid a hand on Isaacs' rein. He halted and bent over, and I heard some whispering. It only lasted a moment, and the figure shot away again. I was sure I heard something like a kiss, in the gloom, and there was a most undeniable smell of roses in the air. I held my peace, though I was astonished. I could not have believed her capable of it. Lying in wait in the dusk of the morning to give her lover a kiss and a rose and a parting word. She must have taken me for his servant in the dark.

"Griggs," said Isaacs as we parted some six or seven miles farther on, — "an odd thing happened this morning. I have left something more in your keeping than money."

"I know. Trust me. Good-bye," and he cantered off.

I confess I was very dejected and low-spirited when I came back into camp. My acquaintance with Isaacs, so suddenly grown into intimacy, had become a part of my life. I felt a sort of devotion to him that I had never felt for any man in my life before. I would rather have gone with him to Kei-tung, for a presentiment told me there was trouble in the wind. He had not talked to me about the

Baithopoor intrigue, for everything was as much settled beforehand as it was possible to settle anything. There was nothing to be said, for all that was to come was action; but I knew Isaacs distrusted the maharajah, and that without Ram Lal's assistance — of whatever nature that might prove to be — he would not have ventured to go alone to such a tryst.

When I returned the camp was all alive, for it was nearly seven o'clock. Kildare and the collector, my servant said, had gone off on *tats* to shoot some small game. Mr. Ghyrkins was occupied with the shikarries in the stretching and dressing of the skin he had won the previous day. Neither Miss Westonhaugh nor her brother had been seen. So I dressed and rested myself and had some tea, and sat wondering what the camp would be like without Isaacs, who, to me and to one other person, was emphatically, as Ghyrkins had said the night before, the life of the party. The weather was not so warm as on the previous day, and I was debating whether I should not try and induce the younger men to go and stick a pig — the shikarry said there were plenty in some place he knew of — or whether I should settle myself in the dining-tent for a long day with my books, when the arrival of a mounted messenger with some letters from the distant post-office decided me in favour of the more peaceful disposition of my time. So I glanced at the papers, and assured myself that the English were going deeper and deeper into the mire of difficulties and reckless expenditure that characterised their campaign in Afghanistan in the autumn of 1879; and when I had assured myself, furthermore, by the perusal of a request for the remittance of twenty pounds, that my nephew, the only relation, male or female, that I have in the world, had not come to the untimely death he so richly deserved, I fell to considering what book I should read. And from one thing to another, I found myself established about ten o'clock at the table in the dining-tent, with Miss Westonhaugh at one side, worsted work, writing materials and all, just as she had been at the same table a week or so before. At her request I had continued my writing when she came in. I was finishing off a column of a bloodthirsty article for the *Howler;* it probably would come near enough to the mark, for in India you may print a leader anywhere within a month of its being written, and if it was hot enough to begin with, it will still answer the purpose. Journalism is not so rapid in its requirements as in New York, but, on the other hand, it is more lucrative.

" Mr. Griggs, are you *very* busy ? "

" Oh dear, no — nothing to speak of," I went on writing — the unprecedented — folly — the — blatant — charlatanism ——

" Mr. Griggs, do you understand these things ? "

—— Lord Beaconsfield's — " I think so, Miss Westonhaugh " — Afghan policy —— There, I thought, I think that would rouse Mr. Currie Ghyrkins, if he ever saw it, which I trust he never will. I had done, and I folded the numbered sheets in an oblong bundle.

"I beg your pardon, Miss Westonhaugh; I was just finishing a sentence. I am quite at your service."

"Oh no! I see you are too busy."

"Not in the least, I assure you. Is it that tangled skein? Let me help you."

"Oh thank you. It is so tiresome, and I am not in the least inclined to be industrious."

I took the wool and set to work. It was very easy, after all; I pulled the loops through, and back again and through from the other side, and I found the ends, and began to wind it up on a piece of paper. It is singular, though, how the unaided wool can tie itself into every kind of a knot — reef, carrick bend, bowline, bowline in a bight, not to mention a variety of hitches and indescribable perversions of entanglement. I was getting on very well, though. I looked up at her face, pale and weary with a sleepless night, but beautiful — ah yes — beautiful beyond compare. She smiled faintly.

"You are very clever with your fingers. Where did you learn it? Have you a sister who makes you wind her wool for her at home?"

"No. I have no sister. I went to sea once upon a time."

"Were you ever in the navy, Mr. Griggs?"

"Oh no. I went before the mast."

"But you would not learn to unravel wool before the mast. I suppose your mother taught you when you were small — if you ever were small."

"I never had a mother that I can remember — I learned to do all those things at sea."

"Forgive me," she said, guessing she had struck some tender chord in my existence. "What an odd life you must have had."

"Perhaps. I never had any relations that I can remember, except a brother, much older than I. He died years ago, and his son is my only living relation. I was born in Italy."

"But when did you learn so many things? You seem to know every language under the sun."

"I had a good education when I got ashore. Some one was very kind to me, and I had learned Latin and Greek in the common school in Rome before I ran away to sea."

I answered her questions reluctantly. I did not want to talk about my history, especially to a girl like her. I suppose she saw my disinclination, for as I handed her the card with the wool neatly wound on it, she thanked me and presently changed the subject, or at least shifted the ground.

"There is something so free about the life of an adventurer — I mean a man who wanders about doing brave things. If I were a man I would be an adventurer like you."

"Not half so much of an adventurer, as you call it, as our friend who went off this morning."

It was the first mention of Isaacs since his departure. I had said the thing inadvertently, for I would not have done anything to increase her trouble for

the world. She leaned back, dropping her hands
with her work in her lap, and stared straight out
through the doorway, as pale as death — pale as only
fair-skinned people are when they are ill, or hurt.
She sat quite still. I wondered if she were ill, or if
it were only Isaacs' going that had wrought this
change in her brilliant looks. " Would you like me
to read something to you, Miss Westonhaugh?
Here is a comparatively new book — *The Light of
Asia*, by Mr. Edwin Arnold. It is a poem about
India. Would it give you any pleasure?" She
guessed the kind intention, and a little shadow of a
smile passed over her lips.

" You are so kind, Mr. Griggs. Please, you are so
very kind."

I began to read, and read on and on through the
exquisite rise and fall of the stanzas, through the
beautiful clear high thoughts which seem to come
as a breath and a breeze from an unattainable heaven,
from the Nirvana we all hope for in our inmost
hearts, whatever our confession of faith. And the
poor girl was soothed, and touched and lulled by the
music of thought and the sigh of verse that is in
the poem; and the morning passed. I suppose the
quiet and the poetry wrought up in her the feeling of
confidence she felt in me, as being her lover's friend,
for after I had paused a minute or two, seeing some
one coming toward the tent, she said quite simply —

" Where is he gone?"

" He is gone to do a very noble deed. He is gone

to save the life of a man he never saw." A bright
light came into her face, and all the chilled heart's
blood, driven from her cheeks by the weariness of
her first parting, rushed joyously back, and for one
moment there dwelt on her features the glory and
bloom of the love and happiness that had been hers
all day yesterday, that would be hers again — when?
Poor Miss Westonhaugh, it seemed so long to wait.

The day passed somehow, but the dinner was dis-
mal. Miss Westonhaugh was evidently far from
well, and I could not conceive that the pain of a temporary parting should make so sudden a change in
one so perfectly strong and healthy — even were her
nature ever so sensitive. Kildare and the Pegnugger magistrate tried to keep up the spirits of the
party, but John Westonhaugh was anxious about
his sister, and even old Mr. Currie Ghyrkins was
beginning to fancy there must be something wrong.
We sat smoking outside, and the young girl refused
to leave us, though John begged her to. As we sat,
it may have been half an hour after dinner, a messenger came galloping up in hot haste, and leaping to
the ground asked for "Gurregis Sáhib," with the
usual native pronunciation of my euphonious name.
Being informed, he salaamed low and handed me a
letter, which I took to the light. It was in *shikast*
Persian, and signed "Abdul Hafiz-ben-Isâk." "Ram
Lal," he said, "has met me unexpectedly, and sends
you this by his own means, which are swift as the
flight of the eagle. It is indispensable that you meet

us below Keitung, towards Sultanpoor, on the afternoon of the day when the moon is full. Travel by
Julinder and Sultanpoor; you will easily overtake
me, since I go by Simla. For friendship's sake, for
love's sake, come. It is life and death. Give the
money to the Irishman. Peace be with you."

I sighed a sigh of the most undetermined description. Was I glad to rejoin my friend? or was I
pained to leave the woman he loved in her present
condition? I hardly knew.

"I think we had all better go back to Simla," said
John, when I explained that the most urgent business called me away at dawn.

"There will be none of us left soon," said Ghyrkins quite quietly and mournfully.

I found means to let Miss Westonhaugh understand where I was going. I gave Kildare the money
in charge.

In the dark of the morning, as I cleared the tents,
the same shadow I had seen before shot out and laid
a hand on my rein. I halted on the same spot where
Isaacs had drawn rein twenty-four hours before.

"Give him this from me. God be with you!" She
was gone in a moment, leaving a small package in
my right hand. I thrust it in my bosom and rode
away.

"How she loves him," I thought, wondering
greatly.

CHAPTER XII.

IT was not an agreeable journey I had undertaken. In order to reach the inaccessible spot, chosen by Isaacs for the scene of Shere Ali's liberation, in time to be of any use, it was necessary that I should travel by a more direct and arduous route than that taken by my friend. He had returned to Simla, and by his carefully made arrangements would be able to reach Keitung, or the spot near it, where the transaction was to take place, by constant changes of horses where riding was possible, and by a strong body of dooly-bearers wherever the path should prove too steep for four-footed beasts of burden. I, on the other hand, must leave the road at Julinder, a place I had never visited, and must trust to my own unaided wits and a plentiful supply of rupees to carry me over at least two hundred miles of country I did not know — difficult certainly, and perhaps impracticable for riding. The prospect was not a pleasant one, but I was convinced that in a matter of this importance a man of Isaacs' wit and wealth would have made at least some preliminary arrangements for me, since he probably knew the country well enough

s

himself. I had but six days at the outside to reach my destination.

I had resolved to take one servant, Kiramat Ali, with me as far as Julinder, whence I would send him back to Simla with what slender luggage we carried, for I meant to ride as light as possible, with no encumbrance to delay me when once I left the line of the railway. I might have ridden five miles with Kiramat Ali behind me on a sturdy *tat*, when I was surprised by the appearance of an unknown saice in plain white clothes, holding a pair of strong young ponies by the halter and salaaming low.

"Pundit Ram Lal sends your highness his peace, and bids you ride without sparing. The *dâk* is laid to the fire-carriages."

The saddles were changed in a moment, Kiramat Ali and I assisting in the operation. It was clear that Ram Lal's messengers were swift, for even if he had met Isaacs when the latter reached the railroad, no ordinary horse could have returned with the message at the time I had received it. Still less would any ordinary Hindus be capable of laying a *dâk*, or post route of relays, over a hundred miles long in twelve hours. Once prepared, it was a mere matter of physical endurance in the rider to cover the ground, for the relays were stationed every five or six miles. It was well known that Lord Steepleton Kildare had lately ridden from Simla to Umballa one night and back the next day, ninety-two miles each way, with constant change of cattle. What

puzzled me was the rapidity with which the necessary
dispositions had been made. On the whole, I was
reassured. If Ram Lal had been able to prepare my
way at such short notice here, with two more days at
his disposal he would doubtless succeed in laying
me a *dâk* most of the way from Julinder to Keitung.

I will not dwell upon the details of the journey.
I reached the railroad and prepared for forty-eight
hours of jolting and jostling and broken sleep. It is
true that railway travelling is nowhere so luxurious
as in India, where a carriage has but two compart-
ments, each holding as a rule only two persons,
though four can be accommodated by means of hanging berths. Each compartment has a spacious bath-
room attached, where you may bathe as often as you
please, and there are various contrivances for venti-
lating and cooling the air. Nevertheless the heat is
sometimes unbearable, and a journey from Bombay
to Calcutta direct during the warm months is a severe
trial to the strongest constitution. On this occasion
I had about forty-eight hours to travel, and I was
resolved to get all the rest in that time that the jolting
made possible; for I knew that once in the saddle
again it might be days before I got a night's sleep.
And so we rumbled along, through the vast fields of
sugar-cane, now mostly tied in huge sheaves upright,
through boundless stretches of richly-cultivated soil,
intersected with the regularity of a chess-board by the
rivulets and channels of a laborious irrigation. Here
and there stood the high frames made by planting

four bamboos in a square and wickering the top,
whereon the ryots sit when the crops are ripening,
to watch against thieves and cattle, and to drive
away the birds of the air.   On we spun, past Meerut
and Mozuffernugger, past Umballa and Loodhiana,
till we reached our station of Julinder at dawn.
Descending from the train, I was about to begin
making inquiries about my next move, when I was
accosted by a tall and well-dressed Mussulman, in a
plain cloth *caftán* and a white turban, but exquisitely
clean and fresh looking, as it seemed to me, for my
eyes were smarting with dust and wearied with the
perpetual shaking of the train.

The courteous native soon explained that he was
Isaacs' agent in Julinder, and that a *tár ki khaber*, a
telegram in short, had warned him to be on the look-
out for me.   I was greatly relieved, for it was evident that every arrangement had been made for my
comfort, so far as comfort was possible.   Isaacs had
asked my assistance, but he had taken every precaution against all superfluous bodily inconvenience to
me, and I felt sure that from this point I should
move quickly and easily through every difficulty.
And so it proved.   The Mussulman took me to his
house, where there was a spacious apartment, occupied by Isaacs when he passed that way.   Every
luxury was prepared for the enjoyment of the bath,
and a breakfast of no mean taste was served me in
my own room.   Then my host entered and explained
that he had been directed to make certain arrange-

ments for my journey. He had laid a *dâk* nearly a hundred miles ahead, and had been ordered to tell me that similar steps had been taken beyond that point as far as my ultimate destination, of which, however, he was ignorant. My servant, he said, must stay with him and return to Simla with my traps.

So an hour later I mounted for my long ride, provided with a revolver and some rupees in a bag, in case of need. The country, my entertainer informed me, was considered perfectly safe, unless I feared the *tap*, the bad kind of fever which infests all the country at the base of the hills. I was not afraid of this. My experience is that some people are predisposed to fever, and will generally be attacked by it in their first year in India, whether they are much exposed to it or not, while others seem naturally proof against any amount of malaria, and though they sleep out of doors through the whole rainy season, and tramp about the jungles in the autumn, will never catch the least ague, though they may have all other kinds of ills to contend with.

On and on, galloping along the heavy roads, sometimes over no road at all, only a broad green track, where the fresh grass that had sprung up after the rains was not yet killed by the trampling of the bullocks and the grinding jolt of the heavy cart. At intervals of seven or eight miles I found a saice with a fresh pony picketed and grazing at the end of the long rope. The saice was generally squatting near by, with his bag of food and his three-sided kitchen

of stones, blackened with the fire from his last meal,
beside him; sometimes in the act of cooking his chow-
patties, sometimes eating them, according to the time
of day. Several times I stopped to drink some water
where it seemed to be good, and I ate a little choco-
late from my supply, well knowing the miraculous sus-
taining powers of the simple little block of "Menier,"
which, with its six small tablets, will not only sustain life, but will supply vigour and energy, for as
much as two days, with no other food. On and on,
through the day and the night, past sleeping villages
where the jackals howled around the open doors of
the huts; and across vast fields of late crops, over
hills thickly grown with trees, past the broad bend
of the Sutlej river, and over the plateau toward Sultanpoor, the cultivation growing scantier and the
villages rarer all the while, as the vast masses of the
Himalayas defined themselves more and more dis-
tinctly in the moonlight. Horses of all kinds under
me, lean and fat, short and high, roman-nosed and
goose-necked, broken and unbroken; away and away,
shifting saddle and bridle and saddle-bag as I left
each tired mount behind me. Once I passed a stream,
and pulling off my boots to cool my feet, the temptation was too strong, so I hastily threw off my clothes
and plunged in and had a short refreshing bath.
Then on, with the galloping even triplet of the
horse's hoofs beneath me, as they came down in quick
succession, as if the earth were a muffled drum and
we were beating an untiring *rataplan* on her breast.

I must have ridden a hundred and thirty miles before dawn, and the pace was beginning to tell, even on my strong frame. True, to a man used to the saddle, the effort of riding is reduced to a minimum when every hour or two gives him a fresh horse. There is then no heed for the welfare of the animal necessary; he has but his seven or eight miles to gallop, and then his work is done; there are none of those thousand little cares and sympathetic shiftings and adjustings of weight and seat to be thought of, which must constantly engage the attention of a man who means to ride the same horse a hundred miles, or even fifty or forty. Conscious that a fresh mount awaits him, he sits back lazily and never eases his weight for a moment; before he has gone thirty miles he will kick his feet out of the stirrups about once in twenty minutes, and if he has for the moment a quiet old stager who does not mind tricks, he will probably fetch one leg over and go a few miles sitting sideways. He will go to sleep once or twice, and wake up apparently in the very act to fall — though I believe that a man will sleep at a full gallop and never loosen his knees until the moment of waking startles him. Nevertheless, and notwithstanding Lord Steepleton Kildare and his ride to Umballa and back in twenty-four hours, when a man, be he ever so strong, has ridden over a hundred miles, he feels inclined for a rest, and a walk, and a little sleep.

Once more an emissary of Ram Lal strode to my side as I rolled off the saddle into the cool grass at

sunrise in a very impracticable-looking country.
The road had been steeper and less defined during the
last two hours of the ride, and as I crossed one leg
high over the other lying on my back in the grass, the
morning light caught my spur, and there was blood
on it, bright and red. I had certainly come as fast
as I could; if I should be too late, it would not be
my fault. The agent, whoever he might be, was a
striking-looking fellow in a dirty brown cloth *caftán*
and an enormous sash wound round his middle. A
pointed cap with some tawdry gold lace on it covered
his head, and greasy black love-locks writhed filthily
over his high cheek bones and into his scanty tangled
beard; a suspicious hilt bound with brass wire reared
its snake-like head from the folds of his belt, and his
legs, terminating in thick-soled native shoes, reminded one of a tarantula in boots. He salaamed
awkwardly with a tortuous grin, and addressed me
with the northern salutation, " May your feet never
be weary with the march." Having been twenty-
four hours in the saddle, my feet were not that portion of my body most wearied, but I replied to the
effect that I trusted the shadow of the greasy gentleman might not diminish a hairsbreadth in the next
ten thousand years. We then proceeded to business,
and I observed that the man spoke a very broken and
hardly intelligible Hindustani. I tried him in Persian, but it was of no avail. He spoke Persian, he
said, but it was not of the kind that any human being
could understand; so we returned to the first lan-

guage, and I concluded that he was a wandering kábuli.

As an introduction of himself he mentioned Isaacs, calling him Abdul Hafiz Sáhib, and he seemed to know him personally. Abdul, he said, was not far off as distances go in the Himalayas. He thought I should find him the day after to-morrow, *mungkul*. He said I should not be able to ride much farther, as the pass beyond Sultanpoor was utterly impracticable for horses; coolies, however, awaited me with a dooly, one of those low litters slung on a bamboo, in which you may travel swiftly and without effort, but to the destruction of the digestive organs. He said also that he would accompany me the next stage as far as the doolies, and I thought he showed some curiosity to know whither I was going ; but he was a wise man in his generation, and knowing his orders, did not press me overmuch with questions. I remarked in a mild way that the saddle was the throne of the warrior, and that the air of the black mountains was the breath of freedom ; but I added that the voice of the empty stomach was as the roar of the king of the forest. Whereupon the man replied that the forest was mine and the game therein, whereof I was lord, as I probably was of the rest of the world, since I was his father and mother and most of his relations; but that, perceiving that I was occupied with the cares of a mighty empire, he had ventured to slay with his own hand a kid and some birds, which, if I would condescend to partake of them, he would proceed to cook. I replied that the light of my countenance would shine upon my faithful servant to the extent of several coins, both rupees and pais, but that the peculiar customs of my caste forbid me to touch food cooked by any one but myself. I would, however, in consideration of his exertions and his guileless heart, invite the true follower of the prophet, whose name is blessed, to partake with me of the food which I should presently prepare. Whereat he was greatly delighted, and fetched the meat, which he had stowed away in a kind of horse-cloth, for safety against ants.

I am not a bad cook at a pinch, and so we sat down and made a cooking-place with stones, and built a fire, and let the flame die down into coals, and I dressed the meat as best I could, and flavoured it with gunpowder and pepper, and we were merry. The man was thenceforth mine, and I knew I could trust him; a bivouac in the Himalayas, when one is alone and far from any kind of assistance, is not the spot to indulge in any prejudice about colour. I did not think much about it as I hungrily gnawed the meat and divided the birds with my pocket-knife.

The lower Himalayas are at first extremely disappointing. The scenery is enormous but not grand, and at first hardly seems large. The lower parts are at first sight a series of gently undulating hills and wooded dells; in some places it looks as if one might almost hunt the country. It is long before you realise that it is all on a gigantic scale; that the quick-set hedges are belts of rhododendrons of full growth, the water-jumps rivers, and the stone walls mountain-ridges; that to hunt a country like that you would have to ride a horse at least two hundred feet high. You cannot see at first, or even for some time, that the gentle-looking hill is a mountain of five or six thousand feet; in Simla you will not believe you are three thousand feet above the level of the Rhigi Kulm in Switzerland. Persons who are familiar with the aspect of the Rocky Mountains are aware of the singular lack of dignity in those enormous elevations. They are merely big, without any superior beauty, until you come to the favoured spots of nature's art, where some great contrast throws out into appalling relief the gulf between the high and the low. It is so in the Himalayas.

You may travel for hours and days amidst vast forests and hills without the slightest sensation of pleasure or sense of admiration for the scene, till suddenly your path leads you out on to the dizzy brink of an awful precipice — a sheer fall, so exaggerated in horror that your most stirring memories of Mont Blanc, the Jungfrau, and the hideous *arête* of the Pitz Bernina, sink into vague insignificance. The gulf that divides you from the distant mountain seems like a huge bite taken bodily out of the world by some voracious god; far away rise snow peaks such as were not dreamt of in your Swiss tour; the bottomless valley at your feet is misty and gloomy with blackness, streaked with mist, while the peaks above shoot

gladly to the sun and catch his broadside rays like
majestic white standards. Between you, as you
stand leaning cautiously against the hill behind you,
and the wonderful background far away in front,
floats a strange vision, scarcely moving, but yet not
still. A great golden shield sails steadily in vast
circles, sending back the sunlight in every tint of
burnished glow. The golden eagle of the Himalayas
hangs in mid-air, a sheet of polished metal to the eye,
pausing sometimes in the full blaze of reflection, as
ages ago the sun and the moon stood still in the
valley of Ajalon ; too magnificent for description, as
he is too dazzling to look at. The whole scene, if no
greater name can be given to it, is on a scale so
Titanic in its massive length and breadth and depth,
that you stand utterly trembling and weak and foolish as you look for the first time. You have never
seen such masses of the world before.

It was in such a spot as this that, nearly at noon on
the appointed day, my dooly-bearers set me down and
warned me I was at my journey's end. I stepped
out and stood on the narrow way, pausing to look
and to enjoy all that I saw. I had been in other
parts of the lower Himalayas before, and the first
sensations I had experienced had given way to those
of a contemplative admiration. No longer awed or
overpowered or oppressed by the sense of physical
insignificance in my own person, I could endure to
look on the stupendous panorama before me, and
could even analyse what I felt. But before long my

pardonable reverie was disturbed by a well-known
voice. The clear tones rang like a trumpet along
the mountain-side in a glad shout of welcome. I
turned and saw Isaacs coming quickly towards me,
bounding along the edge of the precipice as if his
life had been passed in tending goats and robbing
eagles' nests. I, too, moved on to meet him, and in
a moment we clasped hands in unfeigned delight at
being again together. What was Ghyrkins or his
party to me? Here was the man I sought; the one
man on earth who seemed worth having for a friend.
And yet it was but three weeks since we first met,
and I am not enthusiastic by temperament.

"What news, friend Griggs?"

"She greets you and sends you this," I said, taking
from my bosom the parcel she had thrust into my hand
as I left in the dark. His face fell suddenly. It was
the silver box he had given her; was it possible she
had taken so much trouble to return it? He turned
it over mournfully.

"You had better open it. There is probably something in it."

I never saw a more complete change in a man's face
during a single second than came over Isaacs' in that
moment. He had not thought of opening it, in his
first disappointment at finding it returned. He
turned back the lid. Bound with a bit of narrow
ribbon and pressed down carefully, he found a heavy
lock of gold-white hair, so fair that it made everything around it seem dark — the grass, our clothes,

and even the white streamer that hung down from
Isaacs' turban. It seemed to shed a bright light,
even in the broad noonday, as it lay there in the
curiously wrought box — just as the body of some
martyred saint found jealously concealed in the dark
corner of an ancient crypt, and broken in upon by
unsuspecting masons delving a king's grave, might
throw up in their dusky faces a dazzling halo of soft
radiance — the glory of the saint hovering lovingly by
the body wherein the soul's sufferings were perfected.

The moment Isaacs realised what it was, he turned
away, his face all gladness, and moved on a few steps
with bent head, evidently contemplating his new
treasure. Then he snapped the spring, and putting
the casket in his vest turned round to me.

" Thank you, Griggs ; how are they all ? "

" It was worth a two-hundred mile ride to see your
face when you opened that box. They are pretty
well. I left them swearing that the party was broken
up, and that they would all go back to Simla."

" The sooner the better. We shall be there in
three days from here, by the help of Ram Lal's wonderful post."

" Between you I managed to get here quite well.
How did you do it? I never missed a relay all the
way from Julinder."

"Oh, it is very easy," answered Isaacs. "You
could have a dâk to the moon from India if you would
pay for it ; or any other thing in heaven or earth or
hell that you might fancy. Money, that is all. But,

my dear fellow, you have lost flesh sensibly since we parted. You take your travelling hard."

"Where is Ram Lal?" I asked, curious to learn something of our movements for the night.

"Oh, I don't know. He is probably somewhere about the place charming cobras or arresting avalanches, or indulging in some of those playful freaks he says he learned in Edinburgh. We have had a great good time the last two days. He has not disappeared, or swallowed himself even once, or delivered himself of any fearful and mysterious prophecies. We have been talking transcendentalism. He knows as much about 'functional gamma' and 'All X is Y' and the rainbow, and so on, as you do yourself. I recommend him. I think he would be a charming companion for you. There he is now, with his pockets full of snakes and evil beasts. I wanted him to catch a golden eagle this morning, and tame it for Miss Westonhaugh, but he said it would eat the jackal and probably the servants, so I have given it up for the present." Isaacs was evidently in a capital humour. Ram Lal approached us.

I saw at a glance that Ram Lal the Buddhist, when on his beats in the civilisation of Simla, was one person. Ram Lal, the cultured votary of science, among the hills and the beasts and the specimens that he loved, was a very different man. He was as gray as ever, it is true, but better defined, the outlines sharper, the features more Dantesque and easier to discern in the broad light of the sun. He did not

look now as if he could sit down and cross his legs
and fade away into thin air, like the Cheshire cat.
He looked more solid and fleshly, his voice was
fuller, and sounded close to me as he spoke, without a shadow of the curious distant ring I had
noticed before.

"Ah!" he said in English, "Mr. Griggs, at last!
Well, you are in plenty of time. The gentleman who
is not easily astonished. That is just as well, too.
I like people with quiet nerves. I see by your
appearance that you are hungry, Mr. Griggs. Abdul
Hafiz, why should we not dine? It is much better
to get that infliction of the flesh over before this
evening."

"By all means. Come along. But first send those
dooly-bearers about their business. They can wait
till to-morrow over there on the other side. They
always carry food, and there is any amount of fuel."

Just beyond the shoulder of the hill, sheltered from
the north by the projecting boulders, was a small
tent, carefully pitched and adjusted to stand the
storms if any should come. Thither we all three bent
our steps and sat down by the fire, for it was chilly,
even cold, in the passes in September. Food was
brought out by Isaacs, and we ate together as if no
countless ages of different nationalities separated us.
Ram Lal was perfectly natural and easy in his manners, and affable in what he said. Until the meal
was finished no reference was made to the strange
business that brought us from different points of the

compass to the Himalayan heights. Then, at last, Ram Lal spoke; his meal had been the most frugal of the three, and he had soon eaten his fill, but he employed himself in rolling cigarettes, which he did with marvellous skill, until we two had satisfied our younger and healthier appetites.

"Abdul Hafiz," he said, his gray face bent over his colourless hands as he twisted the papers, "shall we not tell Mr. Griggs what is to be done? Afterward he can lie in the tent and sleep until evening, for he is weary and needs to recruit his strength."

"So be it, Ram Lal," answered Isaacs.

"Very well. The position is this, Mr. Griggs. Neither Mr. Isaacs nor I trust those men that we are to meet, and therefore, as we are afraid of being killed unawares, we thought we would send for you to protect us." He smiled pleasantly as he saw the blank expression in my face.

"Certainly, and you shall hear how it is to be done. The place is not far from here in the valley below. The band are already nearing the spot, and at midnight we will go down and meet them. The meeting will be, of course, like all formal rendezvous for the delivery of prisoners. The captain of the band will come forward accompanied by his charge, and perhaps by a sowar. We three will stand together, side by side, and await their coming. Now the plot is this. They have determined if possible to murder both Shere Ali and Isaacs then and there together. They have not counted on us, but they probably expect that our friend will arrive guarded by a troop of horse. The maharajah's men will try and sneak up close to where we stand, and at a signal, which the leader, in conversation with Isaacs, will give by laying his hand on his shoulder, the men will rush in and cut Shere Ali to pieces, and Isaacs too if the captain cannot do it alone. Now look here, Mr. Griggs. What we want you to do is this. Your friend — my friend — wants no miracles, so that you have got to do by strength what might be done by stratagem, though not so quickly. When you see the leader lay his hand on Isaacs' shoulder, seize him by the throat and mind his other arm, which will be armed. Prevent him from injuring Isaacs, and I will attend to the rest, who will doubtless require my whole attention."

"But," I objected, "supposing that this captain turned out to be stronger or more active than I. What then?"

"Never fear," said Isaacs, smiling. "There aren't any."

"No," continued Ram Lal, "never disturb yourself about that, but just knock your man down and be done with it. I will guarantee you can do it well enough, and if he gives you trouble I may be able to help you."

"All right; give me some cigarettes;" and before I had smoked one I was asleep.

When I awoke the sun was down, but there was a great light over everything. The full moon had just risen above the hills to eastward and bathed every object in silver sheen. The far peaks, covered with snow, caught the reflection and sent the beams floating across the deep dark valleys between. The big boulder, against which the tent was pitched, caught it too, and seemed changed from rough stone to precious metal; it was on the tent-pegs and the ropes, it was upon Isaacs' lithe figure, as he tightened his sash round his waist and looked to his pocket-book for the agreement. It made Ram Lal, the gray and colourless, look like a silver statue, and it made the smouldering flame of the watch-fire utterly dim and faint. It was a wonderful moon. I looked at my watch; it was eight o'clock.

"Yes," said Isaacs, "you were tired and have slept long. It is time to be off. There is some whiskey in that flask. I don't take those things, but Ram Lal says you had better have some, as you might get fever." So I did. Then we started, leaving everything in the tent, of which we pegged down the flap. There were no natives about, the dooly-bearers having retired to the other side of the valley, and the jackals would find nothing to attract them, as we had thrown the remainder of our meal over the edge. As for weapons, I had a good revolver and a thick stick; Isaacs had a revolver and a vicious-looking Turkish knife; and Ram Lal had nothing at all, as far as I could see, except a long light staff.

The effect of the moonlight was wild in the extreme, as we descended the side of the mountain

by paths which were very far from smooth or easy.
Every now and then, as we neared the valley, we
turned the corner of some ridge and got a fair view
of the plain. Then a step farther, and we were in the
dark again, behind boulders and picking our way
over loose stones, or struggling with the wretched
foothold afforded by a surface of light gravel, inclined to the horizontal at an angle of forty-five
degrees. Then, with a scramble, a jump, and a little
swearing in a great many languages — I think we
counted that we spoke twenty-seven between us —
we were on firm soil again, and swinging along over
the bit of easy level path. It would have been out
of the question to go in doolies, and no pony could
keep a foothold for five minutes on the uncertain
ground.

At last, as we emerged into the bright moonlight
on a little platform of rock at an angle of the path,
we paused. Ram Lal, who seemed to know the way,
was in front, and held up his hand to silence us;
Isaacs and I kneeled down and looked over the
brink. Some two hundred feet below, on a broad
strip of green bordering the steep cliffs, was picketed
a small body of horse. We could see the men squatting about in their small compact turbans and their
shining accoutrements ; the horses tethered at various
distances on the sward, cropping so vigorously that
even at that height we could hear the dull sound as
they rhythmically munched the grass. We could see
in the middle of the little camp a 1 an seated on a

rug and wrapped in a heavy garment of some kind, quietly smoking a common hubble-bubble. Beside him stood another who reflected more moonlight than the rest, and who was therefore, by his trappings, the captain of the band. The seated smoker could be no other than Shere Ali.

Cautiously we descended the remaining windings of the steep path, turning whenever we had a chance, to look down on the horsemen and their prisoner below, till at last we emerged in the valley a quarter of a mile or so beyond where they were stationed. Here on the level of the plain we stopped a moment, and Ram Lal renewed his instructions to me.

" If the captain," he said, "lays his hand on Isaacs' shoulder, seize him and throw him. If you cannot get him down kill him — any way you can — shoot him under the arm with your pistol. It is a matter of life and death."

" All right." And we walked boldly along the broad strip of sward. The moon was now almost immediately overhead, for it was midnight, or near it. I confess the scene awed me, the giant masses of the mountains above us, the vast distances of mysterious blue air, through which the snow-peaks shone out with a strange look that was not natural. The swish of the quickly flowing stream at the edge of the plot we were walking over sounded hollow and unearthly; the velvety whirr of the great mountain bats as they circled near us, stirred from the branches as we passed out, was disagreeable and heavy to hear. The moon shone brighter and brighter.

We were perhaps thirty yards from the little camp, in which there might be fifty men all told. Isaacs stood still and sung out a greeting.

"Peace to you, men of Baithopoor!" he shouted. It was the preconcerted form of address. Instantly the captain turned and looked toward us. Then he gave some orders in a low voice, and taking his prisoner by the hand assisted him to rise. There was a scurrying to and fro in the camp. The men seemed to be collecting, and moving to the edge of the bivouac. Some began to saddle the horses. The moon was so intensely bright that their movements were as plain to us as though it had been broad daylight.

Two figures came striding toward us — the captain and Shere Ali. As I looked at them, curiously enough, as may be imagined, I noticed that the captain was the taller man by two or three inches, but Shere Ali's broad chest and slightly-bowed legs produced an impression of enormous strength. He looked the fierce-hearted, hard-handed warrior, from head to heel; though in accordance with Isaacs' treaty he had been well taken care of and was dressed in the finest stuffs, his beard carefully clipped and his Indian turban rolled with great neatness round his dark and prominent brows.

The first thing for the captain was to satisfy himself as far as possible that we had no troops in ambush up there in the jungle on the base of the mountain. He had probably sent scouts out before, and was pretty sure there was no one there. To gain time, he made a great show of reading the agreement through from beginning to end, comparing it all the while with a copy he held. While this was going on, and I had put myself as near as possible to the captain, Isaacs and Shere Ali were in earnest conversation in the Persian tongue. Shere Ali told Abdul that the captain's perusal of the contract must be a mere empty show, since the man did not know a word of the language. Isaacs, on hearing that the captain could not understand, immediately warned Shere Ali of the intended attempt to murder them both, of which Ram Lal, his friend, had heard, and I could see the old soldier's eye flash and his hand feel for his weapon, where there was none, at the mere mention of a fight. The captain began to talk to Isaacs, and I edged as near as I could to be ready for my grip. Still it did not come. He talked on, very civilly, in intelligible Hindustani. What was the matter with the moon?

A few minutes before it had seemed as if there would be neither cloud nor mist in such a sky; and now a light filmy wreath was rising and darkening the splendour of the wonderful night. I looked across at Ram Lal. He was standing with one hand on his hip, and leaning with the other on his staff, and he was gazing up at the moon with as much interest as he ever displayed about anything. At that moment the captain handed Isaacs a prepared receipt for signature, to the effect that the prisoner had been

duly delivered to his new owner.   The light was
growing dimmer, and Isaacs could hardly see to read
the characters before he signed.   He raised the scroll
to his eyes and turned half round to see it better.
At that moment the tall captain stretched forth his
arm and laid his hand on Isaacs' shoulder, raising
his other arm at the same time to his men, who had
crept nearer and nearer to our group while the endless
talking was going on.   I was perfectly prepared,
and the instant the soldier's hand touched Isaacs I
had the man in my grip, catching his upraised arm
in one hand and his throat with the other.   The
struggle did not last long, but it was furious in its
agony.   The tough Punjabi writhed and twisted
like a cat in my grasp, his eyes gleaming like living
coals, springing back and forward in his vain and
furious efforts to reach my feet and trip me.   But it
was no use.   I had his throat and one arm well in
hand, and could hold him so that he could not reach
me with the other.   My fingers sank deeper and
deeper in his neck as we swayed backwards and sideways tugging and hugging, breast to breast, till at
last, with a fearful strain and wrench of every muscle
in our two bodies, his arm went back with a jerk,
broken like a pipe-stem, and his frame collapsing
and bending backwards, fell heavily to the ground
beneath me.

The whole strength of me was at work in the
struggle, but I could get a glimpse of the others as
we whirled and swayed about.

Like the heavy pall of virgin white that is laid on the body of a pure maiden; of velvet, soft and sweet but heavy and impenetrable as death, relentless, awful, appalling the soul, and freezing the marrow in the bones, it came near the earth. The figure of the gray old man grew mystically to gigantic and unearthly size, his vast old hands stretched forth their skinny palms to receive the great curtain as it descended between the moonlight and the sleeping earth. His eyes were as stars, his hoary head rose majestically to an incalculable height; still the thick, all-wrapping mist came down, falling on horse and rider and wrestler and robber and Amir; hiding all, covering all, folding all, in its soft samite arms, till not a man's own hand was visible to him a span's length from his face.

I could feel the heaving chest of the captain beneath my knee; I could feel the twitching of the broken arm tortured under the pressure of my left hand; but I could see neither face nor arm nor breast, nor even my own fingers. Only above me, as I stared up, seemed to tower the supernatural proportions of Ram Lal, a white apparition visible through the opaque whiteness that hid everything else from view. It was only a moment. A hand was on my shoulder, Isaacs' voice was in my ear, speaking to Shere Ali. Ram Lal drew me away.

" Be quick," he said; " take my hand, I will lead you to the light." We ran along the soft grass, following the sound of each other's feet, swiftly.

A moment more and we were in the pass; the mist was lighter, and we could see our way. We rushed up the stony path fast and sure, till we reached the clear bright moonlight, blazing forth in silver splendour again. Far down below the velvet pall of mist lay thick and heavy, hiding the camp and its horses and men from our sight.

"Friend," said Isaacs, "you are as free as I. Praise Allah, and let us depart in peace."

The savage old warrior grasped the outstretched hand of the Persian and yelled aloud —

"Illallaho-ho-ho-ho!" His throat was as brass.

"La illah ill-allah!" repeated Isaacs in tones as of a hundred clarions, echoing by tree and mountain and river, down the valley.

"Thank God!" I said to Ram Lal.

"Call Him as you please, friend Griggs," answered the pundit.

It was daylight when we reached the tent at the top of the pass.

CHAPTER XIII.

"Abdul Hafiz," said Ram Lal, as we sat round the fire we had made, preparing food, "if it is thy pleasure I will conduct thy friend to a place of safety and set his feet in the paths that lead to pleasant places. For thou art weary and wilt take thy rest until noon, but I am not weary and the limbs of the Afghan are as iron." He spoke in Persian, so that Shere Ali could understand what he said. The latter looked uneasy at first, but soon perceived that his best chance of safety lay in immediately leaving the neighbourhood, which was unpleasantly near Simla on the one side and the frontiers of Baithopoor on the other.

"I thank thee, Ram Lal," replied Isaacs, "and I gladly accept thy offer. Whither wilt thou conduct our friend the Amir?"

"I will lead him by a sure road into Thibet, and my brethren shall take care of him, and presently he shall journey safely northwards into the Tartar country, and thence to the Russ people, where the followers of your prophet are many, and if thou wilt give him the letters thou hast written, which he may present to the principal moolahs, he shall prosper. And as for money, if thou hast gold, give him of it, and if not, give him silver; and if thou hast none, take no thought, for the freedom of the spirit is better than the obesity of the body."

"Bishmillah! Thou speakest with the tongue of wisdom, old man," said Shere Ali; "nevertheless a few rupees ——"

"Fear nothing," broke in Isaacs. "I have for thee a store of a few rupees in silver, and there are two hundred gold mohurs in this bag. They are scarce in Hind and pass not as money, but the value of them whither thou goest shall buy thee food many days. Take also this diamond, which if thou be in want thou shalt sell and be rich.

Shere Ali, who had been suspicious of treachery, or at least was afraid to believe himself really free, was convinced by this generosity. The great rough warrior, the brave patriot who had shut the gates of Kabul in the face of Sir Neville Chamberlain, and who had faced every danger and defeat, rather than tamely suffer the advance of the all-devouring English into his dominions, was proud and unbending still, through all his captivity and poverty and trouble, and weariness of soul and suffering of body; he could bear his calamities like a man, the unrelenting chief of an unrelenting race. But when Isaacs stretched forth his hand and freed him, and bestowed upon him, moreover, a goodly stock of cash, and bid him go in peace, his gratitude got the better of him, and he fairly broke down. The big tears coursed down over his rough cheeks, and his face sank between his hands, which trembled violently for a moment. Then his habitual calm of outward manner returned.

"Allah requite thee, my brother," he said, "I can never hope to."

"I have done nothing," said Isaacs. "Shall believers languish and perish in the hands of swine without faith? Verily it is Allah's doing, whose name is great and powerful. He will not suffer the followers of His prophet to be devoured of jackals and unclean beasts. Masallah! There is no God but God."

Therefore, when they had eaten some food, Ram Lal and Shere Ali departed, journeying north-east towards Thibet, and Isaacs and I remained sleeping in the tent until past noon. Then we arose and went our way, having packed up the little canvas house and the utensils and the pole into a neat bundle which we carried by turns along the steep rough paths, until we found the dooly-bearers squatting round the embers after their mid-day meal. As we journeyed we talked of the events of the night. It seemed to me that the whole thing might have been managed very much more simply. Isaacs did things in his own way, however, and, after all, he generally had a good reason for his actions.

"I think not," he said in reply to my question. "While you were throwing that ruffian, who would have overmatched me in an instant, Shere Ali and I disposed of the sowars who ran up at the captain's signal. Shere Ali says he killed one of them with his hands, and my little knife here seems to have done some damage." He produced the vicious-looking dagger, stained above the hilt with dark blood, which he began to scrape off with a bit of stick.

"My dear fellow," I objected, "I am delighted to have served you, and I see that since Shere Ali could not be warned of the signal, I was the only person there who could tackle that Punjabi man; yet I am completely at a loss to explain why, if Ram Lal can command the forces of nature to the extent of calling down a thick mist under the cover of which we might escape, he could not have calmly destroyed the whole band by lightning, or indigestion, or some simple and efficacious means, so that we need not have risked our lives in supplementing what he only half did."

"There are plenty of answers to that question," Isaacs answered. "In the first place, how do you know that Ram Lal could do anything more than discover the preconcerted signal and bring down that fog? He pretends to no supernatural power; he only asserts that he understands the workings of nature better than you do. How do you know that the fog was his doing at all? Your excited imagination, developed suddenly by the tussle with the captain, which undoubtedly sent the blood to your head, made you think you saw Ram Lal's figure magnified beyond human proportion. If there had been no mist at all, we should most likely have got away unhurt all the same. Those fellows would not fight after their

leader was down. Again, I like to let Ram Lal feel
that I am able to do something for myself, and that
I have other friends as powerful. He aims at obtaining too much ascendency over me. I do not like it."

"Oh — if you look at it in that light, I have nothing to say. It has been a very pleasant and interesting excursion to me, and I am rather glad I only
broke that fellow's arm instead of killing him, as you
and Shere Ali did your sowars."

"I don't know whether I killed him. I suppose I
did. Poor fellow. However, he would certainly
have killed me."

"Of course. No use crying over spilt milk," I
answered.

So we got into the doolies and swung away. As
we neared Simla my friend's spirits rose, and he
chanted wild Persian and Arabic love-songs, and
kept up a fire of conversation all day and all night,
singing and talking alternately.

"Griggs," he said, as we approached the end of our
journey, "did you have occasion to tell Miss Westonhaugh where I had gone?"

"Yes. She asked me, and I answered that you had
gone to save a man's life. She looked very much
pleased, I thought, but just then somebody came up,
and we did not talk any more about it. I got your
message the evening of the day you left."

"She looked pleased?"

"Very much. I remember the colour came into
her cheeks."

"Was she so pale, then?" he asked anxiously.

"Why, yes. You remember how she looked the night before you left? She was even paler the next day, but when I said you had gone to do a good deed, the light came into her face for a moment."

"Do you think she was ill, Griggs?"

"She did not look well, but of course she was anxious about you, and a good deal cut up about your going."

"No; but did you really think she was ill?" he insisted.

"Oh no, nothing but your going."

His spirits were gone again, and he said very little more that day. As we were ascending the last hills, some eight or nine hours from Simla, the moon rose majestically behind us. It must have been ten o'clock, for she could not have been seen above the notch in the mountains to eastward until she had been risen an hour at least.

"I wonder where they are now, those two," said Isaacs.

"Shere Ali and Ram Lal?"

"Yes. They are probably across the borders into Thibet, watching the moon rise from the door of some Buddhist monastery. I am glad I am not there."

"Isaacs," I said, "I would really like to know why you took so much trouble about Shere Ali. It seems to me you might have procured his liberation in some simpler way, if it was merely an act of charity that you contemplated."

"Call it anything you like. I had read about the poor man until my imagination was wrought up, and I could not bear to think of a man so brave and patriotic and at the same time a true believer, lying in the clutches of that old beast of a maharajah. And as for the method of my procedure, do you realise the complete secrecy of the whole affair? Do you see that no one but you and I and the Baithopoor people know anything of the transaction? Do you suppose that I should be tolerated a day in the country if the matter were known? Above all, what do you imagine Mr. Currie Ghyrkins would think of me if he knew I had been liberating and enriching the worst foe of his little god, Lord Beaconsfield?"

There was truth in what he said. By no arrangement could the liberation of Shere Ali have been effected with such secrecy and despatch as by the simple plan of going ourselves. And now we toiled up the last hills, vainly attempting to keep our horses in a canter; long before the relay was reached they had relapsed into a dogged jog-trot.

So we reached Simla at sunrise, and crawled wearily up the steps of the hotel to our rooms, tired with the cramp of dooly and saddle for so many days, and longing for the luxury of the bath, the civilised meal, and the arm-chair. Of course I did not suppose Isaacs would go to bed. He expected that the Westonhaughs would have returned by this time, and he would doubtless go to them as soon as he had breakfasted. So we separated to dress and be shaved —

my beard was a week old at least — and to make ourselves as comfortable as we deserved to be after our manifold exertions. We had been three days and a half from Keitung to Simla.

At my door stood the faithful Kiramat Ali, salaaming and making a pretence of putting dust on his head according to his ideas of respectful greeting. On the table lay letters; one of these, a note, lay in a prominent position. I took it instinctively, though I did not know the hand. It was from Mr. Currie Ghyrkins.

Saturday morning.

MY DEAR MR. GRIGGS — If you have returned to Simla, I should be glad to see you for half an hour on a matter of urgent importance. I would come to you if I could. My niece, Miss Westonhaugh, is, I am sorry to say, dangerously ill. — Sincerely yours,

A. CURRIE GHYRKINS.

It was dated two days before, for to-day was Monday. I made every possible haste in my toilet and ordered a horse. I wondered whether Isaacs had received a similar missive. What could be the matter? What might not have happened in those two days since the note was written? I felt sure that the illness had begun before I left them in the Terai, hastened probably by the pain she had felt at Isaacs' departure; there is nothing like a little mental worry to hasten an illness, if it is to come at all. Poor Miss Westonhaugh! So, after all her gaiety and all the enjoyment she had from the tiger-hunt on which she had set her heart, she had come back to be ill in Simla. Well, the air was fresh enough now — almost cold, in fact. She would soon be well. Still, it was a great pity. We might have had such a gay week before breaking up.

I was dressed, and I went down the steps, passing Isaacs' open door. He was calmly reading a newspaper and having a morning smoke, until it should be time to go out. Clearly he had not heard anything of Miss Westonhaugh's illness. I resolved I would say nothing until I knew the worst, so I merely put my head in and said I should be back in an hour to breakfast with him, and passed on. Once on horseback, I galloped as hard as I could, scattering chuprassies and children and marketers to right and left in the bazaar. It was not long before I left my horse at the corner of Mr. Currie Ghyrkins' lawn, and walking to the verandah, which looked suspiciously neat and unused, inquired for the master of the house. I was shown into his bedroom, for it was still very early and he was dressing.

I noticed a considerable change in the old gentleman's manner and appearance in the last ten days. His bright red colour was nearly faded, his eyes had grown larger and less bright, he had lost flesh, and his tone was subdued in the extreme. He came from his dressing-glass to greet me with a ghost of the old smile on his face, and his hand stretched eagerly out.

"My dear Mr. Griggs, I am sincerely glad to see you."

"I have not been in Simla two hours," I answered, "and I found your note. How is Miss Westonhaugh? I am so sorry to —— "

"Don't talk about her, Griggs. I am afraid she's g—g—goin' to die." He nearly broke down, but he struggled bravely. I was terribly shocked, though a moment's reflection told me that so strong and healthy a person would not die so easily. I expressed my sympathy as best I could.

"What is it? What is the illness?" I asked when he was quieter.

"Jungle fever, my dear fellow, jungle fever; caught in that beastly tiger-hunt. Oh! I wish I had never taken her. I wish we had never gone. Why wasn't I firm? Damn it all, sir, why wasn't I firm, eh?" In his anger at himself something of the former jerky energy of the man showed itself. Then it faded away into the jaded sorrowful look that was on his face when I came in. He sat down with his elbows on his knees and his hands in his scanty gray hair, his suspenders hanging down at his sides — the picture of misery. I tried to console him, but I confess I felt very much like breaking down myself. . I did not see what I could do, except break the bad news to Isaacs.

"Mr. Griggs," he said at last, "she has been asking for you all the time, and the doctor thought if you came she had best see you, as it might quiet her. Understand?" I understood better than he thought.

People who are dangerously ill have no morning

and no evening. Their hours are eternally the same, save for the alternation of suffering and rest. The nurse and the doctor are their sun and moon, relieving each other in the watches of day and night. As they are worse — as they draw nearer to eternity, they are less and less governed by ideas of time. A dying person will receive a visit at midnight or at mid-day with no thought but to see the face of friend — or foe — once more. So I was not surprised to find that Miss Westonhaugh would see me; in an interval of the fever she had been moved to a chair in her room, and her brother was with her. I might go in — indeed she sent a very urgent message imploring that I would go. I went.

The morning sun was beating brightly on the shutters, and the room looked cheerful as I entered. John Westonhaugh, paler than death, came quickly to the door and grasped my hand.

On a long cane-chair by the window, carefully covered from the possible danger of any insidious draught, with a mass of soft white wraps and shawls, lay Katharine Westonhaugh — the transparant phantasm of her brilliant self. The rich masses of pale hair were luxuriously nestled around her shoulders and the blazing eyes flamed, lambently, under the black brows — but that was all. Colour, beside the gold hair and the black eyes, there was hardly any. The strong clean-cut outline of the features was there, but absolutely startling in emaciation, so that there seemed to be no flesh at all; the pale lips scarcely closed over the straight white teeth. A wonderful and a fearful sight to see, that stately edifice of queenly strength and beauty thus laid low and pillaged and stript of all colour save purple and white — the hues of mourning — the purple lips and the white cheek. I have seen many people die, and the moment I looked at Katharine Westonhaugh I felt that the hand of death was already closed over her, gripped round, never to relax. John led me to her side, and a faint smile showed she was glad to see me. I knelt reverently down, as one would kneel beside one already dead. She spoke first, clearly and easily, as it seemed. People who are ill from fever seldom lose the faculty of speech.

"I am so glad you are come. There are many things I want you to do."

"Yes, Miss Westonhaugh. I will do everything."

"Is he come back?" she asked — then, as I looked at her brother, she added, "John knows, he is very glad."

"Yes, we came back this morning together; I came here at once."

"Thank you — it was kind. Did you give him the box?"

"Yes — he does not know you are ill. He means to come at eleven."

"Tell him to come now. *Now* — do you understand?" Then she added in a low tone, for my ear only, "I don't think they know it; I am dying. I shall be dead before to-night. Don't tell him that.

Make him come now. John knows. Now go. I am tired. No — wait! Did he save the man's life?"

"Yes; the man is safe and free in Thibet."

"That was nobly done. Now go. You have always been kind to me, and you love him. When you see me again I shall be gone." Her voice was perceptibly weaker, though still clearly audible. "When I am gone, put some flowers on me for friendship's sake. You have always been so kind. Good-bye, dear Mr. Griggs. Good-bye. God keep you." I moved quickly to the door, fearing lest the piteous sight should make a coward of me. It was so ineffably pathetic — this lovely creature, just tasting of the cup of life and love and dying so.

"Bring him here at once, Griggs, please. I know all about it. It may save her." John Westonhaugh clasped my hand in his again, and pushed me out to speed me on my errand. I tore along the crooked paths and the winding road, up through the bazaar, past the church and the narrow causeway beyond to the hotel. I found him still smoking and reading the paper.

"Well?" said he cheerfully, for the morning sun had dispelled the doubts of the night.

"My dear friend," I said, "Miss Westonhaugh wants to see you immediately."

"How? What? Of course; I will go at once, but how did you know?"

"Wait a minute, Isaacs; she is not well at all — in fact, she is quite ill."

"What's the matter—for God's sake—Why, Griggs, man, how white you are—O my God, my God—she is dead!" I seized him quickly in my arms or he would have thrown himself on the ground.

"No," I said, "she is not dead. But, my dear boy, she is dying. I do not believe she will live till this evening. Therefore get to horse and ride there quickly, before it is too late."

Isaacs was a brave man, and of surpassing strength to endure. After the first passionate outburst, his manner never changed as he mechanically ordered his horse and pulled on his boots. He was pale naturally, and great purple rings seemed to come out beneath his eyes—as if he had received a blow—from the intensity of his suppressed emotion. Once only he spoke before he mounted.

"What is it?" he asked.

"Jungle fever," I answered. He groaned. "Shall I go with you?" asked I, thinking it might be as well. He shook his head, and was off in a moment.

I turned to my rooms and threw myself on my bed. Poor fellow; was there ever a more piteous case? Oh the cruel misery of feeling that nothing could save her! And he—he who would give life and wealth and fortune and power to give her back a shade of colour—as much as would tinge a rose-leaf, even a very little rose-leaf—and could not. Poor fellow! What would he do to-night—to-morrow. I could see him kneeling by her side and weeping hot tears over the wasted hands. I could almost hear his smothered sob—his last words of speeding to the parting soul—the picture grew intensely in my thoughts. How beautiful she would look when she was dead!

I started as the thought came into my mind. How superficial was my acquaintance with her, poor girl,—how little was she a part of my life, since I could really so heartlessly think of her beauty when her breath should be gone! Of course, though, it was natural enough, why should I feel any personal pang for her? It was odd that I should even expect to—I, who never felt a "personal pang" of regret for the death of any human creature, excepting poor dear old Lucia, who brought me up, and sent me to school, and gave me roast chestnuts when I knew my lessons, in the streets of Rome, thirty years ago. When she died, I was there; poor old soul, how fond she was of me! And I of her! I remember the tears I shed, though I was a bearded man even then. How long is that? Since she died, it must be ten years.

My thoughts wandered about among all sorts of *bric-à-brac* memories. Presently something brought me back to the present. Why must this fair girl from the north die miserably here in India? Ah yes! the eternal why. Why did we go at such a season into the forests of the Terai? it was madness; we knew it was, and Ram Lal knew it too. Hence his warning. O Ram Lal, you are a wise old man, with your gray beard and you mists of wet white velvet and your dark sayings! Ram Lal, will you riddle me, also, my weird that I must dree?

A cold draught passed over my head, and I turned on my couch to see whence it came. I started bolt upright, and my hair stood on end with sudden terror. I had uttered the name of Ram Lal aloud in my reverie, and there he sat on a chair by the door, as gray as ever, with his long staff leaning from his feet across his breast and shoulder. He looked at me quietly.

"I come opportunely, Mr. Griggs, it seems. *Lupus in fabula.* I hear my name pronounced as I enter the door. This is flattering to a man of my modest pretensions to social popularity. You would like me to tell you your fortune? Well, I am not a fortune-teller."

"Never mind my fortune. Will Miss Weston-haugh recover?"

"No. She will die at sundown."

"How do you know, since you say you are no prophet?"

"Because I am a doctor of medicine. M.D. of Edinburgh."

"Why can you not save her then? A man who is a Scotch doctor, and who possesses the power of performing such practical jokes on nature as you exhibited the other night, might do something. However, I suppose I am not talking to you at all. You are in Thibet with Shere Ali. This is your astral body, and if I were near enough, I could poke my fingers right through you, as you sit there, telling me you are an Edinburgh doctor, forsooth."

"Quite right, Mr. Griggs. At the present moment

my body is quietly asleep in a lamastery in Thibet, and this is my astral shape, which, from force of habit, I begin to like almost as well. But to be serious ——"

"I think it is very serious, your going about in this casual manner."

"To be serious. I warned Isaacs that he should not allow the tiger-hunt to come off. He would not heed my warning. It is too late now. I am not omnipotent."

"Of course not. Still, you might be of some use if you went there. While there is life there is hope."

"Proverbs," said Ram Lal scornfully, "are the wisdom of wise men prepared in portable doses for the foolish; and the saying you quote is one of them. There is life yet, but there is no hope."

"Well, I am afraid you are right. I saw her this morning — I suppose I shall never see her again, not alive, at least. She looked nearly dead then. Poor girl; poor Isaacs, left behind!"

"You may well say that, Mr. Griggs," said the adept. "On the whole, perhaps he is to be less pitied than she; who knows? Perhaps we should pity neither, but rather envy both."

"Why? Either you are talking the tritest of cant, or you are indulging in more of your dark sayings, to be interpreted, *post facto*, entirely to your own satisfaction, and to every one else's disgust." I was impatient with the man. If he had such extraordinary powers as were ascribed to him — I never heard him assert that he possessed any; if he could prophesy, he might as well do so to some purpose. Why could he not speak plainly? He could not impose on me, who was ready to give him credit for what he really could do, while finding fault with the way he did it.

"I understand what passes in your mind, friend Griggs," he said, not in the least disconcerted at my attack. "You want me to speak plainly to you, because you think you are a plain-spoken, clear-headed man of science yourself. Very well, I will. I think you might yourself become a brother some day, if you would. But you will not now, neither will in the future. Yet you understand some little distant inkling of the science. When you ask your scornful questions of me, you know perfectly well that you are putting an inquiry which you yourself can answer as well as I. I am not omnipotent. I have very little more power than you. Given certain conditions and I can produce certain results, palpable, visible, and appreciable to all; but my power, as you know, is itself merely the knowledge of the laws of nature, which Western scientists, in their wisdom, ignore. I can replenish the oil in the lamp, and while there is wick the lamp shall burn — ay, even for hundreds of years. But give me a lamp wherein the wick is consumed, and I shall waste my oil; for it will not burn unless there be the fibre to carry it. So also is the body of man. While there is the flame of vitality and the essence of life in his nerves and finer tissues, I will put blood in his veins, and if he meet with no accident he may live to see hundreds of generations pass by him. But where there is no vitality and no essence of life in a man, he must die; for though I fill his veins with blood, and cause his heart to beat for a time, there is no spark in him — no fire, no nervous strength. So is Miss Weston-haugh now — dead while yet breathing, and sighing her sweet farewells to her lover."

"I know. I understand you very well. But do not deny that you might have saved her. Why did you not?" Ram Lal smiled a strange smile, which I should have described as self-satisfied, had it not been so gentle and kind.

"Ah yes!" he said, with something like a sigh, though there was no sorrow or regret in it. "Yes, Griggs, I might have saved her life. I would certainly have saved her — well, if he had not persuaded her to go down into that steaming country at this time of year, since it was my advice to remain here. But it is no use talking about it."

"I think you might have conveyed your meaning to him a little more clearly. He had no idea that you meant danger to her."

"No, very likely not. It is not my business to mould men's destinies for them. If I give them advice that is good, it is quite enough. It is like a man playing cards: if he does not seize his chance it does not return. Besides, it is much better for him that she should die."

"Your moral reflections are insufferable. Can you not find some one else to whom you may confide your secret joy of my friend's misfortunes?"

"Calm yourself. I say it is better for her, better for him, better for both. Remember what you said to him yourself about the difference between pleasure and happiness. They shall be one yet, their happiness shall not be less eternal because their pleasure in this life has been brief. Can you not conceive of immortal peace and joy without the satisfaction of earthly lust?"

"I would not call such a beautiful union as theirs might have been by such a name. For myself, I confess to a very real desire for pleasure first and happiness afterwards."

"I know you better than you think, Mr. Griggs. You are merely argumentative, rarely sceptical. If I had begun by denying what I instead asserted, you would by this time have been arguing as strongly on my side as you now are on yours. You are often very near degenerating into a common sophist."

"Very likely, it was a charming profession. Meanwhile, by going to the very opposite extreme from sophistry, I mean by a more than Quixotic veneration for an abstract dogma you hold to be true, and by your determination to make people die for it, you are causing fearful misery of body, untold agony of soul, to a woman and a man whom you should have every reason to like. Go to, Ram Lal, adept, magician, enthusiast, and prophet, you are mistaken, like all your kind!"

"No, I am not mistaken, time will show. Moreover, I would have you remark that the lady in question is not suffering at all, and that the 'untold agony of soul' you attribute to Isaacs is a wholesome medicine for one with such a soul as his. And now I am going, for you are not the sort of person with whom I can enjoy talking very long. You are violent and argumentative, though you are sometimes amusing. I am rarely violent, and I never argue: life is too short. And yet I have more time for it than you, seeing my life will be indefinitely longer than yours. Good-bye, for the present; and believe me, those two will be happier far, and far more blessed, in a few short years hence, than ever you or I shall be in all the unreckonable cycles of this or any future world." Ram Lal sighed as he uttered the last words, and he was gone; yet the musical cadence of the deep-drawn breath of a profound sorrow, vibrated whisperingly through the room where I lay. Poor Ram Lal, he must have had some disappointment in his youth, which, with all his wisdom and superiority over the common earth, still left a sore place in his heart.

I was not inclined to move. I knew where Isaacs was, where he would remain to the bitter end, and I would not go out into the world that day, while he was kneeling in the chamber of death. He might come back at any time. How long would it last? God in his mercy grant it might be soon and quickly over, without suffering. Oh! but those strong people

die so deathly hard.   I have seen a man — No, I was
sure of that.   She would not suffer any more now.

I lay thinking.   Would Isaacs send for me when
he returned, or would he face his grief alone for a
night before he spoke?   The latter, I thought; I
hoped so too.   How little sympathy there must be
for any one, even the dearest, in our souls and hearts,
when it is so hard to look forward to speaking half-
a-dozen words of comfort to some poor wretch of a
friend who has lost everything in the wide world
that is dear to him.   We would rather give him all
we possess outright than attempt to console him for
the loss.   And yet — what is there in life more sweet
than to be consoled and comforted, and to have the
true sympathy of some one, even a little near to us,
when we ourselves are suffering.   The people we do
not want shower cards of condolence on us, and
carriage-loads of flowers on the poor dead thing; the
ones who could be of some help to the tortured soul
are afraid to speak; the very delicacy of kind-
heartedness in them, which makes us wish they
would come, makes them stay away.

I hope Isaacs will not send for me, poor fellow.

If he does, what shall I say?   God help me.

CHAPTER XIV.

THE hours came and went, and though worn out with the exertions of the past days, and with the emotions of the morning, I lay in my rooms, unable to sleep even for a moment. I went down once or twice to Isaacs' rooms to know whether he had returned, but he had not, nor had any one heard from him. At last the evening shadows crept stealthily up, darkening first one room, then another, until there was not light enough to read by. Then I dropped my book and went out to breathe the cold air on the verandah. Wearily the hours went by, and still there was no sign of my friend.

Towards eleven o'clock the moon, now waning, once more rose above the hills and shed her light across the lawn, splendid still, but with the first tinge of melancholy that clouds her departing glory. Exhausted nature asserted herself, and chilled to the bone I went to bed, and, at last, to sleep.

I slept peacefully at first, but soon the events that had come over my life began to weave themselves in wild disharmony through my restful visions, and the events that were to come cast their lengthening shadows before them. The world of past, present,

V

and future thoughts, came into my soul, distorted, without perspective, nothing to help me to discern the good from the evil, the suffering gone and long-forgotten from the pain in store. The triumph of discrepancy over waking reason, the fancied victories of the sleep-dulled intellect over the outrageous discord of the wakeful imagination. I passed a most miserable night. It seemed rest to wake, until I was awake, and then it seemed rest to sleep again, until my eyes were closed. At last it came, no dream this time; Isaacs stood by my bed-side in the gray of the morning, himself grayer than the soft neutral-tinted dawn. It was a terrible moment to me, though I had expected it since yesterday. I felt like the condemned criminal in France, who does not know the day or hour of his death. The first intimation is when the executioner at daybreak enters his cell and bids him come forth to die, sometimes in less than sixty seconds from his waking.[1]

How gray he looked, and how infinitely tried. I rose swiftly and took his hands, which were deadly cold, and led him to the outer room. I could not say anything, for I did not know how such a terribly sudden blow would affect him; he was so unlike any one else. Why is it so hard to comfort the afflicted? Why should the most charitable duty it is ever given us to perform be, without exception, the hardest of tasks?

I am sure most people feel as I do. It is far less painful to suffer wounds and sickness in one's own

---

[1] A fact, as is well known.

body than to stand by and see the cold clean knife go through skin and flesh and cartilage; it is surely easier to suffer disease than to smooth daily and hourly the bed and pillows of some poor tormented wretch, calling on God and man to end his misery. There is a hidden instinct — of a low and cowardly kind, but human nevertheless — which bids us turn away from spectacles of agony whether harrowing or repulsive, until the good angel comes and whispers that we must trample on such coarse impulse and do our duty. "Show pity," said the wise old Frenchman, "do anything to alleviate distress, but avoid actually feeling either compassion or sympathy. They can lead to no good." That was only his way of making to himself an excuse for doing a good action, for Larochefoucauld was a man who really possessed every virtue that he disclaimed for himself and denied in others.

I felt much of this as I led Isaacs to the outer room, not knowing what form his sorrow might take, but feeling in my own person a grief as poignant, perhaps, for the moment, as his own. I had known he would come, that was all, though I had hoped he would not, and I knew that I must do my best to send him away a little less sorrowful than he had come. I was not prepared for the extreme calm of voice and manner that marked his first words, coming with measured rhythm and even cadence from his pale lips.

"It is all over, my friend," he said.

"It has but begun," said the solemn tones of Ram Lal, the Buddhist, from the door. He entered and approached us.

"Friend Isaacs," he continued, "I am not here to mock at your grief or to weary your strained heart-strings with such petty condolence as well-nigh drove Ayoub of old to impatience. But I love you, my brother, and I have somewhat to say to you in your trouble, some advice to give you in your distress. You are suffering greatly, past the power of reason to alleviate, for you no longer know yourself, nor are aware what you really think. But I will show to you three pictures of yourself that shall rouse you to what you are, to what you were, and to what you shall be.

"I found you, not many years ago, a very young man, most exceptionally placed in regard to the world. You were even then rich, though not so rich as you now are. You were beautiful and full of vigour, but you have now upon you the glow of a higher beauty, the overflowing promise of a more glorious life. You were happy because you thought you were, but such happiness as you had proceeded from without rather than from within. You were a materially thinking man. Your thoughts were of the flesh, and your delights — harmless it is true — were in the things that were under your eyes — wealth, power, book knowledge, and perhaps woman, if you can call the creatures you believed in women.

"You gathered wealth in great heaps, and your

precious stones in storehouses. You laid your hand
upon the diamond of the river and upon the pearl of
the sea, and they abode with you, as the light of the
sun and the moon. And you said, 'Behold it is my
star, which is the lord of the dog-heat in summer, and
it is my kismet.' You also took to yourself wives of
rare qualities, having both golden and raven black
hair, whose skin was as fine silk, and their breath as
the freshness of the dawning, and their eyes as jewels.
Then said you, rejoicing in your heart, that you were
happy; and so you dwelt in peace and plenty, and
waxed glad.

"Therefore you accomplished your first destiny,
and you drank of the cup that was filled to overflowing. And if it had been the law of nature that from
pleasure man should derive permanent lasting peace,
you had been happy so long as you lived. But,
though you have the faultless life of the body to enjoy
all things of the earth, even as other men, though in
another degree, you have within you something more.
There is in your breast a heart beating — an organ so
wonderful in its sensitiveness, so perfect in its consciousness of good, that the least throb and thrill of
pleasure that it feels is worth years and ages of mere
sensual life enjoyment. The body having tasted of
all happiness whereof it is capable, and having found
that it is good, is saturated with its own ease and
enjoys less keenly. But the heart is the borderland
between body and soul. The heart can love and the
body can love, but the body can only love itself; the

heart is the wellspring of the love that goes beyond self. Therefore your heart awoke.

"Shall I tell you of the first early stirrings of your love? Think you, because I am gray and loveless, that I have never known youth and gladness of heart? Ah, I know, better than you can think. It is not sudden, really, the blossoming out of the tree of life. The small leaves grow larger and stronger though still closely folded in the bud, until the bright warmth of the spring makes them burst into bloom. The little lark in the nest among the grass grows beneath the mother's wing and idly moves, now and then, unconscious of the cloud-cleaving gift of flight, until all at once, in the fair dawning, there wells up in his tiny breast the mighty sense of power to rise.

"The human heart is like the budded folded leaves, and like the untaught lark. The quiet sleep before the day of blooming is, while it lasts, a state of happiness. But it is not comparable with the breathing joy of the leaf that feels and sees the wonderful life around it, whispering divine answers to the wooing breeze. The humble nest where it has first seen light is for many days a happy home to the tender songster, soon left behind, when the first wing-strokes waft the small body upwards to the sky, and forgotten as the first glad trill and quaver of the new-found voice roll out the prelude to the glorious life-long hymn of praise. The heart of man — your heart, my dear friend — gave a great leap from earth to sky, when first it felt the magic of the other life. The grosser scales of material vision fell away from your inner sight on the day when you met, and knew you had met, the woman you were to love.

"I found you again, a different man, a far happier man, though you would hardly allow that. A sweet uncertainty of the future half-tinged your joy with a shadow of sadness, which you had not known before: but love sadness is only the shading and gentle pencilling in love's wondrous picture, whereby the whole light of the painting is made clearer and stronger. A new world opened out before you in endless vistas of untold and undreamed bliss. You looked back at your former self, so careless and sunny, so consciously happy in the strong sense of life and power, and you wondered how you could have been even contented through so many years. The good and evil deeds of your past life lost colour and perspective, and fell back into a dull, flat background, against which the ineffable vision of beautiful and immortal womanhood stood forth in transcendent glory. The eternal womanly element of the great universe beckoned you on, as it did Doctor Faustus of old. You had hitherto accepted woman and ignored womanhood, as so many of the followers of the prophet have always done. Henceforth there was to be a change, entire, complete, and enduring. No doubts now, or careless scepticism; no cant about women having no souls and no individual being; you had made a great step to a better understanding of the world you live in. Filled with a new life, you

went on your way rejoicing and longing to do great
deeds for her who had come into your destiny. From
dawn to sunset, and from evening to dawn, one
picture ever was before you leading you on. You
were ready to run any risk for a smile and a blush of
pleasure, you were willing to sacrifice anything and
everything for her praise. And when, down there
among the mango-trees in the Terai, your lips first
touched hers and your arm pressed her to your side,
the joy that was yours was as the joy of the im-
mortals."

Ram Lal paused, and Isaacs, who had been sitting
by the table, stony and dry-eyed, hid his face in his
hands, clutching with his white fingers among his
bright black hair — all that seemed left to him of life,
so dead and ashy was his face. He remained thus
without looking up, as the old man continued.

"Think not, dear friend and brother, that I have
come here to dwell needlessly on your grief, to rouse
again the keen agonies that have so lately burned
through and through you to the quick. I love you
well, and would but trace the past in order to paint
the future. All that you felt and knew in those
short days of perfect love on earth was good and true
and noble, and shall not be forgotten hereafter. But
last night closed the second of your three destinies
— as true love always must close on earth — in bitter
grief and sorrow because the one is gone before.
Rather should you rejoice, Abdul Hafiz, that she is
gone in virgin whiteness, whither ere long you shall

follow and be with her till time shall chase the crumbling world out over the broad quicksands of eternity, and nought shall survive of all this but the pure and the constant and the faithful to death. There is before you a third destiny, great and awful, but grand beyond power of telling. Body and heart have had their full cup of happiness, have enjoyed to the full what has been set in their way to enjoy. To the full you have enjoyed wealth and success and the sensuality of a refined and artistic luxury; to the full, as only a few rarely-gifted men can, you have enjoyed the purest and highest love that earth can give. Think not that all ends here. The greatest of destinies is but begun, and it is the destiny of the soul. Two days ago if I had told you there was something higher in you than the loving heart, you would not have believed me; now you do. It is the ethereal portion of the heart, that which longs to be loosed from the body and floating upwards to rejoin its other half.

"Your love has been of the best kind that falls to the lot of man. Not a single shadow of doubting fell between you. It has been sweet if it has seemed short — but it has really lasted a long time, as long as some people's lives. You are many years older than you were when it began, for a month or two ago — or whenever it was that your heart first awoke — you were entirely immersed in the material view of things that belonged naturally enough to your position and mode of life. Now you have passed the critical border-land wherein love wanders, himself not knowing whither he shall lead his followers, whether back to the thick green pasture and heavy-scented groves of sensual existence or forward to free wind-swept heights of spiritual blessedness, where those who are true until they die walk forth into truth everlasting. Yours is the faith and the truth that abide always, yours henceforward shall be the perfect union of souls, yours the ethereal range of the outer firmament. Take my hand, brother, in yours, and seek with me the path to those heights — to that pinnacle of paradise where you shall meet once more the spirit elected to yours."

Ram Lal stood beside Isaacs, whose face was still hidden, and laid his hand with tender gentleness on the weary head. The old man looked kindly down as he touched the thick black hair, and then raised his eyes and looked out through the door at the brightening landscape over which the morning sun was shedding warmth and beauty once more.

"Brother," he continued, "come forth with me. You have suffered too much to mix again with the world, even if you wished it. Come forth, and your soul shall live for ever. Your grief shall be turned to joy, and the sinking heart shall be lifted to heights untried. As now the sun steadily rises in his unerring course, following the pale footsteps of the fleet dawning, and fulfilling her half spoken promises a million-fold in his goodness; as now the all-muffling heaviness of the sad dark night is forgotten in the gladness of day — so shall your brief time of dark-

ness and dull distress perish and vanish swiftly at
the first glimpses of the heavenly day on which follows no creeping night nor shadow of earthly care.
I come not to bid you forget; I come to bid you
remember. Remember all that is past, treasure it in
the secret storehouse of the soul where the few flowers
culled from life's abundant thorn are laid in their
fragrance and garnered up. Remember also the
future. Think that your time is short, and that the
labour shall be sweet; so that in a few quick years
you shall reap a harvest of unearthly blooming. Fear
not to tread boldly in the tracks of those who have
climbed before you, and who have attained and have
conquered. What can anything earthly ever be to
you? What can you ever care again for gold, or
gem, or horse, or slave? Do with those things as it
may seem good in your eyes, but leave them behind.
The weight of the money-bags is a weariness and
soreness to the feet that toil to overtake eternity.
The flesh itself is weariness to the spirit, and soon
leaves it to wing its flight untrammelled and untiring. Come, I will give you of my poor strength what
shall carry your uncertain steps over the first great
difficulties, or at least over so many as you have not
yet surmounted. Be bold, aspiring, fearless, and
firm of purpose. What guerdon can man or Heaven
offer, higher than eternal communion with the bright
spirit that waits and watches for your coming? With
her — you said it while she lived — was your life,
your light, and your love; it is true tenfold now, for

with her is life eternal, light ethereal, and love spiritual.   Come, brother, come with me!"

Slowly Isaacs raised his head from his hands and
gazed long on the old man.   And while he gazed it
was as if his pale face were transparent and the whiteness of the burning spirit, dazzling to see, came and
went quickly and came again as flashes in the northern sky.   Slowly he rose to his feet, and laying his
hand in the Buddhist's, spoke at last.

"Brother, I come," he said.   "Show me the way."

"Right gladly will I be thy guide, Abdul," Ram
Lal gave answer.   "Right willingly will I go with
thee whither thou wouldest.   Never was teacher
sought by more worthy pupil; never did man embrace
the pure life of the brethren with more single heart
or truer purpose.   The way shall be short that leads
thee upward, the stones that are therein shall be as
wings to lift thy feet instead of stumbling-blocks
for thy destruction.   The hidden forces of nature
shall lend thee strength, and her secrets wisdom;
the deep sweet springs of the eternal water shall
refresh thee and the food of the angels shall be thine.
Thy sorrows shall turn from bitter into sweet, and
from the stings of thy past agonies shall grow up the
golden flowers of thy future crown.   Thou shalt not
tire in the way, nor crave rest by the wayside."

"Friend, tell me what I shall do that I may attain
all this."

"Be faithful to her who has preceded you, and
learn of us, who know it, wherein consists true hap-

piness. You need but little help, dear friend. Banish only from your thoughts the human suggestion that what you love most is lost, gone irrevocably. Rejoice, and mourn not, that she has entered in already where all your striving is to follow. Be glad because she looks on those sights and hears those sounds which are too bright and strong yet for your eyes and ears. Some of these unspeakable things you shall perceive with your perishable body; but the more perfect and glorious remain hidden to our mortal senses, be they ever so keen and exquisite. Believe me, you shall reach that state before I do. My poor soul is still bound to earth by some slender bonds of pleasure and contemptible pain, fine indeed as threads of gossamer, and soon, I trust, to be shaken off for ever. Yet am I bound and not utterly free. You, my brother, have been wrenched suddenly from the life of the body to the life of the soul. In you the vile desire to live for living's sake will soon be dead, if it is not dead already. Your soul, drawn strongly upward to other spheres, is well nigh loosed from love of life and fear of death. If at this moment you could lie down and die, you would meet your end joyfully. Very subtle are the fast-vanishing links between you and the world; very thin and impalpable the faint shadows that mar to your vision those transcendent hues of heavenly glory you shall so soon behold. Look forward, look upward, look onward —never once look back, and your waiting shall not be long, nor her watching many days. She stands before you, beckoning and praying that you tarry not. See that you do her bidding faithfully, as being near the blessed end, and fearful of losing even one moment in the attainment of what you seek."

"Fear not, Ram Lal. My determination shall not fail me, nor my courage waver, until all is reached."

The light of another world was on the beautiful brow and features as he looked full at his future teacher. What strange powers these adept brethren have! What marvellous magnetism over the souls of lesser men — whereby they turn sorrow into gladness, and defeat into triumph by mere words. I myself, bound by thought and word and deed to the lesser life, was not unmoved by the glorious promises that flowed with glowing eloquence from the lips of that gray old man in the early morning. They moved toward the door. Ram Lal spoke as he turned away.

"We leave you, friend Griggs, but we will return this evening and bid you farewell." So I was left alone. Another comforter had taken my place; one knowing human nature better, and well versed in the learning of the spirit. One of that small band of high priests who in all ages and nations and religions and societies have been the mediators between time and eternity, to cheer and comfort the broken-hearted, to rebuke him who would lose his own soul, to speed the awakening spirit in its heavenward flight.

*   *   *   *

As I sat in my room that night the door opened and they were with me, standing hand in hand.

"My friend," said Isaacs, "I have come to bid you farewell. You will never see me again. I am here once more to thank you, from the bottom of my heart, for your friendship and kind offices, for the strength of your arm in the hour of need, and for the gold of your words in time of uncertainty."

"Isaacs," I said, "I know little of the journey you are undertaking, and I cannot go with you. This I know, that you are very near to a life I cannot hope for; and I pray God that you may speed quickly to the desired end, that you may attain that happiness which your brave soul and honest heart so well deserve. Once more, then, I offer you my fullest service, if there is anything that I still can do."

"There is nothing," he answered, "though if there were I know you would do it gladly and entirely. I have bestowed all my worldly possessions on the one man besides yourself to whom I owe a debt of gratitude — John Westonhaugh. Had I known you less well, I would have made you a sharer in my forsaken wealth. Only this I beg of you. Take this gem and keep it always for my sake. No — do not look at it in that way. Do not consider its value. It is to recall one who will often think of you, for you have been a great deal to me in this month."

"I would I might have been more," I said, and it was all I could say, for my voice failed me.

"Think of me," he continued, and the bright light shone through his face in the dusk, "think of me, not as you see me now, or as I was this morning, bowed beneath a great sorrow, but as looking forward to a happiness that transcends this mortal joy that I have lost, even as the glory of things celestial transcends the glory of the terrestrial. Think of me, not as mourning the departed day, but as watching longingly for the first faint dawn of the day eternal. Above all, think of me not as alone but as wedded for all ages to her who has gone before me."

Ram Lal laid his hand on my arm and looked long into my eyes.

"Farewell for the present, my chance acquaintance," he said, "and remember that in me you have a friend. The day may come when you too will be in dire distress, beyond the skill of mere solitude and books to soothe. Farewell, and may all good things be with you."

Isaacs laid his two hands on my shoulders, and once more I met the wondrous lustre of his eyes, now veiled but not darkened with the last look of his tender friendship.

"Good-bye, my dear Griggs. You have been the instructor and the genius of my love. Learn yourself the lessons you can teach others so well. Be yourself what you would have made me."

One last loving look — one more pressure of the reluctant fingers, and those two went out, hand in hand, under the clear stars, and I saw them no more.

THE END.

www.ingramcontent.com/pod-product-compliance
Lightning Source LLC
Chambersburg PA
CBHW060521030726

47498CB00004B/1033